To my wife, my family and all those who gave me valuable
input and support

# FROM DUST TO DNA

## RJ Hogarth

## SELECTED REVIEWS

★★★★★ **Exceptional!**, December 9, 2014 , By Erik – Amazon Reviewer

This was an amazing read, I definitely got a "Da Vinci Code" vibe from it. That is NOT to say that this is a copy cat, not at all. I loved the individuality and inspiration of this book. Those who have strong beliefs about anything should always be willing to listen to the opposition, how else can you be sure unless you've truly investigated? How can you practice loyalty if you do not understand the whole picture? I will be reading this again. I received a copy of this book in exchange for an honest review.

★★★★★ **Engaging, thought-provoking** on November 16, 2014 , Ronnie, Amazon Reviewer

An excellent book. It is well written and seems to have been thoroughly researched. It gave both sides and gave excellent arguments for both sides. At first I thought there was an agenda or the book was going to be preachy. It wasn't, it was thought-provoking and engaged the reader to think.

★★★★★ **Thought provoking and entertaining!**, December 27, 2014 ,ZP, Amazon Reviewer

This book was thought provoking and intriguing. I like when a work of fiction makes you think and opens your mind to other possibilities and From Dust to DNA certainly did that. The book was fast-paced and full of adventure so most nights I'd find myself staying up late to read even just a few more pages. I'd recommend this book to anyone looking for an interesting and unique read. Those who enjoy books like the Da Vinci Code would like From Dust to DNA, in my opinion. I received a free copy in exchange for an honest review.

**Many more 5 star reviews can be viewed at the *From Dust to DNA* pages at the Goodreads and Amazon books web sites**

## AUTHOR'S NOTE TO THE READER

Since this book was first published, numerous reviews and a great deal of interesting philosophical discussion followed.  A principle emerging from the book came to be known as the *Infinite Wall Principle* - a solution to the problem of  evil. The principle shows how reality is, in essence, insoluble with irrationality and chaos preventing perfection. Many found the book of great benefit with its inspiring worldview.

In 2021 a paper was published in an international philosophical journal presenting the *Infinite Wall Principle* which can be viewed at:
https://cloverleaf.spiritualeducation.org/v4n1/god-choice

Although the principle is explained in this book in relation to whether perfection is possible in defining omnipotence and omniscience it is not referred to as the *Infinite Wall Principle* which later became a convenient name for this underlying philosophy.

ISBN: 978-0-646-93295-8

# FROM DUST TO DNA
# BY R.J. HOGARTH

**Dramatis Personae**
*(in order of appearance)*

Sir Ernest Eveleigh—university lecturer
Antiquities Foundation – Trust Fund associated with Sir Ernest
Hakeem Khan—antiquities dealer in Kabul
John Rowntree—student undertaking arts at Oxford
Bill Rose—fellow teacher and friend of John Rowntree
Basil Rumsden—headmaster at John's school
Jane Thornton—John's girlfriend, former journalist and university student
Pip – school friend of Jane
Arthur Briggs—heckler from the theology faculty
Professor Cedric Simons—Oxford professor and challenger to debate Sir Ernest
Brendan Everleigh—first boyfriend of Jane and eldest son of Sir Ernest
Peter Castle—friend of Jane
Anne Rochester—friend of Jane
Martin Crawford—student who goes missing
Kenneth Hardwick— publisher
Norton & Sykes—publishers
Alistair Thornton—ex-vicar of Morgrove
Professor Ian Cummings—leading geneticist, rejected by two other scientists

Rev. Basil Rowntree—John's father, an associated priest at St. Mary's Church, Oxford

Horace Wilkins—student who argues that God exists against problem of evil

Joe Carter—student who argues that God exists against problem of evil

Alison Cooper—student who argues that God exists against problem of evil

James Dunkley—parson rescuing John

Mrs Dunkley—parson's wife

Paul Sanders—ex-Royal Marine coming to John's aid

Detective Chief Inspector Townsend—Detective from Oxford City Centre Police Station

Detective Chief Inspector Braun— Detective from Oxford City Centre Police Station

Val – mentor of Jane

Thomas Everleigh—youngest son of Sir Ernest Everleigh

Thistlewaite & Hazelhurst, solicitors—lawyers on the biotech case

John Hazelhurst—solicitor and partner of Thistlewaite & Hazelhurst

Count Christian Nansen—secretary of the Nobel Foundation

Warren Tolhurst III—editor of *Landmarks in Science* magazine

Jim Alsop—biomedical partner of Professor Cummings

Ted McEwen—biologist partner of Professor Cummings

Alsop McEwen Biomedical Ltd- public company founded by Alsop & McEwen

AMB - Alsop McEwen Biomedical Ltd

Andrew Faulkner—paleontologist

Derek Hanson—MI5 operative

Gordon Hudspeth—MI5 operative

Arnold Taylor—MI5 operative

Yousef Rahmaan—smuggler

Amar Kalim—smuggler

Omar—impersonator of Hakeem Khan

Hassan Sahib—courier/bank manager at the State Bank of Afghanistan

Martin De Jersey—director, Greater Baxendale Bank

Abdul Khan—brother of Hakeem Khan

Father Ian Augustus, SJ—Jesuit

Father Joe Campbell, SJ—Jesuit
Father Lombardo Fezzalo, SJ—Jesuit
Leo—Italian commando
Ahmed—Iraqi soldier at Tallil Air Base
Sayeed—Iraqi flight mechanic Tallil Air Base
Sergeant Taylor—US soldier in Iraq
Walid—archaeologist employed by Mr. Khan
Arthur Frost—art dealer at Frost Artefacts
Gunter Keller –senior stockbroker in funds management
Mary – secretary to Gunter Keller
Catherine Tonkin—TV news reporter for BusiStream business channel
Douglas Cory-Smith—executive director of stockbrokers Heydon Capital Markets
Heydon Capital Markets—stockbrokers, underwriters of AMB
Nadia—clerical assistant to Douglas Cory-Smith at Heydon Capital Markets
James Barden—lawyer to Heydon Capital Markets
Robert Prasad- manager, London Stock Exchange
Lester Cruickshank—lawyer to AMB
Arun Kumar—project manager, Origin of Life project; mathematician and biologist
Frederico Cesare – elusive billionaire owner of Zelacorp Media
Zelacorp Media—Italian conglomerate owned by elusive billionaire Frederico Cesare

# PROLOGUE

Oxford Don Sir Ernest Everleigh spoke tensely upon answering the telephone in the study of his country mansion in Oxfordshire.

"Mr. Everleigh," said the voice, "my name is Hakeem Khan, and I am phoning from Kabul in Afghanistan. I have had one of your students here, a Mr. Martin Crawford, who also mentioned the Antiquities Foundation. I believe you are the chairman?"

"Oh, yes. I have not heard from Martin."

"Well, he is missing," said Khan.

A short silence followed, and Sir Ernest continued: "That's a worry. Martin has been helping us and the Foundation search for a certain relic. Were you aware of that?" asked Sir Ernest.

Sir Ernest reached into the library that adorned his sumptuous study and pulled a sheet of paper from a book in his glass bookcase. He glimpsed his own reflection in the glass bookcase: a distinguished, blue-eyed, slightly tanned, and gray-haired professor type in his fifties, but tall and well-built enough to intimidate most people.

A large painting of Charles Darwin hung on the wall, illuminated by special lights in the dimly lit study. A side table, almost resembling a shrine, sat beneath it. On the table was a reprint of Darwin's scientific masterpiece *The Origin of the Species*, together with other Darwin memorabilia. Sir Ernest's goal in life was to disprove God's existence, and he believed he was onto something in Afghanistan that would be a death-blow to believers. He pursued his goal with religious fervor.

"Yes, Martin gave me some pictures, and in fact I have located the relic. However, it will be quite expensive and dangerous to get it," replied Khan.

"I hope Martin did not go after it himself," said Sir Ernest. "It's possible; he's a very motivated young man. How much would it cost to get the relic?"

"You tell me," goaded Khan. Another short silence followed.

"One hundred thousand pounds," offered Sir Ernest.

"Ooo! You joke with me. We are looking at over one million dollars," replied Khan.

"Look, that is a huge sum. I will have to consult the Foundation about that. Where can I call you?" asked Sir Ernest.

Khan gave his number, and Sir Ernest scribbled it on his paper before hanging up. He stood up and walked to the window and stared into the darkness.

**

John Rowntree was the type of teacher who wanted a cause, and today he had one. As he walked toward the school where he taught, his friend and fellow teacher Bill Rose stood in the pathway blocking his way, hands held up high.

"Don't do it, John!"

"Out of my way, Bill."

"John, you are throwing your job away!"

John stepped around him and continued his way into the classrooms. He walked into the large entrance hall, up a flight of stairs, and wheeled into the second classroom on that wing, where he had taught a class called Religious Knowledge. In his pocket a crumpled letter read:

Important Notice to all Staff

Following the findings of the Everleigh Committee regarding the teaching of Religion in Schools, all teaching of religious studies shall cease as of first day of next month. This will also apply to the teaching of the dubious subject "intelligent design" in science studies. Studies in ethics will replace all religious knowledge subjects.

BY ORDER
Basil Rumsden, Headmaster

John entered his classroom of sixteen-year-old boys and went to the blackboard, where he wrote the word "ethics" on the board. At the back of the classroom sat an inspector from the Department of Education.

John then crossed out the word "ethics" and wrote "God," to which the whole class burst into laughter. All eyes spun around to the inspector, who wrote something on the clipboard he had on his lap, and then promptly left the room.

John then turned to the class and said, "How many of you believe in God?"

About three quarters of the class put up their hands.

"How many are not sure?"

A few boys put up their hands.

"I take it, then, the rest of you do not, and so what I would like to do is to ask you why I should not teach you one of the most fascinating subjects: theology."

One hand rose slowly. A boy of curly hair and dark complexion replied, "Well, sir, if I do not believe in God, then why should I have to learn about Him?"

"Do you believe in war?"

"No" said the boy.

"Does that mean you should not learn about it?"

"That's not the same, is it?" the boy replied.

"Haven't I always provided you with a balanced view of everything? I have not tried to convince you of God's existence. But if God exists, what ramifications does this have? Surely an atheist must say that God's existence is one of the most important theories in the world, even if he does not accept that theory. We learned about the earth being flat, even though we now reject that theory because we learned from it."

The door opened and the headmaster entered the classroom. "Mr. Rowntree, can I see you outside, please?"

Outside the classroom, the headmaster said, "Well, you have gone too far this time, Rowntree. You *are* dismissed as a teacher at this school. You received the Everleigh directive, as all schools have. This is the future and you must accept it."

"A future without God?" said John.

"Oh, don't be a hypocrite. Rowntree. You *are* an agnostic."

"It's the principle of the matter, headmaster. It goes beyond my beliefs," replied John.

The headmaster turned on his heel and left John alone to ponder his position. John reentered the classroom, and before he reached the front, he noticed that half of the students were standing.

"Why are you standing?" said John.

"We do this as a mark of support for *you*, sir."

John stopped and then continued to the front of the classroom. He announced, "As you may have guessed, I will be no longer teaching at the school, but I will make a vow to you that I will return."

"Will you fight this?" asked one of the boys.

"Yes, but first you must know your enemy."

A wave of curious looks and raised eyebrows swept the room.

"Let me thank you for your patience in this class when it was called by its rightful name, "Religious Knowledge."

With that, the boys clapped and John, feeling emotional, nodded, shrugged his shoulders, and left the room with mixed feelings. His life was now to take a different course.

**

J ane Thornton, the rebel reporter, hopped out of the London cab and onto the sidewalk outside the British Museum.

"Jane!" a voice cried out.

She spun around and was embraced by another young woman.

"Pip, what are you doing here, of all places?" said the redhead wearing a green jump suit and carrying a rucksack and helmet.

"I'm working as a trainee archaeologist. I was just on my way to a dig with some of the gurus from the museum. What about you, Jane? Haven't seen you since they kicked you out of school—oops, I shouldn't have said that, sorry."

"That's all right. Look, I'm a first-year journalist cadet, and they've sent me on some boring political story. There's some stuffed-shirt Oxford don who's making some government announcement or something." Jane looked at her watch. "I'd better run. They're starting."

They parted ways and she walked onto the polished floors of the museum. It was because of Val that she was in journalism, but that was another story. A crowd of people surrounded three silver-haired men sitting at a long table. Behind the table was a screen with the seal of the "Department of Education" behind it. Television cameras were about to shoot, and journalists were checking their microphones.

"Are we ready?" muttered Sir Ernest Everleigh. "We are here to deliver our full report on the abolishment of religious teaching in all schools in Great Britain. I would like to offer my sincere thanks and congratulations for the fine work that the committee has done, and to all staff who worked tirelessly to meet our deadlines. This report heralds a new landmark for the modernization of our education system. Thank you, ladies and gentlemen. Are there any questions?"

A senior, bespectacled gentleman in a gray tweed suit raised his hand.

"Yes," said Sir Ernest, pointing at the man.

"Don't you think that you, being an atheist, disqualifies you to preside over this report, Sir Ernest?"

"No, I do not. We live in a secular society, so my beliefs are of no relevance to presiding over the report. Next question."

A flurry of questions followed, but Jane could not get a question in, despite catching Sir Ernest's attention at the end of the conference. The committee's publicist cut her question short as being out of time. The crowd broke up, and Jane sat down at the empty conference table to ring her newspaper to file a report. At least she had taped the press conference and was able to upload it to her office by phone. As she hung on the phone, she noticed a business card lying on the ground and picked it up. It read:

Sir Ernest Everleigh

Philosopher

Oxford University

As she talked, she flipped it over and saw the scribbled words "relic…antiquities found…one million dollars US…Khan." Her eyes widened. She hung up the phone abruptly and picked up the card again, peering at it front and back.

Just then she saw Sir Ernest walking toward the entrance. She thrust the card into her brief case and ran. She appeared in front of Sir Ernest, asking, "Sir Ernest, I missed asking you a question at your press conference in there. Can I ask you a couple of questions now?"

Sir Ernest looked at his watch and walked around her curtly and smiled. She came up behind him and said, "Why are you paying a million dollars for a relic?"

The rushing Sir Ernest froze. Jane froze also. Sir Ernest turned around slowly, and this time his smile was nicer.

"What do you know?" asked Sir Ernest.

"I'm the reporter, Sir Ernest, I ask the questions."

"Who told you about the relic?" Sir Ernest was insistent.

"Sir Ernest, you know I can't reveal my source," replied Jane smugly.

Sir Ernest took on a look of submission and paused.

"Yes?" prompted Jane.

"How would you like a cup of coffee?"

# From Dust To DNA

"I magine there is a garden deep in the forest. It is a very neat garden, and you wait to see the gardener…and you wait, a very long time. In fact, you wait millions of years, but no gardener comes. What would you conclude?"

A silence shrouded the Harris lecture theater at Oriel College, Oxford, as Sir Ernest Everleigh's words hung in the air.

"You would conclude that there is no gardener, would you not?"

The students nodded.

"Well, that, ladies and gentlemen, is the demolition of religion's favourite argument for the existence of God, courtesy of the great Scottish philosopher David Hume. In other words, believers in God say that the world has all the hallmarks of intelligent design, and therefore there must have been a designer."

Looks of admiration and intense loyalty circled among the mixture of colorful bohemian students and city types as a premature clap uncorked some of the enthusiasm.

Sir Ernest cut in. "This might have had some weight before Darwin, but—"

A shout from the side door rang out. "Not the same drivel, Everleigh! We're sick of it!"

A couple of athletic students tackled the interjector to the ground as he shouted more.

"That's right, muzzle me again. Why don't you accept my challenge?"

He had almost been bundled out of the door when Sir Ernest shouted back, "Challenge! We have a jester among us!"

The two students stood their captive up to face Sir Ernest for his parting shot.

"Bring him here!" barked Sir Ernest.

The heckler was now on his feet, adjusting his brown jacket and doing up the tie that had been pulled halfway around his neck. He was escorted to the podium.

"What do you want to say, my friend?" asked Sir Ernest.

"Only that I can debate you anytime on God's existence—right here and right now, if you wish. Unless you don't want to be embarrassed in front of your worshippers."

He replied, "All right, we"ll start you off on something easy. We have just been learning about David Hume's debunking of the argument of design. Let's not bore our audience. David Hume's other argument against the existence of God was based on the fact that if God is all powerful, then why would He permit so many religions to flourish all over the world that are plainly inconsistent and incompatible?"

The heckler tilted his head. "What does that prove?"

"Only that your brain does not exist," retorted Sir Ernest.

The students burst out laughing.

At that moment John Rowntree appeared at the side door and made his way up the aisle toward a seat. Sir Ernest glared at him and said, "Stop!"

John stopped and blushed, unaware of the spectacle that was taking place.

"Are you with him?" Sir Ernest said, pointing at the heckler.

"No, I'm just joining your class, Mr. Everleigh."

"Sir Ernest to you. What is your name?"

"John Rowntree, Sir Ernest."

"Well, Mr. Rowntree, watch and learn."

John's jet-black hair and squarish but handsome face gave him an almost priestly air. His father was the vicar of the university church at Oxford. As a former teacher, John's inclination was for the law; but his presence in Sir Ernest's class was no accident, for Sir Ernest was the chairman of the Everleigh Committee, which had effectively abolished religious education in all schools in the United Kingdom.

John sat down next to a female student. He glanced at her maiden-like curves, hazelnut eyes, brown hair and innocent face, but he could only imagine himself pushing her on a swing of flowers in a garden as he sat down. *Silly thought!*

She pulled John aside and said, "Jane Thornton."

John shook her hand, replying, "John Rowntree."

Jane whispered, "That's Arthur Briggs from the theology faculty—he's a tutor there—and he's always causing trouble."

"Free will," answered Briggs, more defiant at Sir Ernest's flippancy.

"Free to worship false gods or burn people at the stake, kill in God's name, or free to do evil. Is this your loving God, Briggs?

Briggs was silent, but Sir Ernest turned to John.

"And Mr. Rowntree, your baptism will be to pronounce the winner of this impromptu debate, since Mr. Briggs has found silence to be golden."

Something stirred inside John. He felt pity for Briggs, who appeared outmatched by Sir Ernest.

"Well, Sir I can only pronounce that Briggs's anger has been outdone by your venom."

Sir Ernest's face changed. "Well, I will have to watch you, Rosetree."

"Rowntree, Sir Ernest."

Sir Ernest grimaced. A small crowd had gathered at the entranceway to the theater, and a middle-aged gentleman in green tweed and crimson tie stepped forward, caressing his beard.

"I will debate you at any time and any place," he proclaimed.

"On what topic?" responded Sir Ernest, reveling in the heated atmosphere.

"Your favorite topic, Sir Ernest: God's existence. Shall we say, the faculty of theology in two weeks? Say, Thursday the 21st of April?"

"I wouldn't set foot in the place. Make it the Oxford Union. Check the availability."

The lecture broke up, and John followed Jane Thornton outside the Harris lecture theater, which formed part of the "Island Site," a complex cluster of buildings in Oriel College that had been developed over six hundred years. The Harris lecture theater was formerly Oriel Court, a tennis court where King Charles I played tennis with his nephew, Prince Rupert, in 1642.

"Is philosophy always like that?" asked John.

"Why don't you come to lunch with some friends of mine, and I'll tell you all about it?" "Fine" replied John.

"By the way, who was the fellow that challenged Sir Ernest to the debate in two weeks?"

"That's Cedric Simons. He's a biblical scholar and professor from the theology faculty. He's very astute, not like that hothead Briggs!"

They walked through the labryrinth of the Island Site and outside into Oriel Square, alongside a row of castlelike buildings. Oriel College was one of the smaller colleges at Oxford, and it created a closer-knit community. They entered a three-story turreted building known as Porter's Lodge, crowned by the Oriel College flag, before crossing the quadrangle to the Junior Common Room. The JCR gave undergraduates a place to "chill out."

A young couple chatting in the lounge stood up as they approached. Jane introduced John, and a young man replied, "Peter Castle. Pleased to meet you. This is Anne Rochester."

"Castle's a good name to have around here," replied John.

They arranged some tea and sandwiches, and Jane opened the discussion.

"Peter, we've just come from Sir Ernest's class, and you wouldn't believe the scene that some of the staff from the theology faculty made."

"What happened?" said Anne.

"Well, a number of them barged into the lecture led by that mad dog Briggs, whom Sir Ernest has always refused to debate. In short, Sir Ernest is going to debate one of them. I believe he is a professor in philosophy or theology or something – Professor Cedric Simons," said Jane.

"Ooh, this is exciting. When is the debate?" said Anne.

"Next Thursday—on the existence of God, of course," replied Jane.

Peter turned to John. "What do you think of Sir Ernest Egoist, John?"

Jane interjected, "John just joined the class."

"Oh, I'm sorry," said Peter. "Philosopher or philanthropist?"

"Neither, actually. I hope to study law."

Peter looked at John, and replied, "Well, that's good, because philosophers make dreams, not money."

"Are you staying at Oriel College?"

"Yes, they've given me a room overlooking…well, the quadrangle, of course." John smiled.

Peter replied, "That's great; there's a lively social scene here, so you should enjoy it." The conversation soon turned to how much money lawyers in London made. John found himself staring at Jane's good looks until he was awoken from behind by a young man in a tennis outfit.

"Jane? I thought you might be here. Ready for our game?" said the young man, gripping his racket.

"Oh, Brendan! I'm so sorry. In all this excitement, I forgot. How stupid of me," said Jane.

Soon they were all gone except for John and Peter. John's curiousity for Jane was growing.

"So Jane and Brendan are…?" John groped for words.

"What would you like them to be?" smiled Peter.

John smiled back. Peter leaned forward and said, "I'll give you a tip, if you want to compete. Are you religious?"

"I have an open mind," replied John.

"She's a true believer in Sir Ernest, and I think you know where he stands. And one more thing: Brendan is Sir Ernest's son."

Peter pulled a card from his pocket and showed it to John.

"Since you have just joined Sir Ernest's class, why don't you go to his dinner party this Friday night? It's by invitation only, but I can't make it, so you might as well have mine."

John's father was an Anglican minister who had wanted John to follow in his footsteps. He had rigorously taught him theology and philosophy to the extent that the pupil outstripped the master; but John, being the defiant and rebellious type, rejected his father's plan for him. Furthermore, the Bible seemed no longer relevant to modern society despite the many good ethical principles that could be distilled from it. Key questions remained unanswered. Why was there evil and suffering in a world that God had designed, and why did God not intervene to stop evil and suffering? Christ's appearance in the world was puzzling. Why had He not come sooner—perhaps at the beginning of civilization? Why had He not visited more frequently to more effectively spread His message, especially in the Far East, which evolved in different religious pathways? Why weren't His miracles enduring so that they could be verified today? The whole system of humans playing the game of life and going to the afterlife seemed implausible. John became an agnostic. He stopped short of becoming an atheist because the possibility of a God without the religious inconsistencies remained to be tested in his mind. It seemed to John that your model of God determined your belief (or not) in God. Was God a kinglike figure with white hair, or a cosmic or intelligent entity? These questions are what fascinated John and led him to teaching religion, despite being an agnostic.

His debating skills and analytical mind attracted him more to being a teacher, but this came to an abrupt end when he was dismissed for teaching religion after Sir Ernest's committee's ban on religious teaching in all UK schools. An unemployed John became adventurous, embraced Eastern religions, and attended a Buddhist monastery in Bhutan that was carved into the side of a cliff. It was where John had sought his "Shrangri-La" and (he believed) experienced enlightenment. It was there that he had arranged to meet the mysterious Martin Crawford, who was now missing in Afghanistan. He had sought him out to learn more about the man who had destroyed his career. Martin had told him about Sir Ernest, and this had prompted John to finally seek out Sir Ernest—to bring his own karma to Sir Ernest.

John's time in Bhutan, and his knowledge of philosophy, imbued in him a clarity of thought. After travelling south from Bhutan through

India, and after observing many religions with different gods, John re-membered Scottish philosopher David Hume's famous theory that a multiplicity of religions implies that it is more likely that God does not exist. John's earlier doubts on religion and the puzzle of Christ, com-bined with David Hume's theory, transformed John into an atheist. Not even miracles moved him, because the great philosopher David Hume had pronounced, "There is not to be found in all history, any miracle attested to by a sufficient number of men, of such unquestioned good sense, education, and learning, as to secure us against all delusion in themselves."

However, on the way back to England, John came across something that occurred after David Hume's time. John's curiosity had led him to Portugal, where he encountered the strange story of the children of Fatima. The reported miracles at Fatima in Portugal in 1917 were wit-nessed by a crowd of seventy thousand to one hundred thousand people, and was later reported in the antireligious government newspaper *O Século*. Three children reported a series of visions of a religious figure. The children maintained their story even after being imprisoned and threatened with being tortured in a pot of burning oil. The miracles reported were that of a dancing and spinning sun, and cures for the disabled people present.

What explained this? The pendulum had swung back, and John again became an agnostic. Apart from his thoughts of retribution, he started to hope that Sir Ernest might provide him with answers.

# TWO

Kenneth Hardwick was a successful newspaperman turned publisher. He had met Sir Ernest before jumping into publishing, initially acting as Sir Ernest's book agent before later offering him a book advance after he joined Norton & Sykes, Publishers. He had boldly put forward Sir Ernest's provocative book *God Does Not Exist* as a sure seller on the mass market. He was right. Advertisements for *God Does Not Exist* adorned the sides of buses running around London.

Hardwick, dressed impeccably in a pinstripe suit, walked into the dimly lit oak panelled reception of Norton & Sykes to collect his messages and caught Sir Ernest behind the *Financial Times* newspaper.

"How much money did you make yesterday, Ernie?" began Hardwick.

"Not enough to pay your royalties, Mr. Hardwick."

"Come in anyway, Ernie. We've got a problem."

Sir Ernest followed Hardwick into a wood-panelled office that more resembled a barrister's chambers than a publisher's office. Hardwick's success had been rewarded with a makeover, including rare artworks cluttering the walls of his office. Picasso splashed alongside Matisse and more modern masters. A sculpture of Our Lady sat religiously on his inlaid red leather desk next to his banker's lamp.

They both sat in the brown leather chesterfield lounge backing onto Hardwick's impressive library.

Sir Ernest sank into the chesterfield and peered at Hardwick. "Well…out with it!"

Hardwick tilted his head back and said, "The vicar of Morgrove is waiting in the boardroom."

"You mean the *ex*-vicar of Morgrove. Isn't that why we backed his book?" replied Sir Ernest. "But what is his problem?"

"He received our letter of offer, and says he is insulted by the offer…"

Sir Ernest smiled. "He'll come 'round. Did he say anything else?"

"No, just that he wanted to meet with us about his book."

Hardwick stood up, approached the door, and Sir Ernest followed, adding, "Let's hear what he has to say."

Hardwick entered the sunlit boardroom and greeted the ex-vicar of Morgrove..

"Alistair! Glad you could come in. You remember Sir Ernest?"

Alistair stood and walked over to both men, shook hands, and they all were seated at the large walnut table flanked with sixteen black leather chairs. The name NORTON & SYKES and their coat of arms was inlaid across the board table as light danced on it, reflected from morning traffic in the busy street below.

"Did you get my edits on your manuscript?" asked Sir Ernest.

"Look, I did, but before talking about that, I don't think I can proceed with your book deal."

Sir Ernest shrugged, and Hardwick replied, "Alistair, you didn't explain much on the phone. You might expound your position for our benefit."

Alistair leaned forward and joined his hands as if in prayer.

"Well," he said, "after I was expelled from the church for my criticism of the Archbishop of Canterbury, I knew my book denouncing all religions would be a best seller. I was contacted by every newspaper, yet your company has offered me a 3 percent gross royalty on sales of my book, which is well under the 10 to 15 percent I would have expected. But what is more galling is that Sir Ernest is to receive 10 percent gross just because he is to go on as a co-writer with me. And that's a joke. He is just going to edit it."

Sir Ernest's face went red. "Who do you think you are? You've never published, and from what I've read, you need me not only to edit it but also to add plenty to it. There are three hundred thousand books written every year, and only a tiny fraction ever get published. You are going to ride on my coattails; and moreover, my name will guarantee you heavy sales, which means big dollars."

Alistair frowned and looked indignant as an awkward silence crept in. Hardwick rescued him.

"Come now, Alistair, you admitted to me that none of the other publishers offered you a deal. On a brighter note, however, I was going to give you some good news."

Alistair's eyes widened.

"If you sign this deal, I can give you a twenty-thousand-pound advance against royalties—and you'll do a lot better than that. What does it matter what Sir Ernest makes?"

Sir Ernest cut in. "See here, I have better things to do. Why don't we just forget it?" He stood up as if to go.

Alistair scratched his head and said, "Wait!"

Sir Ernest turned toward him and said, "Shall I sit down?"

"Yes," he replied.

"Before we go on, there is an important matter to clear up. Have you read my book *God Does Not Exist?*" asked Sir Ernest.

"Yes, I have," replied Alistair.

"And what do you think of it?" continued Sir Ernest.

"It is very well argued, especially those criticisms of the church." Alistair was hesitant.

"Good, I was worried there might have been a problem with you and I being compatible, you being a former vicar. What do you think, Kenneth?"

"I don't see any problems, as long as Alistair allows me to handle the publicity and promotional spin."

"I have no problem with that," replied Alistair.

Sir Ernest rose again. "Good, that's settled. Look, you must excuse me. I have another meeting. Can I leave you both to settle this? I assume it will go off to the lawyers now."

"Yes. Thank you, Sir Ernest," replied Hardwick formally.

# THREE

Arrowfield Manor had been in Sir Ernest's family for generations. It was originally owned and built by the Earl of Arrowfield, a retired soldier who survived the battle of Trafalgar. After some speculative business deals and a spendthrift second wife, the Earl of Arrowfield was forced to sell the manor to Sir Ernest's ancestor. Sir Ernest's newfound publishing wealth had been ploughed into a new wing of the manor. The wing contained a ballroom that doubled as a private debating theater. Sir Ernest's critics dubbed it a place for a mutual admiration society of atheists and scientists. A five-hole golf course had also been built.

The manor served Sir Ernest well because important guests he wished to influence were always impressed with the bluestone walls, labyrinthian garden, and former chapel (now a shrine to humanity). Organic farming was practiced, in keeping with the practices applied at Highgrove by the Prince of Wales. What need of heaven, when Sir Ernest had his own?

Guests had started arriving in the magic twilight of this autumn Friday night for a formal dinner party. The ballroom was alive with chatter flowing from colorful satins and velvets amid black ties and white. John showed the invitation to the doorman, and was ushered in by attendants in black tie and coattails. One of them thrust a glass of champagne in his hand.

He had been told to wear a suit, but many guests had worn black tie. He knew no one.

"John Rowntree, Esquire!"

It was Alistair Thornton. "You don't remember me, do you?"

John shook his head.

"I remember you when your father was the parson with me at my rectory."

John did not know that Thornton was an ex-vicar or that a scandal had occurred. John was pleased to know someone.

"What church was that?" replied John.

"Morgrove. Where is your father stationed now"? asked Thornton.

"He's an associated priest at St. Mary's, Oxford. The University Church."

Thornton smiled "Good old Basil. He always wanted a position there. I assume you're going to Oxford, perhaps following Basil's footsteps?"

"Not quite. I am currently doing an arts degree, but I want to switch to law if I can," replied John.

Jane appeared and kissed Thornton on the cheek.

"Hello, Daddy," she said, to John's surprise.

"Oh, Jane! I thought you might be here." Thornton turned to her. "You look pretty tonight."

"Jane, this is John Rowntree. He's the son of a friend of mine."

Jane was about to speak, but John was quicker. "Reverend, by coincidence I met Jane at lectures this week."

"You're both in Sir Ernest's philosophy class?"

Jane and John nodded. Thornton turned to Jane and commented, "I hope he doesn't make an atheist of you, Jane."

Jane looked coy. "I'm afraid it's too late, Daddy. I'm converted. Anyway, after your criticism of the church, I would have thought you've come to the same view."

"No, I have not," replied Thornton, "and I hope my views on the church have not influenced you."

"Well, no one can explain to me why bad things happen. Anyway, I made my own mind up," she replied.

"Your mother will not be happy, and I daresay I will get the blame. Look, let me get you both a drink."

"I'm fine," replied John, lifting his champagne glass.

As Thornton left, Jane and John caught each other's eyes. John spoke first.

"It looks as though we both have fathers who are in the church."

"You don't know?" asked Jane.

"Know what?" asked John.

"My father was asked to leave his position at his church because he criticized the power brokers in the church. A real no-no, as you would know! Excuse the pun!"

"Oh, I'm sorry. I didn't know," John said sheepishly.

"But that's the bad news. The good news is that he's publishing a new book," Jane continued.

"What about?" asked John.

"Well, actually, it is on the same stuff he was sacked over," Jane pondered and paused. "I suppose it will sell well then." She laughed.

"Yes, controversy sells," said John.

Thornton returned with some drinks and the conversation meandered for a while until they were joined by other students. One of them stood in front of John in an almost confrontational way.

"Brendan Everleigh," announced the student.

"John Rowntree." John recognized him as the student who seemed to be going out with Jane. Curiously, Jane left with some other students when Brendan Everleigh had arrived, leaving John and Brendan awkwardly together.

"Are you related to Sir Ernest?" asked John.

Brendan smiled "Yes, of course! He's my father!"

"I haven't seen Lady Everleigh—your mother?" continued John.

"It was my younger brother, you see…how he was born. My mother died," replied Brendan.

"I'm sorry. Difficult childbirth?" commented John.

"No, it was my brother's condition that led to her suicide."

John's curiosity was heightened but interrupted when a bell rang in the ballroom.

"Oh, good!" said Brendan, relieved to change the subject. "Dad is giving one of his impromptu speeches."

The ballroom was now packed with guests, and Sir Ernest's staff had raised a podium at the end of the room, where he stood gulping some champagne before handing the empty glass to a waiter.

"Ladies and gentlemen, welcome here tonight. And to all my new students, welcome to the end of the first week of term. I have a little poem to read to you:

There once was a girl called Goldilocks

Who thought of life as building blocks

Of complexity without destiny
Of heresy without clarity
But through Darwin's eyes
Oh what a prize!
Seeing all of life's perfection

'Twas caused by natural selection."

A round of clapping quickly followed, but the tapping of an empty champagne glass cut it short. John unexpectedly blurted out his own poem as a mass of heads craned to see this maverick poet:

"Tiger! Tiger! burning bright
In the forests of the night,
What immortal hand or eye
Could frame thy fearful symmetry?"

A few chuckles were muffled as Sir Ernest's smiling face turned ashen, but he pulled on his lapels, ignoring the interjection, to launch his soliloquy: "Thank you all. And now I say, is it too harsh to see God as some type of vicious schoolmaster hovering over us as His pupils?"

Sir Ernest's hands hovered in front of him, as if to simulate God.

"And we, having no escape from His wrath, for He reads our every thought!"

Sir Ernest was now pointing at his temple.

"And yet He is omnipotent and omniscient and knows our fate—but!"

His finger was now pointing upward.

"We have free will, and although He made us, He had no hand in our decisions. And so He is not a vicious schoolmaster, but we *will* be punished if we do not exercise our free will in a certain way, or do evil before judgment day."

Another round of clapping quickly followed, and Sir Ernest stepped from the podium. An uneasy silence gathered, and this time heads turned slowly to the back of the room to see John deliver his riposte:

"Thou Great First Cause, least Understood!

Who all my Sense confin'd

To know but this—that Thou art

Good, And that my self am blind:

Yet gave me, in this dark Estate

To see the Good from Ill

And binding Nature fast in Fate

Left free the Human Will."

Sir Ernest was not accustomed to being upstaged. He glared at John, but paused before reacting. His own sense of mischievous humor rose up, and he burst out laughing.

"A toast, to William Blake, sir, and to our young poet up the back!"

Everyone was soon drinking champagne and puffing, "To Blake!

Jane nestled up to John. "I see your flair for poetry, but I didn't recognize the other poet."

"Alexander Pope," replied John.

Although John had defied Sir Ernest's apparent hegemony among Oxford's philosophical elite, Jane found herself attracted to John. Very soon they were kissing on Sir Ernest's ornate terrace, but unfortunately this caught the eye of Brendan Everleigh, who discreetly avoided them. Later, Jane agreed to see John for a night of joint study and wine.

Sir Ernest was still standing at the podium when a middle-aged man with brown hair, glasses, and black tie approached him.

"Professor," declared Sir Ernest. "Thank you for coming!"

"Sir Ernest, please call me Ian," replied Professor Ian Cummings, another Oxford don who specialized in genetics.

"Tell me, Ian, whatever happened to the wonderful work you were doing on mapping the human genome?" asked Sir Ernest.

Ian's face dropped, but he said, "Ran into a spot of trouble. My two colleagues, Jim Alsop and Ted McEwen, have left the university and set up a biotech company."

"That should be good for you, surely?" asked Sir Ernest.

"Except that I was given no shares in the company, and they have stolen my technologies!" replied Ian.

"What! That's preposterous! How did it come to that?" exclaimed Sir Ernest.

"Well, we were arguing. I wanted our human genome project to be our flagship, and they had promised that it would be, and then they reneged and I was furious. They basically walked out and left the university and formed the company. One of their financier friends raised them five million pounds, and they now have a state-of-the-art biotech facility in an industrial estate, with twenty-five staff and world-class facilities. What is galling is that they have the very equipment we could not afford at the university to run my human genome project. And not only that, but they are also running the genome project themselves, without me!" Ian's face was now red with anger. "These chaps have the hides of elephants," commented Sir Ernest. "You know, I have a human genome project myself."

"Oh, and what is that?" frowned Ian.

"Well, I wish to prove a philosophical point, namely, that man was an accident and not created by God," replied Sir Ernest.

"But doesn't Darwin do that by showing that man evolved by natural selection?" said Ian. "Not quite. Natural selection can only occur through mutation of the genes in DNA, and thus the DNA mechanism itself is said to be God's creation. Thus, chaos or randomness must be shown to be the father of DNA; and to do that, we need mathematics applied to biology," postulated Sir Ernest.

"Yes, I see. The equipment they have would be ideal for that project, and that is a multimillion-pound project," observed Ian.

Sir Ernest stared through Ian as if his mind was a thousand miles away. Sir Ernest was soon surrounded by other guests, but before he joined them he took Ian aside and said, "Ian, I would like you to ring me next week. We'll have a proper chat. Something should be done about this."

# FOUR

A few days had passed since the party, and John strolled eagerly to his second lecture with Sir Ernest. The sun sparkled through a line of oaks and elms, throwing speckled shadows along the historic stone wall that lined his path. Oxford made you feel part of something great, with its rich history and aura. John turned off the pathway toward his lecture theater and was surprised to hear his father's voice a short distance behind him.

"John! John!" His voice was earnest and puffing.

"Hello, father. Look, I'm off to lectures."

John kept walking, and the Reverend Basil Rowntree caught up.

"John, I just heard that you have joined Sir Ernest Everleigh's philosophy class. Why have you defied me on this?"

John stopped and faced his father. "I have a mind of my own, you know. I don't understand you! First you say you understand that I don't go church. It's my decision, and I am agnostic, so why would you worry about Sir Everleigh?"

"I do accept that, but the man is ruthless and anti-all religions. He will only turn you into a church-hating atheist," pronounced his father.

"No one will turn me into anything. I will be totally impartial in approaching his views, but I will have an open mind…. I will be late."

John started to walk again, with his father keeping pace.

"It's not only you I worry about. I confess that I worry how it will look if I, as a member of the clergy, can't even maintain the spiritual needs of my own son!"

"Don't put that on me. I would have thought the damage is already done in that regard."

His father stopped to let him go on, but added, "John, there is something I must warn you about."

John stopped and turned toward him, saying, "What now?"

"Well, I received a call from that Alistair Thornton, which I confess was a great surprise after what he has done to the church. In any event, we had a peculiar chat. He seemed very curious as to why my son had joined Sir Ernest's class. I told him that you wanted to be a teacher and had a natural affinity for philosophy, which I have always said you do, if you use it wisely. Now, with you wanting to study law, this gives an unstable picture, I suppose. Anyway, he told me about some young, brash fellow reciting Blake, which spoiled some atheistic jaunt of Sir Ernest. But he warned that this fellow would be sorry he crossed him. The word 'destroyed' was even used. Do you get the gist of that?"

"John looked at the ground and replied, "This is going to be fun!"

His father groaned, and John sped off to his lecture.

John almost bumped into Sir Ernest coming out of the staff common room just before he reached Harris lecture theater.

"Good morning, Sir Ernest," muttered John.

"Morn-eeng!" screeched Sir Ernest, brushing past him.

Intense conversation resonating from students in the main quad spilled into the lecture theater. Sir Ernest was busy at the whiteboard, scribbling some points. He wrote *The problem of evil* on the board. The conversation died down naturally, and Sir Ernest moved gracefully to face his students. John sat at the back of the lecture theater, as if to place himself out of harm's way. Still, Sir Ernest's confident voice filled the lecture theater:

"One of the key issues grappled by theologians and philosophers was the problem of evil. Who can tell me what this problem is?"

An enthusiastic young man at the front remarked, "If God is good, why does He allow evil in the world?"

"Mmm, yes. And the usual answer is?" hummed Sir Ernest.

Another voice responded, "To have free will, you need both good and evil."

Sir Ernest walked back to the podium, picked up what appeared to be a Bible, and continued, "Well, in precise terms, the issue is of great significance because it is more than just a question that one might put to God—if one is able to question God. It is a major factor in many people's minds as to whether God exists at all."

Sir Ernest now was looking at his Bible. "In fact, the Bible itself, in the book of Job, relates Job challenging God in many ways, but generally the question 'Why is there suffering?' I quote what God says to Job: 'Where were you when I laid the earth's foundations?' or, further on, 'Who endowed the heart with wisdom or gave understanding to the mind?'

What is God's defense here?"

The same young man responded, "God is saying that Job is not in the business of creating, and therefore cannot judge the creator."

"Yes, that's good," said Sir Ernest, "but what I would like to do now is gauge where you all lie on this issue. Hands up, those who agree that the problem of evil is defensible?"

A few hands went up.

"I would like those people to come up the front."

Four students arrived at the front.

"Oh, I see our poet believes the problem can be defended."

Sir Ernest was referring to John, who had joined the group of defenders.

"The last person standing wins the debate. Each of you must provide an arguable defense against the argument from evil. By evil, I include suffering of any type. You will then defend it against me. The students will vote on who wins each debate. Are you ready?"

They nodded. The first student, Horace Wilkins, was a plump, boyish young man with black woolly hair who seemed keen to try his luck. "No pain, no gain," he pronounced and stepped back, folding his arms.

"Is that it?" replied Sir Ernest. "Doesn't this paint God as a nasty tyrant, putting man through suffering sometimes approaching torture? As Einstein wondered, 'Did God have any choice in the way He made the world?' 'If God exists, then He is surely omnipotent, and therefore powerful enough to give us gain with no pain or less pain, but He has not. It is more likely, therefore, that He does not exist."

Sir Ernest turned to the class. "All those in favour of Mr. Wilkins?

A few hands went up.

"Against?"

A majority of hands rose.

"Take your seat, Mr. Wilkins," directed Sir Ernest, with a smug look on his face.

The second student, Joe Carter, wore thick spectacles with an old green pullover and jeans, and generally appeared as though he had slept in what he was wearing. He stepped forward. "If we suffer in this lifetime," he said, "it is but a second in the span of eternity that will follow this life, which will engrave its wise marks on us forever. God is a wise teacher."

"Is God omnipotent in your model, Mr. Carter?"

"Why, yes He is," replied Carter.

"Then in etching this lesson on our eternal soul, what lesson did the elephant man learn by being horribly deformed, and then kicked and spat on all his life?"

Carter was silent. Shortly afterward he sat down.

Alison Cooper was freckled, with wavy red hair and a blue cotton blouse and medium-length olive green skirt.

She opened her argument: "Everything happens for a reason, but we may never know what that is. Everything is connected by a large plan: God's plan. Yes, evil exists, but it is a metamorphosis—some type or process where the human race will eventually come good and join with God."

Sir Ernest paused and then replied, "Yes, that is a nice thought, but did fifty-five million people have to die in our last great war? And is it necessary for children to starve to death in many parts of the world, to improve the world? Surely a great designer of worlds could have designed a more elegant method of improving the world. Why could not the world be built without evil, but still with a learning process without suffering?"

Ms. Cooper replied, "The greatest achievements in history have risen from great hardship. Climbing Mount Everest is a daring feat because many die in the process. Peace is beautiful for the billions because of the millions that die. God may have other methods, but this is the best method to create the most noble being."

Sir Ernest smiled. "Surely the most noble being is the one created out of love, not evil?"

The hand count proceeded, and Ms. Cooper was narrowly defeated and sat down with a compliment from Sir Ernest: "Well fought, Ms. Cooper. Thank you."

Sir Ernest then turned to John Rowntree with the look of a cat who had swallowed the canary. "Well, our poet, what have you got to say for yourself?"

"Einstein had the key," said John. "He wondered whether God had any choice in the type of world that was created. If He did not, then God was not responsible for evil in the world. Or, to put it a better way, the probability of God existing is not diminished by the presence of evil. Thus the question is whether God had any choice. He would only have no choice if He were not omnipotent." At this, a gasp went around the theater. "A creator who made billions of stars is still God if He could only do it one way," responded John.

Sir Ernest interjected, "You assert that God is not omnipotent, then?"

"In the sense that He could not have made a perfect world, Yes," John replied.

"Prove it!" blurted Sir Ernest.

A low "oooh!" swept across the theater.

John moved to the blackboard and drew two circles. "The word *omnipotence* has an unknown meaning to us. This is because it is a man-made concept that has not been tested by logic or evidence. If God is omnipotent, then He can create a God identical to himself." John then wrote the word *God* inside each circle. "If so, then if God number one does something inconsistent with what God number two is doing, then both gods are not omnipotent. It could be objected that God number one could remove God number two, and then do what could not be done with two gods, but so could God number two."

Sir Ernest injected, "A clever logic twist, Mr. Rowntree. This is like saying God cannot make a God that is more powerful than He is. This is merely a nonsense, like saying God cannot make two plus two equal five. What do you say to that?"

"I say that God cannot make two plus two equal five, but why is God relieved from being able to change logic? Is not good the opposite of evil in logic? Even the most pain-free world would contain people who, with free thought, could think and do evil by logical possibility in our world. How can we understand a strange pain-free world well enough to make any comment about it in this world?"

Sir Ernest interjected again, "It is not good enough to say God is not omnipotent because two plus two cannot equal five. You must say something that is not a logic trap."

"But Sir Ernest, God creating a second God is logically consistent because they are both equally powerful. I don't think *omnipotent* means that there cannot be two gods. In fact, in Christian religion, they believe in a trinity of three gods in one. Which is most powerful? Let me put another quality of God to you. God could not diminish His power if He were omnipotent, because then He would not be omnipotent."

"Mr. Rowntree, this is another circular logic trap. Can God make lightning if He turns off His lightning-maker?"

John was defiant. "What I am demonstrating is that, with or without logic, the meaning of omnipotent sits in uncharted waters, and you cannot say whether a world without evil is its own logic trap anyway. If we all use a reasonable meaning of 'omnipotent' such as 'omnipotent' means the power to do what is logically possible and not absurd then God is omnipotent, and therefore Einstein's question can be answered 'no'— because it was not possible to have chosen a better world."

Sir Ernest paused and then said, "For the benefit of everyone, that means?"

"Well, that means that God probably had no choice in the way He created the universe, but it remains awesome whichever way you look at it." John folded his arms and grinned before continuing: "What impudent creatures we are! Someone creates something of such extraordinary beauty and majesty, but because of historical religious fervor about omnipotence, people conclude that God does not exist. Omnipotence is the luxury atheists use to disprove God's existence—including you, Sir Ernest."

There was a chuckle or two from the students as John stood awaiting the verdict. Sir Ernest asked for a show of hands. "All those in favour of Mr. Rowntree?" A sea of hands rose in the lecture theater, with Sir Ernest's loyal followers strangely abstaining, prompting Sir Ernest to dispense with the "no" vote and storm out of the lecture theater in fury.

# FIVE

J ohn saw Jane leave the lecture theater quickly, and he briskly followed her. However, someone else blocked his way, outstretching his hand to greet him.

"Cedric Simons. I believe you are John Rowntree"

John shook his hand with surprise, but recognized him as the professor who challenged Sir Ernest during his first lecture.

"I watched your performance today. You have extraordinary talent as a debater, and you have an excellent grasp of theology."

John blushed and replied, "I see myself as more a philosopher. My father is a theologian, and I follow a different path than he does."

Cedric pulled him away from the flow of students leaving the theater and continued, "You may be aware that I have challenged Sir Ernest to a debate next Thursday. Sir Ernest has himself and two students on his debating team. I would like you to join Arthur Briggs and myself as the third member of our debating team. What do you say?"

John was nonplussed. "Professor Simons, don't take my debate inside to mean that I am strongly religious. Again, that is the path my father has taken. I am a philosopher, not a staunch defender of theology.

Professor Simons smiled. "Look, think it over. Here is my card. Come over and visit us at the theology faculty anytime."

They shook hands and parted ways.

John caught up with Jane. They had met two days earlier in John's room at Oriel College for some philosophical study, but the first glass of wine led to their romantic entwinement.

"What's the hurry?" called out John.

Jane glared at John.

"Well?" pressed John.

"You see, you've ruffled some feathers, and Brendan says you shouldn't be in Sir Ernest's class."

"Brendan! I thought he was history," protested John.

"He's still my friend. Look, John, I don't know. I am in two minds. Let me be."

John held her hand and she gently broke away, adding, "For now."

John stood still as Jane moved reluctantly on her way, without John seeing the tear that ran down her cheek.

Later that day John made his way over to the faculty of theology and was soon waiting outside Professor Simons' office. Half an hour went by, and he stood up to go. He went over to the secretary and said, "Can you tell the professor that he can count me in on his debating team for this Thursday?" The secretary gave him a mischievous glance and replied, "He'll be happy, as he was counting on you."

The day before the debate John received a phone call on his mobile phone from Professor Simons.

"John, I received your message. Thank you for your support. Can you come over today to go over the debate material?"

"What's the topic of the debate?" asked John

"Existence of God," replied Professor Simons.

"I mean, what aspect are we debating?" asked John.

"Darwin versus intelligent design, and of course Sir Ernest is on Darwin's side."

"That's a tough debate. We will need every ounce of skill," replied John.

"Can you be at my office after lunch, say at three?" proposed the professor.

"See you there," agreed John.

Thursday, the day of the debate, had arrived. John had met the professor and Arthur Briggs to train for the debate and looked forward to the challenge. The debate was at 7:00 p.m. After an early dinner at 5:30 p.m., John decided to walk for half an hour to cool his nerves. He had walked around the grounds and was about twenty meters from the Oxford Union building when he came upon a group that appeared to be approaching the Oxford Union for the debate. No one else was around, and it was now dark.

They appeared to be walking toward him rather than the debating chamber, and as they came closer he could see four males dressed in black or brown ski jackets, each with the hood over his head. John's adrenalin rushed, but he thought, "This is Oxford!" Two of them carried a large sack. As they shuffled passed him, he felt a little uneasy, and then without warning he found the sack had been pulled over his head as he was tackled rugby-style and thrown to the ground, with a number of them on top of him.

John struggled and shouted, "Get off! You bastards!" but to no avail. As he called for help again, he was punched hard and it winded him, causing him to fall silent. His struggling died out as he felt himself being tied up and carried away. They ran, carrying him to the street, where he was thrown into the back of a vehicle. It must have been a four-wheel-drive or van, as he found himself lying on a flat surface.

None of them spoke, but at least two of them kept him confined to the back of the van. He struggled again but was punched, and he became still. He then protested, "Hey, you chaps must have the wrong guy!" but he received no response. He could feel someone loosening the rope allowing him to breath more easily. A feeling of dread overcame John as his mind raced with the horrible possibilities. Still, they had not shown their faces or spoken, and he was still alive. He reasoned that it must be a nasty university prank taken too far.

He could smell alcohol around him as the vehicle wound its way across the countryside to its unknown destination. The vibration of the chassis soothed his nerves, and he waited. He suddenly realized:

*the debate.* He was going to miss it and let down Professor Simons and Briggs. A feeling of intense disappointment now replaced the dread.

Back at the Oxford Union, the debate was about to begin. The Oxford Union debating chamber was housed in a freestanding cluster of ornate red brick buildings with fairy-tale turrets and slate roofs dating from the nineteenth century and renowned as a training ground for future politicians. The debating chamber itself, with its salmon pink walls, high ceilings, and cold, polished wooden floors, was reminiscent of a school hall with church pews to house the audience. A piano stood in the corner not far from the podium, in front of a projector screen for presentations. Behind the audience stood a series of busts of former Prime Minister Edward Heath, the first Marquess Curzon of Kedleston, and others. This night the "pews" were full, with many standing, and the upstairs gallery was also full.

Professor Simons had elected to continue the debate, with only two on his team, against Sir Ernest. Professor Simons was well into the debate:

"And there are gaps in Darwin's theory. I am not asserting that Darwin's theory is wrong. It is a sound theory, and evidence mounts to support it, but the principle of irreducible complexity is an anomaly to Darwinists. Darwin postulates that mutations in a species result in both weaker and stronger variants of that species, and that the weak die and strong survive—survival of the fittest. However, the morphological changes that take place in some species are inexplicable by Darwin's natural selection process. For example, the development of the eye. A Darwinist has to say that a blind animal had offspring that had mutations which became eyes. It is a giant leap that an instrument as intricate as the eye arose out of malformed body parts. The inference is that another process is at play. Science has no explanation as to what it is. God is the explanation."

The van came to rest, and John was then marched across soft grass when his captors stopped dead.

"What's that?" one of them said.

"Shh!" came the reply. They stood still.

John saw his chance. "Help! Help!" he shouted.

John felt them shaking and squeezing his arms. Suddenly, John heard a heavy punch and shriek of pain, but John felt nothing. Perhaps he was suffering shock. A second heavy punch was heard, and gasping for breath by one of his winded captors. He felt their grip vanish, and he fell to the ground. He could hear them running away in the dark as he lay on the cold grass.

John struggled on the ground shouting again, "Help!" when a voice said, "Settle down. Settle down. They've gone!"

John realized that a Good Samaritan had arrived on the scene. Soon the hood was off and John saw that he was in the grounds of a country church, with two men quickly removing the rope and sack that bound him. One of the men appeared to be a parson. The other man was well built with sandy red hair.

"Come inside, and we will call the police," said the parson.

John was led slowly inside, feeling groggy from the ordeal, and soon was sitting in the rectory sipping tea given to him by the parson's wife.

"The police are on their way. Do you know who did this?" said the parson.

"No idea. By the way, where am I?" asked John.

"Chipping Norton," said the parson's wife. "Seems like a university prank?" mumbled John.

"My name is James Dunkley, and this is my wife," said the parson.

The second man then entered the rectory, announcing, "They've cleared out in their van. I couldn't get the number plate. They must have smashed the lamp." He came up to John and introduced himself. "Paul Sanders."

The parson then explained, "Paul interrupted your kidnapping with some sharp blows to…"

John nodded. "I think I heard your handiwork. I'm indebted to you and Mr. Dunkley." He shook Paul's hand.

"I found this mobile phone on the grass. Is it yours?" The parson was holding a silver mobile phone.

John took it in his hand and activated the screen. "No."

"You shouldn't touch it. The police could get fingerprints," advised Paul.

John put it on the table. The police arrived as they were still speaking.

"Detective Chief Inspector Townsend," announced a dark-haired man with moustache. He was dressed in plainclothes. "And this is Detective Chief Inspector Braun. DCI Braun was a well-dressed woman with fair hair.

"Now who was kidnapped?" asked DCI Townsend.

"I was," said John.

DCI Braun sat down at the table and began writing notes. John quickly related the story and handed over the mobile phone.

They soon left, and Paul said to John, "Why don't I drive you back to Oxford?"

"Thanks, that would be great," replied John.

The debate at the Oxford Union had raged, and Sir Ernest was giving his address.

"Creationism is long dead. This cancer is creeping back into society and our schools. Scientists are again battling the forces of ignorance that push intelligent design. These forces even wish intelligent design taught in schools as part of the science curriculum. It is bad enough that it is taught in religious studies. However, more precisely I refer to this curious term 'irreducible complexity.' This insidious term is an unwelcome guest in the Darwinist vocabulary and should be turned away.

"Our opponents postulate that complex organs such as the eye could not have developed without divine intervention. However, I would like to refer to the excellent work Professor Suzuki of Canada has done in postulating how natural selection could have produced the eye. His work has been shown around the world on television, and without the footage I can only describe the elegant explanation he has given for emergence of the eye. A mutation appears, and some light-sensitive tissue appears on the skin. It provides some advantage to the mutant, who finds the ability to sense light an advantage in the habitat that it finds itself in. Mutants with a light-sensitive piece of tissue survive more than other non mutants of the species. Later, a further mutation occurs at the light-sensitive spot, where this spot is enhanced in some way that provides a little improvement.

"Other mutations occur that are not so good, and these mutants do not survive. The improved mutation of the light-sensitive spot provides more information to the animal than previously, and again an advantage emerges. This process goes on countless times, until a crude eye becomes the mutation, and still there is a long way to go. But the functionality of that crude eye is enough to give a great advantage as an improved sensor to that animal, and gradually the advantage increases as a multitude of further mutations occur and only one with a real eye emerges.

"This is the elegance of natural selection: over millions of years, mutations can produce complexity that is reducible into these iterations. So I reject the term 'irreducible complexity' as invalid when applied to this context.

"Man and apes are 98 percent similar, genetically. This missing 2 percent difference was the only stumbling block to showing common ancestry. However, a discovery explaining the chromosome difference occurred. Man has forty-six chromosomes, or twenty-three pairs; and apes have forty-eight chromosomes, or twenty-four pairs. Scientists discovered that human chromosome number two is, in fact, a fusion of chromosomes explaining the difference. This type of evidence continues to fortify Darwin's theory of evolution."

Professor Simons gave his reply, but the debate was over, in the judges' minds. Sir Ernest's team had won.


John had thanked the parson and his wife, and was now being driven in Paul's Jaguar back to Oxford, which was over twenty kilometres on the return journey by expressway. Paul was a former Royal Marine who had served in Northern Ireland some years ago before joining the British SAS to serve in Afghanistan some years after 9/11. Like many veterans he had returned to his hometown of Chipping Norton to find everything foreign to him. Horrible images possessed him that he could not forget. He had tried. His psychiatrist had given him heavy medication. This did the job—too well. He could not hold a single thought. The pills found their way down the sink. Having no wife to help him,

Paul had approached Reverend Dunkley that night for counseling after hearing that Reverend Dunkley had moved from Northern Ireland, where he had served as an army chaplain. Veterans needed someone who understood—someone they could trust. Reverend Dunkley had urged Paul to "move on" and let the "grass grow" over these thoughts of war, when John descended on the church grounds. Unwittingly, John was to become the key to Paul's recovery.

"What do you do?" asked Paul.

"I'm at Oxford doing an arts course," replied John.

"What does being at Oxford mean, exactly?" Paul was being coy.

"Oh, well, I stay in Oriel College, where I go to lectures and study."

"So you have left home and you don't work?"

"That's partly right, except I can go home after term."

"Why do you think they picked on you?" said Paul.

"Wrong place at the wrong time, I guess," replied John.

The traffic was streaming by, dazzling John's eyes with their headlights.

"Have you got under anyone's skin lately?" asked Paul.

"I have been a little more vocal than usual…. I mean, in my philosophy course, the students worship this pompous lecturer. He's quite a famous writer, and he's wealthy. His name is Sir Ernest Everleigh. Heard of him?"

"Yes" said Paul, keeping his gaze on the road ahead.

"I have caused a bit of stir, because I am going out with Jane Thornton, who is Sir Ernest's son's old girlfriend."

Paul smiled and whistled.

John continued, "To make matters worse, I have been a bit provocative a couple of times. But I don't think…." John stared into space.

"Don't think what?" asked Paul.

"Well, there are some fanatics, but I wonder if they are capable of doing what was done to me tonight."

"Was there any advantage in them doing that to you tonight?" Paul was coming to life.

"No, except I didn't turn up for a major debate with Sir Ernest," John spoke quickly.

"You mean 'yes' then, don't you? You were neatly sidelined in a key debate. Kidnappings like the one tonight don't happen to people like you for nothing. Someone drove you over twenty kilometers. You were not robbed, and you were not really hurt, at least physically." Paul drove on into the night.

"What's your background?" asked John.

Paul explained his military background.

"And you are a member of the parson's church?"

"Well, yes and no. Before the war I was a Catholic priest at a near-by church. Strangely, our paths crossed in the local community, and we became friends. We both saw so many lives in tatters. It was a real challenge to try and help these people. I've fought in Afghanistan, but this was a different type of fight. We were fighting pain and suffering. Unfortunately it got to the parson, and he began to drink. Keep this to yourself. He would say to me, 'Paul, what are we doing here?' And I would say, 'To help them and to bring God to them—that's our job.'

"Sometimes it got tough. One day I got a call from a mother whose son was born a quadriplegic. I went to the hospital to give them moral support because they were members of our parish. The father says to me 'Why?' I responded that God felt their pain also, and would help. 'How?' said the father. I would just say, 'He will,' but what do you say?

"It got worse. They came to me and said that there could be grounds for euthanasia if they took their son to Switzerland. The father said, 'God has not provided comfort for my son. It is too much of a cross to bear. Surely this is not part of God's plan.'"

"What did you say?" asked John.

"I said, 'It's tough, but we cannot play God.'

"The old question always comes up: 'Why do bad things happen?'" said John. "You reminded me of a true story I heard about a hanging in Auschwitz. As the executed man was hanging in front of the prisoners, someone shouted, 'Where is God in all this?' and someone replied, 'He is hanging up there.'"

Paul was silent.

"This is one the subjects of my work: the philosophy of theology," added John. The questions those parents raised with you remain unanswered, but they are not unanswerable." Paul glanced curiously at John, prompting the latter to continue: "Well, one possible answer is that God doesn't want this any more than you or I, but this is the best of all possible worlds. There is plenty of evidence for this. Man has many defects. In fact, the famous intellectual Arthur Koestler once said, ; 'Man has a design defect.' Man can have mental illnesses that prevent him from choosing right from wrong—a pretty fundamental ability if you were going to create a world. Likewise all the other disabilities. They can't be explained away by saying that they were put there to test us or to make the world nobler. There would be better ways to do this in a perfect world by a God who made the world in seven days.

"Take even communicating between God and man. We have no telephone to God, and then there is the multiplicity of religions that are not really consistent with each other. God's plan would surely involve one religion, even in an imperfect world. This is was one of the reasons I am agnostic."

"You're agnostic!" exclaimed Paul.

"Yes," replied John.

"Yet you study theology," smiled Paul.

"Well, yes. My father is an associated priest at St Mary's of Oxford," replied John.

"Like father, like son, but not really," joked Paul.

"What about you, Paul? You've been through the mill. Are you still religious?"

Paul paused while he accelerated past a truck and settled back in the left lane once ahead. "To answer your question, I will have to tell you a strange story. I wanted to discuss the big issues with my superiors in the church. I needed answers. People were leaving my church unless I could provide convincing answers to all these difficult questions. There's too much anti-religious movement now in our media to lecture the public with parables that don't answer their basic questions, or at least provide intelligent, *possible* answers.

"So I went down to London to see the archbishop. Of course, I didn't get to see him; but I did meet with a bishop, but he gave me no answers. I was on my way out of his office when a young priest stopped me. He said, 'Okay, you didn't hear it from me, but contact this man.' I looked at the card he gave me with surprise. It was the card of a priest based in the Vatican."

"Did you contact him?" asked John.

"Yes, I did; but look, we're here now. Let's leave it for another time."

Paul dropped John off at Oriel College. As he left the car, John said "Paul, thanks a lot for your help. If you are ever near Oxford, drop in. Here's my mobile." John wrote his mobile number on the back of a card and gave it to Paul, who thanked him and went on his way.

# SIX

The next morning, John couldn't wait to visit Cedric Simons and Arthur Briggs to explain to them what had happened.

"That's disgusting," said Professor Simons.

"It's beyond a university prank; it's a police matter," proclaimed Briggs, with a mad look in his eyes.

"Well the police came, actually," explained John.

"I hope they investigate that unholy bunch from top to bottom," said Briggs.

"I agree," said Professor Simons.

"They left no clues except for a mobile phone, but the police have that now," said John.

"Oh, that will finish them. That's good news," smiled Briggs.

John nodded before saying goodbye and left for class.


John entered his philosophy class that Friday morning feeling some humiliation at what they had done to him—whoever it was. As he sat waiting for Sir Ernest, his mobile rang.

"Detective Chief Inspector Townsend here, Mr. Rowntree. I trust you are feeling better today."

"Yes, thank you," replied John.

"We have found the identity of the person who owns the phone," said DCI Townsend. "It's Jane Thornton"

John felt sick but composed himself. "That's not possible."

"There's no doubt. DCI Braun has already contacted her, and she's confirmed it was stolen last night. We will be investigating the matter further. Anyway, I just thought you might like to know."

Jane Thornton was "too wild" or "too hard to handle," as her distraught mother had said when Jane was expelled from boarding school, after she had "run off with a rich Arab." This included flying over London, sipping champagne in his private jet, before sneaking back through the hospital infirmary hoping that no one would notice. Unfortunately, an impromptu medical examination revealed a heavy intoxication that exposed her folly.

At home she grew restless. She knew better than her mother—"simple woman," Jane thought—and who did not understand the world like she did. After slapping her mother when she was drunk, Jane was sent to a boot camp "for brats." After a month of suffering from cold nights in a wilderness setting, she still refused to say sorry to her mother. Another month went by, and she was allowed to speak to her parents but still refused to say sorry.

The boot camp had a special lady experienced in such cases. Her name was Val, and she arrived in the third month. Val was a big lady with a big determination and a unique understanding of the rebellious. Val explained to Jane that her parents loved her, but Val did not, and issued a challenge. Jane could rebel against Val as much as she liked, providing she survived a *little* test.

Val would march three girls, including Jane, deep into the forest, where there was a real danger of becoming lost. Whoever arrived back in camp first would be sent home. Jane had smiled at the thought, as she was the best athlete of the three girls chosen; but on turning for home, Val fell to the ground clutching her chest gasping, "My heart pills!"

One of the girls went through Val's rucksack and secretly pocketed the pills. Val exclaimed, "You must go to camp and return with my pills—quickly!"

The three girls rushed back toward the camp, when they stopped together, puffing heavily. The girl who had taken the pills held them up, laughing, "Well, that's the end of that old cow!" Jane, disgusted, snatched the pills away from her, screaming "Are you mad?"

The other girls laughed and said, "This is our chance. We'll be rid of that bitch! Keep moving!" But Jane stopped and let the others return. Jane retraced her steps to Val and gave the pills to her.

As she did, Val took the pills from her and said, "So you stole the pills, Jane!"

Jane's face went white. "I didn't! They took them."

Val smiled "I know. I told them to. It was part of your test." She then hugged Jane, who had burst into tears. "You do have a heart, Jane."

Jane replied, "Aren't you going to take your pills?"

"I think I would rather die than see you rude to your mother again," said Val. "All right, all right, I'll do it!" and Val took her pills.

Later, Jane reconciled with her mother and father, and was quietly happy that it had happened. What she did not know was that Val had never suffered a heart attack and had arranged for two outside girls to pose as "brats" to tempt Jane.

Jane had started to heal her emotional wounds. It was Val's advice to her that led her to become a journalist, as she had an outspoken but eloquent debating style.


"Didn't see you at the debate last night. Weren't you meant to debate?" said Jane as she sat next to John.

John was defiant. "No…thanks to you."

Jane looked puzzled. "What on earth do you mean?"

John was silent, and at that moment Sir Ernest entered the lecture theater.

John whispered, "Your friends kidnapped me last night and dropped your mobile phone in the process."

Jane's face went red. She composed herself and whispered back, "How dare you accuse me of such a thing!"

John returned her steely glare before being interrupted by Sir Ernest:

"Mr. Rowntree, you might share your thoughts with us."

John stared at Sir Ernest, shook his head, and said, "I have feelings of intense anger at this moment."

A round of laughter rang around the lecture room before Sir Ernest said, "You had better see someone about unwanted thoughts!"

A second round of laughter circulated. John continued to ignore Sir Ernest, whispering through clenched teeth to Jane, "Explain to me how your mobile phone ended up in their hands?"

Jane said, "I don't think anyone I know could even do this. Clearly you are *wrong*," Jane replied.

The two sat in an uneasy state before they received another irritated glare from Sir Ernest.

Sir Ernest continued, "And so many philosophers used theoretical proofs for the existence of God, rather than empirical proofs…"

After a while Sir Ernest paused and then said, "I am announcing an expedition to Afghanistan in search of empirical proof that God does not exist. I am not at liberty to reveal what I hope to find in Afghanistan that will accomplish this task, but I am calling for volunteers to accompany me on the expedition. I believe that there are good prospects for success. Obviously the trip has its dangers, and I certainly would not travel to Afghanistan by choice. The artifact I seek is in that country. Well, is there anyone willing to go?"

A chorus of chatter broke out as everyone discussed his offer.

"Again…are there any volunteers?" Sir Ernest asked.

No one raised his hand. Sir Ernest eyed everyone and pronounced, "Oh, ye of little faith." He shrugged, turning to wipe the whiteboard.

"I'll go!" said John.

Jane put her hand on John's arm, whispering, "Are you mad, John?"

Sir Ernest wheeled around. "You would come as a skeptic, Mr. Rowntree."

John replied, "Well, does your offer stand?"

"Yes."

"I'll come too!" announced Jane. John glared with puzzlement at her.

"That's good. Are there any others?"

The lecture room was silent.

John left abruptly, again leaving Jane in the lecture theater. The next day he called into Sir Ernest's office. Finding Sir Ernest out, he spoke to Sir Ernest's secretary about the trip.

"Sir Ernest has left this travel itinerary, ticket, and notes for everyone who is travelling on the trip."

"Thank you, but that is just Jane Thornton and myself, isn't it?" said John.

No, Sir Ernest has some others travelling with him."

"Can I ask who?"

"You may ask, but you will find out on the trip. By the way, hotels and food are paid for, but you had better arrange for spending money."

John took his travel pouch and left. He was keen to telephone Paul Sanders, who had served as a Royal Marine in Afghanistan. Paul was pleased to hear from John, and they met the following day at a local Oxford pub.

"Explain this madness to me, John," began Paul as he sipped his beer and spoke loudly due to the noisy patrons, who were more intoxicated than they were.

"Sir Ernest has been commissioned by the British Museum—no one else would go—to return several tons of antiquities that have been looted by criminal gangs in the past few years to Afghanistan. Our government has also promised to allocate some of our armed forces there to protect certain rare sites, and Sir Ernest will have a role in selecting those sites. In return, the Ministry of Culture in Afghanistan has allowed Sir Ernest a limited right to collect some artifacts himself. Apparently Afghanistan is so rich in history that you can dig anywhere and find an artifact."

A rowdy group abruptly left the pub, and it was easier for the two of them to hear each other. John grabbed a map and showed Paul the location of the rare sites.

Paul stared closely at the map and then frowned. "Helmand province. Yes, we fought in Sangin, where one of the sites is. This site in Dishu, near the Pakistan border, would be surrounded by smugglers and poppy fields. I read about the antiquities. Looters have even fought on airplanes over who owned what."

John craned his neck to see the sites on the map and said, "The British Museum has a treasure of the stuff under lock and key that has to be returned. Sir Ernest must be well connected to pull this off."

Paul smiled "He has to live to enjoy it, and that goes for you too. If you want my advice, John, it is one thing to watch Afghanistan on CNN, but another to have bullets whistling above your head."

"Paul, I know the risks, but we will be protected by British troops, and maybe I can write a book or something, or become a journalist. It's a huge opportunity!"

Paul went to buy another beer for them both, and soon returned, placing the drinks on the dull wooden bench where they were sitting. John nodded in thanks and said, "Paul, you intrigued me with your story about the Vatican. Did you go to the Vatican to meet this mystery man?"

Paul took a gulp of beer and replied, "Yes. I travelled to a villa outside Rome and met a priest who ran one of the church's vineyards. Only the best wine is used for church services—you know, when they use it in ceremony by celebrating the Roman Catholic mass. He said to me, 'You can call me Mr. Chairman,' which was quite strange. I later learned his real name was Father Lombardo Fezzalo, SJ, and that he was chairman of the Vatican Guild for Church Ideology. I thought at first this was just one of the hundreds of committees that exist in the Catholic Church, but he explained to me that it was a secret committee, not officially sanctioned, but backed by senior officials of the Catholic Church. I asked whether the pope knew, and his reply was ambiguous. He said, 'These people advise the pope.' He also said that I had been chosen as someone they could trust. Their main work was to attack serious ideological threats the church faced, such as the debate on teaching intelligent design in schools, or replacing religious education with secular ethics classes—"

"Pretty harmless stuff?" John interrupted.

"So I thought," Paul said. "But a more serious function of the committee emerged. It seemed the committee had access to huge funding and could dispatch its staff to pursue dangerous or controversial affairs, such as priest kidnappings by terrorists or anti-religious government policies.

Atheists were also monitored by them; and, in fact, Sir Ernest's name did come up in the conversation."

"How?" asked John.

"It seems that Sir Ernest has spent some time trying to debunk one of the church's greatest miracles: the events relating to the children of Fatima. The focus of Sir Ernest's attention surrounded the third of three messages from the children. You've got to understand what happened to understand Sir Ernest's interest. These three children claim that they were visited by a lady who called herself the "Lady of the Rosary," referring to a Catholic prayer. She gave three messages to the children. The children came under intense pressure to change their story, and were even imprisoned and under threat of torture if they refused to change their story.

"Finally, in July 1917, seventy thousand people turned up at the spot where the children claimed they were visited by the supernatural lady. During that day the sun changed colors, rotated like a fire wheel, and, to some, appeared to fall from the sky. The phenomenon was seen from many miles away, yet some saw nothing. This was even reported by Portugal's most influential newspaper, *O Seculo,* which was anti-religious. In fact, Portugal was then a socialist regime with a strongly anti-Catholic agenda.

"The day this happened, rain had fallen steadily all day, people were drenched, and it was muddy. However, when the sun stopped its dancing, an unusual wind blew through the area, and in a few seconds everyone was dry and comfortable, and there was no mud or puddles anymore. There is no scientific explanation for what happened."

"What were the messages, then?" asked John.

"Apparently, the children were shown a sea of fire, with humans and demons, as the first message. The second message was that the war was going to end, but if people did not cease offending God, a worse war would break out; and when a strange light appeared at night it was a sign that God was about to punish the world for its crimes. However, to prevent this, if Russia was converted to Christianity, then there would be peace. If not, Russia would spread her errors throughout the world, spreading wars and persecutions of the church.

"It's interesting that there was the Second World War, which was triggered in the three -way conflict between Germany, Russia, and Poland. In 1952 the pope consecrated Russia to prompt its conversion. Even looking later at the Cuban missile crisis indicates how close the world went to war. Perhaps the sea of fire represents the nuclear holocaust that would have followed, and the demons were the monsters caused by genetic mutation.

"The third message is spoken of as a mystery in some quarters. The Vatican published the third secret in 2000, which related religious men and women ascending a mountain and dying beneath a cross at the hands of soldiers who fire bullets and arrows to kill them. Two angels then collect the blood of those fallen, which is used to assist souls making their way to God. Others believe that the Vatican is hiding a further secret, and that it is the Apocalypse."

"And what did Father Fezzalo believe?" asked John, who remained fascinated with the story.

"He knew more than he let on. He did tell me that he travelled to London to see a minister who was helping Sir Ernest write a book," replied Paul. Thirsty from talking, Paul sipped his beer. John's eyes glazed over as he pondered what Paul had told him.

# SEVEN

The next day, John took the train to London and visited the British Museum to learn all he could about the looted treasures. John walked into the Parthenonlike building, past two stairways, and into the Great Room, with its vast spiderweb ceiling. He browsed the various books as he wandered around the white polished floor. He encountered one of the museum staff, who soon told him that the "Afghanistan expert" was in a meeting.

John continued his visit, walking around the ornate reading room to pass the time, when he saw Sir Ernest strolling across the Great Room toward the exit. John stood still, not wishing to engage in small talk with Sir Ernest. Sir Ernest left the museum and was soon walking briskly down the street. Something made John follow him.

Sir Ernest was walking briskly around the museum toward Russell Square. John mingled among the many Londoners scurrying about, and soon saw his target cross Southhampton Row. After a series of left and right turns, he saw Sir Ernest enter the narrow Great Ormond Street and proceed into the monolithic Great Ormond Street Hospital, with its peach bricks and steel railings. Great Ormond Street Hospital was a children's hospital rich in history, and it boasted the largest center for treatment of childhood illness outside the United States.

John waited outside, with care not to be seen, and soon slipped cautiously inside. A nurse behind the reception desk gazed curiously at John as he approached her.

"Excuse me, I just saw my university lecturer here a moment ago—Sir Ernest Everleigh. You didn't see him pass here, by any chance?"

"Yes, he's visiting his son."

"Oh, yes," John replied softly, hitting his head and moving past reception as if he knew the way. He weaved in and out of the wards, asking staff regarding a young patient with the surname "Everleigh." He was soon directed to the right ward and an unattended nurses' station, where he sat on a visitor's chair. He picked up a newspaper to read. A nurse soon returned.

"Can I help you?" she asked.

"I'm just waiting for my sister," John said.

"Who are you visiting?" the nurse asked.

"Well, actually, my sister is visiting a friend here. I'm just meeting her here."

John sat for about twenty minutes, reading.

The nurse asked again. "Maybe you're waiting in the wrong ward?"

At that moment, John saw Sir Ernest walking toward the nurses' station, so he pulled the newspaper over his face without answering.

"Sir!"

Sir Ernest stopped at the nurses station. John kept the paper over his face.

Sir Ernest replied, "Yes, what do you want?"

John dropped the paper to see Sir Ernest's back as the nurse said, "No, sir, not you. I was talking to the gentleman over there."

John raised the paper and cried out, changing his voice so that Sir Ernest would not recognize it. "No, this is it!"

Sir Ernest glanced across to where John sat hidden and shrugged, moving off quickly.

A few moments later, John got up and walked in the direction where Sir Ernest had been standing. He looked in the first room, and it was vacant. The second room housed a little girl. In the third room he could only see the back of the head of a child who was lying down, facing the window looking onto Great Ormond Street. He was drawn into the room and saw a clipboard with the name THOMAS EVERLEIGH.

The boy turned toward him, and John gasped in horror. He saw the room melting, and he felt sick. The boy was badly deformed and had a huge head. John recalled seeing photos of Joseph Merrick, the elephant man, who lived in the 1800s.

The boy spoke in a beautiful voice, "Are you a friend of Daddy's?"

John tried to speak, but he could not utter a word.

"Are you all right?" asked the boy.

"I was thinking the same thing," said the nurse, who had come to investigate John's visit.

John composed himself and replied, "I just thought—"

"Look, I had a thought. Why don't you go to the next nurse's station? Straight down this corridor and turn right."

John nodded and quickly walked down the corridor. Turning to the right, he froze as he saw Sir Ernest and a doctor in lime green surgical garb heavy in discussion.

"Just tell me what happened, Doctor," barked Sir Ernest.

"Well, I received an emergency call that Thomas was having a cardiac arrest," explained the doctor. They thought it might have been a reaction due to change in medication, so at first we thought it was an allergic reaction, but we treated it with extreme urgency, in any event. When I arrived, I took over from the nurse, who was giving your son a heart massage, and she informed me that his heart had stopped for four minutes. They wheeled in the defibrillator, and I set to work. After five minutes I had revived him."

"Yes, I understand all that, but after speaking to the staff here, there is something you're not telling me," objected Sir Ernest.

The doctor paused, looked at the ground, and then looked Sir Ernest directly in the face: "Thomas had a near-death experience."

Sir Ernest's face went red. "You're not telling me he went to heaven and back!"

"Sir Ernest, I only report on what the patient told us. He reports hovering over the nurses, and later myself trying to revive him, while his heart had stopped," said the doctor.

"Go on" asked Sir Ernest.

"He reported some the classic features of an NDE. He went up a dark tunnel and came into a blinding light. He met certain people and reported a feeling of great joy. He says someone told him that he had to return to bring you a message, but he was brought back before he could be told," said the doctor.

"I got the message," replied Sir Ernest.

"I would like to know myself," urged the frowning doctor.

"The message is that there is a soul and an afterlife, but my own research shows that these type of events are hallucinations. You did say he was on heavy medication," said Sir Ernest.

"What research is that, Sir Ernest?" asked the doctor.

"I understand that ketamine can cause out-of-body experiences just like some other drugs" explained Sir Ernest.

"We weren't using ketamine or anything hallucinatory," the doctor countered.

"What are you saying?"

"I'm just giving you the facts, Sir Ernest. It is a major anomaly for medical science. You see, when the heart stops, the oxygen is cut off from the brain, which is not active during such a crisis. This rules out dreams and hallucinations. What is inexplicable is how the person has memory of the event, when the brain couldn't have been functioning without oxygen."

John had heard enough and started to withdraw to avoid Sir Ernest. He passed the first nurses' station, smiling, as he left the hospital. The nurse smiled back with a puzzled look.

Back in his lamp-lit room at Oriel College that night, John switched on his computer, fired up the Internet, and searched for information on Joseph Merrick. He thought about Sir Ernest and mused, *That is why Sir Ernest does not believe in God! How could a loving God allow that to happen to a child? It would test anyone.*

John saw that Joseph Merrick's congenital condition was the subject of medical controversy, but most likely it was neurofibromatosis type 1. Apparently, Merrick would visit a hospital for the blind to find a woman who would not be repulsed by his appearance. *Yes, two beautiful souls together, without the deformity preventing their love*, thought John. John read further and found that Merrick used to end his letters with a poem by Isaac Watts:

Tis true my form is something odd,
But blaming me is blaming God.
Could I create myself anew,
I would not fail in pleasing you.

If I could reach from pole to pole,
Or grasp the ocean with a span,

I would be measured by the soul,

The mind's the standard of the man.

John's own thoughts were reflected in this poem, and as he read it he felt his being tingle as if with static electricity. John then remembered the debate in Sir Ernest's class, and Einstein's query, "Did God have any choice in the way He made the world?"—or, put another way, "Did God have any choice in the way Merrick or the young Everleigh looked?"

John stared out the window across the neat lawn to the vine-covered stone walls. Three students stood laughing, their voices echoing around the quadrangle. He saw Professor Simons walk the path toward his building, look up, and nod. John lifted his hand as he approached the building. A knock at the door followed soon after, and John let him in.

"I just thought I would stop by and see how you are, John."

"Thank you, Professor, I'm all right….I'm…"

"Continue please, John."

"I found out today that Sir Ernest has a severely disabled son. It explains his anti-religious stance."

Professor Simons sat on the bed without replying.

"Professor, why does God permit disabled children?"

"Difficult…. The problem of evil and suffering, as you and I have discussed the question, assumes that God is omnipotent and all-loving.

If He is all-loving then He could not be omnipotent, as He would not design the world to permit so much suffering, or He does not exist. Man simply does not know whether God is omnipotent or not. Sir Ernest certainly assumes that an omnipotent and all-loving God could not exist, because otherwise God would not permit disabled children to be born. But once you accept that God is not omnipotent in the sense of being unable to make a perfect world, mathematical logic gives you the answer. It is the same answer as to why God does not intervene to stop evil and suffering. Although I would add that both man's free will and the freedom of events must, by logical necessity, permit the possibility of evil, but not necessarily suffering, if there were a perfectly designed world."

"Well, what is this mathematical logic?"

"Let's not put the cart before the horse. First, is God omnipotent? Taking theology, Jewish scholars refer to the famous Book of Job, where Job puts God on trial.

Job challenges God as to why He permitted evil in the world, and God's ultimate response was, in effect, 'Where were you when I laid the foundations of the earth? Who determined its measurements?' This suggests that either it was difficult to make the world (which is not consistent with an omnipotent God), or that evil was a necessary part of the world, and Job does not understand why it is necessary. Would an omnipotent God struggle with making a world, or permitting evil? This implies an acknowledgement by God that the world is imperfect because evil is a necessity of creation."

"Of course, people judge God as though He was human," replied John.

"Yes," said the professor. "That is another aspect that arises from Job—that is, whether God sees these issues through human eyes. If God is not a 'white-bearded man on a throne,' then what is God? Is He some cosmic force that is at great pains to communicate and empathize with us? 'Love' is the communicated message, but does 'love' mean to God what it means to man? Of course, God in the Bible says we were made in His image. I cannot see God in His realm as having a human image. Perhaps being 'made in His image' refers to man's soul."

The professor smiled as he spoke. "Let's explore something else. Let us say that God is not omnipotent in the sense that He had no choice in the way He made the world, but is omnipotent in every other way. Would He choose to communicate such a fact?"

"One good thing would be that Sir Ernest and his followers couldn't rely on omnipotence to disprove God!" exclaimed John.

The Professor continued, "I believe that if God is not omnipotent. Then it may be that while man can ask the question, 'Is He omnipotent?' man may not be able to comprehend the answer. Already the complexity of the world, with quantum mechanics, genetics, the cosmos, et cetera, is mind-boggling, and it may be that we need a lot more knowledge to comprehend God and the work He has done. The true answer to 'What is God's precise power?' will not likely be made in human concepts."

"Professor, let's not limit it to one issue. Why does not God communicate more often, and in clearer terms?"

"A good question; but on omnipotence, complexity may be the hurdle. But the answer is probably wrapped up in this issue of intervention, which I am getting to. What I mean is that His ability to intervene is limited, which I will explain. If so, intervention to communicate or to send religious figures is limited. But let me finish my point and respond to Einstein's famous question, 'Did God have any choice in the way He created the world?' Regardless of the answer to that question, I myself trust God to have made the world in the best way He could, and because I am not in the business of creating worlds, I do not judge God harshly as others do."

"Professor, they judge God harshly to dismiss God's existence, but it is interesting to consider whether the atheist's harsh judgment of God remains if God is not omnipotent. In summary, you are saying that— let's call Him the 'classic God' in the same way that the Genesis version of world creation in seven days is considered 'classical' but only figuratively—God should be seen as perhaps a supernatural entity or the 'real God.'"

"Yes," replied Professor Simons.

"Professor, the most tantalizing model of God derives from the French Jesuit Teilhard de Chardin's concept, where the complexity and consciousness of the world evolve to end in the 'omega point' outside space and time. To take this one step further, the omega point joining with God at the end of an evolutionary process would imply a God that could be a collective of souls with collective consciousness. A collective God would be very different from an individual God.

"Okay, Professor, let's assume then that God is not omnipotent. You mentioned that both the issue of *intervention* and the issue of *evil* and *suffering* are solved by mathematical logic?" asked John.

"You mean, even though God created the best universe He could have created, why does He not intervene to prevent evil, such as to prevent genocide?"

"Yes, that's the issue."

"Well, it is helpful to think in terms of *event freedom* versus *event control*. We know the earth operates with event freedom. I suppose someone calls this 'free will,' but if you think in terms of events, we can examine it in terms of mathematics. God's universal systematic intervention would result in what I call the Event Tree Conundrum. Let me explain. Scientists tell us that the universe was created in the big bang, say thirteen billion years ago, and outside the universe there is no space or time as we know it. The entire fabric of space and time was created in that instant, and expanded to create the universe as one system.

"Our model of God is that He stands outside the universe, in another dimension. By definition, God's dimension stands outside time and space because our physics tells us that time and space are embedded in our universe. In this sense, we have a timeless God looking into a time-streamed universe, which is a conundrum in itself. In fact, some argue that God could not exist before time existed, and thus God does not exist at all.

"But to continue my concept, for my timeless God observing from outside the universe, there is a constant stream of time and events inside the universe. There are thousands of injustices taking place in our imperfect world, every hour or minute, requiring this intervention. Intervention by God in our stream of time would require interventions along this time stream for all time that we have lived. Such interventions would cause multiple ripples, changing events hour by hour or instant by instant along the time stream, increasing exponentially to infinity—event numbers so large that no clear picture of each future outcome can be relied on to make just one intervention.

"In other words, you must envision events approaching infinity if you plan to stop more bad events. If you wait for the outcome, you are too late. Remember, if it were possible to go back in time, paradoxes can occur. Elementary mathematics will tell you that when you have exponential growth to infinity, not even a supercomputer has the power to calculate the permutations and combinations that would result from the myriad divine interventions, each spawning a new 'event tree' along the time stream—let alone manage the new events and perform new interventions for each new branch of that event tree (and I include natural events caused by each intervention).

"An alternative demonstration of the difficulty with divine intervention is seen in the turbulence of liquids and the unsolvable mathematical equations that apply to them. The best they can do is to model the behavior of liquids. If I see my event tree unfolding with *event turbulence*, my intuition tells me that predicting precise human event outcomes is unsolvable also. In fact, human interaction is probably more unpredictable than that of liquids!

"Anyway, getting back to our supercomputer, this exponential growth in the event tree would reach infinity quite quickly, crashing our supercomputer (which is merely tracking events, not altering them). Those who postulate God having classical omnipotence would say that God can do these trillions of interventions, because they ignore the rules of logic and mathematics."   John interrupted: "Professor, in my recent clash with Sir Ernest during a lecture debate I put to him a more reasonable definition of omnipotence as the power to do what is logically possible and not absurd... do you agree?"   The Professor nodded and continued:

" However, systematic intervention is mathematically impossible, because each of the thousands of event trees spawned by each intervention must reach infinity, and therefore could not have been predictable. In other words, it is not mathematically possible for God to predict the ultimate result of multiple interventions and the possible paradoxes that can occur from conflicts between event trees. Like the unsolvable liquid behavior, future events could be modeled for an approximation of what could occur. But that's hardly a basis for precision event control.

"This, in itself, proves that God's omniscience cannot include knowledge in respect of these possible future events (depending on how you define an 'all knowing' God). If you consider the trillions (likely many more) of interventions required—including event trees and consequent ripple effects throughout the history of time—these interventions would create unknown results because the results are unpredictable mathematically, and God is not classically omniscient in a strict definition of omniscient."

"The church would not like to hear that, Professor!" objected John. "No….If I adopt a similar reasonable definition to your definition of 'omnipotence' for 'omniscience' we can indeed retain God's 'omniscience' –let me explain. Take the Catholic Church as an example. Perhaps their greatest philosopher and theologian is St. Thomas Aquinas, who spoke of God's omniscience. I happen to have our own course textbook in my pocket, with selected passages from his work, as it something we teach." The Professor reached into his green tweed coat and pulled out a well-worn paperback that bore a monk's face on its cover. He flipped through to a marked page and read: "God is called omniscient because He knows everything knowable; false things not knowable He does not know."

He flipped to another page and read, "'In the theories of sciences we always base ourselves on something already known, whether we are proving propositions or discovering definitions. But we can't go on this way forever; that would spell the death of all science, its proofs, and its definitions, since *you can't bridge the infinite.*' I analogize 'false things' to be in the same category as unsolvable or unknowable things. So you can see that even St. Thomas Aquinas saw infinity as a barrier to knowledge, and that is what I am saying here about infinity preventing the predictability of possible future events. St. Thomas also said that God could not make a triangle that did not have three angles equal to two right angles, and so he saw mathematical limitations on God's power such as infinity. Otherwise, paradoxes would result. And so he would agree with our views on God's omnipotence and John, to give you your reasonable definition of 'omniscience' it is knowing what is logically possible to know and that excludes the absurd."

"Why would trillions of interventions be required?" asked John.

"God not only has to change events but also to manage outcomes to avoid further bad events, and so on. He must ensure no conflicts between outcomes (producing paradoxes), which requires in-depth future knowledge of events approaching the infinite in number. Divine intervention might cause butterfly effects for each intervention, with 'multiple event ripples' that crisscross, producing further exponential event trees with similar predictability problems. The butterfly effect observed by mathematician Edward Lorenz recognizes small changes in the initial conditions can result in large changes in the outcomes of events. Again, this is hardly a sound basis for good outcomes. The world must be sustainable on its own steam to avoid this event tree conundrum. That is, event freedom is sustainable, but event control is not.

"However, this is not to say that there have not been interventions. The sending of religious figures, or other events that spawned different religions, may have been interventions to produce good outcomes—but without knowledge by God of the possible future infinite outcomes. This would explain the succession of interventions. People ask that if Christ was God, then why did He come relatively late in history? The answer is, probably, 'He was not the first intervention.' Once the event trees in human history took the trend they did, there was sufficient cause for Christ to be sent as an intervention. You see, in terms of predicting history, even if there was intervention, the ultimate results are unknown and unknowable in advance."

"Fascinating, Professor, but surely there would be some interventions that merely allow the ripple effect to flow to its unknown destiny?" said John.

"This is what I am saying to explain some of the interventions, such as emergence of religious leaders in history. Note the ripple effects from these interventions have resulted in a substantial segment of the world's population being religious."

"One more thing: we discussed God's omniscience, but can He know the future?" asked John.

"While the precise future cannot be known due to this indeterminacy caused by infinite possible events, I believe a probable future could be predicted but not known. Our timeless God may see the outcome of future events as He stands outside time. Presumably He sees flows of time, or even the end result, the omega point (allowing limited interventions 'with the benefit of hindsight'). So there may be an outcome-based omniscience, rather than the paradoxical omniscience that allows knowledge of unsolvable problems."

"Sorry, but I did have another question, Professor. Your Event Tree Conundrum is quite a hypothesis, but can you prove it?"

"John, I don't have to prove it!" laughed the professor. "You've got Everleigh running around saying to everyone, 'If God exists, then what *possible reason* is there in the world for evil and suffering? It is simply inexplicable.' All I need to do is use mathematical intuition to give my hypothesis as the *possible reason*. John, there are many great mathematical propositions that have been formulated on intuition. Some are still not proven but are still very useful."

John nodded as Professor Simons got up.

"John, I believe you decided to go on Everleigh's expedition to Afghanistan. Why?"

John opened the door and replied, "Professor, if something is happening on this issue on the world stage, then I want to be there as a counterbalance to Everleigh."

Professor Simons looked at John and said, "Perhaps, but I hope you know what you are doing. If you need help, let me know. I was going to say, 'Have a safe trip,' but...you know what I mean! Oh, John, I forgot to mention one thing. Did you know that Jane Thornton's father is writing a book to be co-authored by Sir Ernest?" John looked incredulous. "You're surprised," said the professor.

"Well, I happen to know that her father is not an atheist. What on earth is the book about?"

"The rumors are that it is an anti-church establishment rant by Alistair Thornton, with Sir Ernest taking the classic David Hume philosophical line that a multiplicity of religions implies they are all wrong—with a sprinkle of other contemporary atheists to argue that religion damages people."

The Professor left as John's mind puzzled over Sir Ernest's new book.

******

Cedar bookcases lined with Kings and Queens Bench law reports, All England reports, and *Halsbury's Laws of England* stood like two pillars guarding a huge glass door next to the reception desk. A large, polished brass plate bearing the embossed name THISTLEWAITE & HAZELHURST, SOLICITORS glistened above the receptionist, whose impeccable red hair, designer clothes, and slim-line glasses suggested something more flamboyant than a legal office. Sir Ernest sat in the brown leather chair opposite Professor Cummings, who was calmly reading the *Financial Times* newspaper.

The lift pinged as a man arrived on the floor and entered the reception. John Hazelhurst, solicitor—whose grandfather founded the law firm—was bald and a little overweight in his pinstripe suit.

"Sorry about that gentlemen. Just follow me."

"Oh Mr. Hazelhurst, a Mr. Sandhurst rang for you," said the receptionist, handing him a message.

Hazelhurst punched in the security code in the lock on the glass door, which buzzed open. He walked passed numerous workstations and a row of offices, each housing a lawyer who looked up as they walked by—some smiling, others too stressed to see them. They soon reached Hazelhurst's huge corner office and were shown to a couple of plush client chairs behind his antique desk. His phone rang, but he ignored it and walked to an open shelf, pulling a file off it and opening it on his desk.

"So, you must be Professor Cummings?" asked Hazelhurst, realizing he had forgotten to introduce himself beforehand.

"Yes I am. I am glad to meet you."

"Sir Ernest has given me your story, but you might want to repeat it for my own benefit," said Hazelhurst.

With that, Professor Cummings related his story again—about his two scientist partners starting a new company and stealing his technology. After he heard the story, Hazelhurst looked through his file, rustling the papers.

"How can you prove you own the technology?" asked Hazelhurst.

"Well, I invented the main product, leading to a patent family over a particular gene," replied the professor.

"And how did that lead to a product?" asked Hazelhurst.

"It allowed me to develop a diagnostic test for the propensity of various cancers and other diseases, which is now used by hundreds of hospitals around England."

"And who developed the diagnostic test?" asked Hazelhurst.

"Jim Alsop," came the reply.

"Well, doesn't Jim Alsop own the technology?" asked Hazelhurst pointedly.

"I gave him the concept. It was my idea," replied the professor.

"Yes, but the notebooks, the e-mails—will that show it was your concept?" pressed Hazelhurst.

With that, the professor dug into his briefcase, pulled out a manual, and handed it to Hazelhurst, who started flipping through it. "I have recorded the concept and noted the development and instructions I gave to Alsop," said Professor Cummings. "I have now found out that Alsop lodged patents without my knowledge. I was even helping with drafting the patents, but I was unaware that the patent attorney had been patenting them in the name of this company that I had never heard of: Alsop McEwen Biomedical Ltd.

"When I did find out, they said that they had planned to give me a third of the shares, but I was so unreasonable that we could not longer work together. I asked, then, why my name was not in the company name, and I received no sensible explanation. You see, my main work was the development of a mathematical model explaining the human genome. I had developed many algorithms, but they were more interested in diagnostic tests and designer drugs. I even helped them develop some of these new drugs.

"We argued about my focus on the human genome, and they said that it would never make money. My point was that a biotech company needed prestige and products," explained the professor.

"And Ted McEwen?" asked Sir Ernest.

"He was more a businessman than a biologist. He was already making contacts with various hospitals, universities, labs, and so on to distribute the test. I understand that he had even approached a firm of stockbrokers about floating a company on the stock exchange. Well, Mr. Hazelhurst, what do you think?"

"Thank you Professor. I think you could have a valid claim, but in your type of case, tactics are often more important than black-letter law. I am looking for any edge that you may have. What I would like to do is to make some inquiries of my own and ponder on your case. Sir Ernest, I think you and I can have a chat as well, later?"

# EIGHT

Rain trickled down the windows of the Norton & Sykes boardroom, where Kenneth Hardwick sat again with Alistair Thornton. Sir Ernest sat at the head of an oak table that had spiral legs and ornate inlaid red leather.

"We have a title for the book, Alistair," said Hardwick.

"Well, I hope you liked the title I gave you," replied Thornton.

"Not enough," said Hardwick "How does *The Fall of the Church* sound?"

Thornton's eyebrows raised, and he commented, "The book does not contain anything that dramatic."

"It will," replied Sir Ernest.

"Is that the secret last chapter we have been expecting?" asked Thornton.

"Yes. I am going to Afghanistan to collect a relic; and once it is in our hands, this will feature in the last chapter to the book," Sir Ernest spoke with great enthusiasm.

"And you're taking my daughter with you, I believe. Don't you think that is a little dangerous?" Thornton was beginning to get angry.

"Now, now, Alistair, there are British troops in Afghanistan, and we won't be in any combat zone. Anyway, you can withdraw your consent to her going at any time. She volunteered without any prompting from me."

"I have already forbidden her, but it makes no difference. She's a wild girl."

"Do you want me to stop her?" suggested Sir Ernest.

"No, her stubbornness would make her do something more stupid if I did that. You know what the young are like. But surely, as your co-author, I should know what it is going to say."

Sir Ernest sat forward, informing him solemnly, "Alistair, it is imperative that it be secret until I return." Sir Ernest looked at his watch and continued, "All right. We have another meeting now."

Thornton rose reluctantly and nodded to Sir Ernest as Hardwick showed him out. On the way out he brushed past a tall, Nordic-looking man with white hair.

The distinguished gentleman in pinstriped suit and gold silk tie emblazoned with multiple motifs entered the room.

"Count Christian Nansen, meet Sir Ernest Everleigh."

Sir Ernest shook hands and bowed.

"No formalities are needed, Sir Ernest."

"It is not often that we entertain a dignitary of your stature," remarked Hardwick, taking Count Nansen to his seat. The phone buzzed and Hardwick picked up the receiver before leaving the room. He returned soon after with another well-dressed gentleman, also gray-haired, who spoke with an American accent.

"Count Nansen and Sir Ernest, may I present Warren Tolhurst III, the editor of *Landmarks in Science* magazine, one of the most prestigious magazines in the world." The introductions finished and they all took a seat around the table.

"I've read the literature on your relic. Quite fascinating," remarked Tolhurst.

"Thank you, but will you publish the article?" asked Sir Ernest.

"I'd like to hear what Count Nansen believes first. Our technical consultants have reviewed everything, but we believe that the relic must be returned to London for testing in an independent laboratory. We cannot afford a mistake. Relics can be fakes. We don't know the authors of the previous reports, and the lab work was done in Cairo. Our people have not heard of the lab.

"The relic must be tested, retested, and triple tested. There must be no mistake. The relic will cause a worldwide sensation. It may even cause riots, and so we need to be very sure before we back it."

Sir Ernest sat forward in his chair, appearing agitated, and said, "But the relic is in Afghanistan in a war zone. What do you expect me to do?"

"I'm afraid our interest is based on testing. Mr. Tolhurst, what do you think?"

"That is our feeling also. Landmarks in Science is the most prestigious journal in its class in the world. If the relic was not so unique, we would require more peer review, but our editorial board realize we are missing out on the find of the century," answered Tolhurst.

"Gentlemen, we thought that might be your answer, and thus we have booked a trip to Afghanistan." Both visitors appeared surprised. Sir Ernest then pressed them. "And so, if I test it, then you will both honor your commitments?"

"If the test results are satisfactory," the count explained.

"Meaning?" asked Sir Ernest.

"It would have to mean the old report is confirmed beyond reasonable doubt," said Tolhurst.

"Well I take that as a yes from both of you," said Sir Ernest. "I will get you what you want. What can I get from you at this stage? Because I am putting my money and life on the line for this."

"You have my word" said the count.

Sir Ernest peered at Tolhurst, who said, "Likewise for me. I've got 'in principle' approvals from my committee, but the test results must corroborate the historical report."

After a few moments of contemplation, Sir Ernest stood up, prompting the others to stand as well, before concluding, "Gentlemen, our work is cut out for us. We are all in for exciting times. I am sure of it!"

They shook hands and left.

**

S ir Ernest and Professor Ian Cummings were sitting again in John Hazelhurst's corner office while he was on the phone:

"Yes, Sir Peter I don't believe that's the issue here. It's a question of tactics. Look, I'll have to ring you back, as I have some clients with me." Hazelhurst hung up the phone and turned to Sir Ernest and Ian. "That was Sir Peter Finlay, QC. He believes we have good prospects for success in this case. The problem is that it will cost over five hundred thousand pounds in legal fees to win it."

Ian groaned.

"Okay, there might be a more elegant solution. Ian, what do you want? Money or shares in the company?"

Ian looked out the window and said, "Well, I suppose money is a consolation prize. I really want what is rightfully mine: my proper share in the company."

"Including a board seat?" asked Hazelhurst.

"A board seat and full laboratory facilities. That is my dream," replied Ian.

"Yes, I thought so. Perhaps, then, my elegant solution could work for you. I have found out through my stock exchange contacts that your friends plan to float Alsop McEwen Biomedical on the London Stock Exchange in a twenty-five-million-pound float. It seems they plan to acquire some of the most advanced biotech equipment in the world to fulfill technology licensing contracts to major pharmaceutical companies. During a float, a company is very vulnerable to legal action, as it delays the float or can even result in the underwriter pulling out because it can make investors nervous. In Ian's case, the claim goes to the very ownership of the company's assets, and so it would definitely impact the float greatly. Thus, by spending only a fraction of your total legal budget for the full life of the case, you can grind your friends to a halt. Then they must deal with you," explained Hazelhurst.

**

Sir Ernest sat in the boardroom of Alsop McEwen Biomedical, examining the annual report he'd picked up in the reception area of the massive laboratory complex. The building had a magnificent tapestry of green-and-blue-tinted glass joined in helical and other shapes that resembled a giant DNA molecule. Ironic that they used DNA as their theme, when they refused to pursue Ian's DNA project.

Two men soon appeared: one in a lab coat, and the other in a pin-stripe suit with a pink tie with little DNA segments all over it.

"Jim Alsop," said the man in the white coat.

Ted McEwen introduced himself. "Sir Ernest Everleigh! I saw your interview the other day concerning the change in school policy through-out England. A very daring recommendation to ban religion being taught in schools, and for it to succeed. Quite amazing."

Sir Ernest just smiled as Ted McEwen continued: "You're not here to agnosticize us, are you?"

"Not exactly, but I do have a proposition for you. I'm working on a project that aims to explain the missing link between man and the apes through DNA analysis," replied Sir Ernest.

"Is there any other way?" asked Jim Alsop.

"No need to be flippant. This is a serious offer, so listen carefully," insisted Sir Ernest. "You have the full spectrum of facilities here to un-dertake the project."

"Let me understand this: You intend to answer one of the greatest questions in biology using our facilities? How?" asked Alsop.

"I already have evidence that human DNA was genetically engi-neered using techniques that can be recognized as outside natural evolu-tionary processes," replied Sir Ernest.

"Meaning?" asked Alsop.

"Meaning that God did not create man, but some advanced race— perhaps the original man who walked this earth—did. Ergo, God does not exist."

"Where is this evidence?" pressed Alsop.

"A paleontologist, Andrew Faulkner, postulates this, and has in-vited me to travel to the Middle East with him to get it. That is all I can tell you. Until then, I will remain as skeptical as you are," replied Sir Ernest.

"What is your proposition, then?" asked McEwen.

"I believe you are soon to float on the stock exchange," began Sir Ernest.

"Where did you hear that?" asked Jim Alsop.

"My broker, of course. I understand that your underwriters are building their investors, and my proposition is that I can invest now, without you listing."

"How much did you have in mind?" asked McEwen.

"I was thinking of five million pounds for 30 percent of the company."

"With the greatest respect, you have some nerve, Sir Ernest. Don't you know we propose to issue only 25 percent of the company for twenty-five million pounds? Why should we accept your offer, and with strings attached?" objected McEwen.

"Well, you have the expense and risk of going through the listing process, which is many months away. If you accept my offer, you get the cash after I return from the Middle East, and you can still float when you need to. And if your float is delayed for any reason—stock market meltdown or whatever—at least you have a bird in the hand," explained Sir Ernest.

Jim Alsop looked at McEwen, who looked irritated, and replied, "You are really offering me private equity with strings attached. I could get that tomorrow for much better terms. Yes, if there were a meltdown, we would have to delay our float, but I could probably still do a better private equity deal without strings. Your project only rewards you, and gives us no revenue."

" I would give you royalties from a book I'm about to publish."

McEwen smiled. "I thought philosophers were dreamers. Let me give you a counteroffer that works for us. We'll do the project for five million pounds, in fees payable to us. What do you say to that?"

Sir Ernest now looked irritated. "Why, I could buy the equipment for that."

"You know you couldn't. This equipment is worth over twenty million pounds, and you know it. We only have it under a strategic alliance with a major corporation, and I don't think they would like us handing it over to you for nothing."

Sir Ernest shrugged, got up, and said, "Looks like we have to do this the hard way. I'll show myself out."

# NINE

John crawled over the forest floor, camouflaged by his jungle greens. Paul was meters away, gesturing for him to stay still. They waited… and waited. John started to move again, and Paul again stopped him. Just then two men carrying their weapons flashed in front of them, and Paul fired his weapon, followed quickly by John.

"You're dead!" shouted Paul, who stood up. The two men were covered in paintball hits. John followed as well. They marched them off to the base to record their "kills." Paul had taken John to a weekend of war games to give him some basic combat training. A visit to a mock Afghan village at a military base was also part of the training.

The following day, John was sitting in the departure lounge at Heathrow Airport. Paul had accompanied him for moral support. John's mobile phone rang.

"John, DCI Townsend here. Can you come into the station?"

"Why?" replied John.

"We've found something interesting on the tape," he said.

"Look, Inspector, I'm at Heathrow, about to catch a plane. Can't you tell me now?"

"No, proper procedure…. Also, you don't know where Paul Sanders is, do you?" asked the inspector.

"As a matter of fact, he's here with me, Inspector." John passed the phone to Paul. Paul spoke with the inspector, hung up, and handed the phone back to John.

"What's the story?" asked John.

"Dunno. He wants to see me."

Just then, John saw Sir Ernest, Jane, and famous paleontologist Andrew Faulkner—on the way to board the plane. John's stomach churned, and he remarked to Paul, "See that chap? That's Andrew Faulkner. He's one of the bastards who sat on the committee with Everleigh."

"What committee?" asked Paul.

"That's the whole reason I lost my job. He and Everleigh both recommended banning religion being taught in schools."

Paul stared at Faulkner hard.

"Paul, looks like this is it. I'd better run."

"Remember what I told you. Keep your head down, and if you hear anything like bullets, you eat dirt."

They shook hands, and John joined the queue some way behind the others as the air hostess took their boarding passes. John fumbled with his Afghan visa and passport, and soon found his boarding pass. He shuffled his way into the aircraft. Sir Ernest was already seated in first class at the front of the British Airways 747 jumbo jet, and greeted John.

"Mr. Rowntree, you continue to surprise me. Did you read my briefing paper on our trip?"

"Well, I intend to make good use of our flight time"

"In that case, you might like to read the real briefing paper."

Sir Ernest handed John a black folder, which John tugged from a grinning Sir Ernest, who held it a little longer than he should have. John sat in the row adjacent and in front of Sir Ernest and his team.

"Who gave me the aisle seat? I don't want to miss the scenery," remarked John.

"Didn't you arrange your own seat allocation?" said a voice.

John looked down and saw that Jane was sitting on the window seat.

"No, it was prebooked for me, of course," replied John, trying not to look surprised at Jane being seated next to him. The tension between them had melted somewhat, but a frosty atmosphere remained as both grabbed reading material as the plane readied itself for takeoff.

The plane took off, and John felt turbulence as they passed through the clouds. Ten minutes later the seatbelt sign pinged off and John's eye caught the black brief Sir Ernest had given him tucked into the seat pocket in front of him. Air hostesses had commenced handing out drinks at the front of the plane as John opened the folder with intense curiosity:

"The land of Babylon was only known from the Bible, until archaeological discovery confirmed its existence," John read a brief history of Babylon. The story continued: "Babylon was thought to be the first civilization in the history of the world, but a discovery in 1850 by Edward Hincks changed that assumption. He theorized that Akkadian, the international language of the Akkad in Mesopotamia over four thousand years ago, evolved from an earlier language that was later confirmed by 'bilingual' clay tablets. Later it was suggested that a people from Sumer (present-day Iraq) preceded the Akkadian-speaking Babylonians, dubbed the Sumerians. The Sumerians were the world's first known civilization, with a sophisticated society consisting of doctors, lawyers, judges, teachers, mathematicians, etc.

They had laws, courts, schools, and used writing as part of their system of living. The Sumerians, who had developed mathematics and astronomy, had appeared on earth without any clue as to their origin. What bridged the gap between caveman and this civilization? Scholars have no explanation for the origin of the Sumerians."

John read on until the last page of the brief, which ended,

"Certain writings discovered on clay tablets in Afghanistan pointed to undiscovered archaeological sites of great significance in Iraq, Egypt, and other lands. These sites are believed to also have theological implications of greater magnitude than the discovery of the dead sea scrolls. See Addendum."

John flipped through various ancient maps and diagrams to a page headed ADDENDUM. He turned the page, which bore only the words CONFIDENTIAL DOCUMENT RETAINED BY SIR ERNEST EVERLEIGH. He found a similar tab marked Relic, which also bore the same words.

John got out of his seat, stepped over to Sir Ernest's seat, and said, "Sir Ernest, thanks for the brief. However, I am missing the addendum, and I still don't know what the relic is."

"It's all for your protection. The disclosure of this information could render you liable to a lawsuit."

John's face dropped. "Well, how can I participate in this trip, then?"

"It's being worked out, and I hope to have a solution when we land in Afghanistan. A little patience…" smiled Sir Ernest, to which John grinned back and returned to his seat.

Paul had taken a cab back to the police station to see DCI Townsend, and now sat in his office.

DCI Townsend entered the room holding a cup of coffee and sat down. He picked up the mobile phone.

"We have found that a text message was sent from Jane Thornton's phone to Sir Ernest Everleigh's eldest son, Brendan. Normally I wouldn't disclose this, but I am only doing it to ease John's concern, because those thugs were not after John. They were after Sir Ernest's son."

"How do you know that?" asked Paul.

"Well, we know those thugs had the phone, and the text message to Brendan said, 'Meet me at the Oxford Union tonight at 5:30 p.m.' Obviously, Brendan would have thought it was Jane Thornton…had he received the message."

"He didn't receive it?" Paul raised his eyebrows.

"We tried to contact him, and he's in the United States. And so, we assume, he still doesn't know anything. If you could pass this on to Mr. Rowntree from us, I would be grateful. Oh, there is something I wish to warn you about." The inspector tabled a set of photographs of bearded men wearing Afghan caps. "We believe that these are the four men who kidnapped John."

Paul grabbed the photos and exclaimed, "These are no pranksters. What's going on here?"

"That's what we would like to know" replied the DCI Townsend. He got up. "Thank you, Mr. Sanders, for coming in. Oh, there is someone who would like to meet you."

Paul stood up and said, "Yes?"

The inspector opened the door and pointed to a man in the pinstripe suit in the waiting room. Paul nodded and walked out to meet him.

"Mr. Sanders, Derek Hanson, MI5. Why don't I drive you home?"

Paul realized he was travelling in an MI5 operative's Jaguar, with the countryside blurring by and the sun setting.

"It seems young Rowntree was fortunate a person of your caliber stopped these kidnappers," said Hanson, his eyes fixed on the road.

"Who are they?" asked Paul, throwing his hands in front of him in exasperation.

Hanson's face tensed into a technical smile before he replied. "We were watching four men whom we thought were terrorists. We had tapped their phones. I won't go into the whole story, but I will tell you what you need to know. They were Asians, probably from Afghanistan. To date we have no evidence of terrorism to support their arrest, but we have strong suspicion of foul play and imminent threat, but something was different. They don't live here. They shuttle to and from Pakistan, Iran, and Afghanistan. We believed their cover was as art dealers because they have imported many crates of antiquities from these countries. To our surprise, we taped a conversation of what appeared to be genuine negotiations for the sale of a valuable antiquity." Hanson paused, as if deep in thought, as he weaved through traffic on the expressway they were on.

Paul interjected, "Between whom?"

Hanson regained his train of thought: "The conversation occurred between Sir Ernest Everleigh and one of the four dealers, a man named Yousef. They talked about selling Sir Ernest a relic for one million dollars. Our people could not discern what the relic was, as they both were reviewing something on a computer screen. The sale was set up, until a further phone call between the parties resulted in a nasty dispute. This

Yousef claimed Sir Ernest had misled him as to the value of the relic, which Yousef argued was priceless. Yousef said the price was now ten million dollars."

"No mention of what the relic was?" asked Paul.

"The only clue was that they began referring to it as some ancient fabric; but other than that, nothing. Then there was the threat. They said that harm would come to Sir Ernest's son if the deal didn't go through. Sir Ernest stated he did not have the ten million dollars in cash and would need time to raise it, and so on. It was at this point that we interviewed Sir Ernest and warned him. He assured us that his eldest son was in the United States at an unknown location, and the other son was safe because he was disabled but no one knew his location either. He did not want to talk about the affair any further. He's a fairly arrogant and independent type."

"Yes, so I have heard," agreed Paul.

"Anyway, nothing happened until the kidnapping. DCI Townsend had been able to locate a witness who saw a car drop them off to the van, which was stolen. The witness took down the number plate because they were acting suspiciously. Our four art dealers turned up, and I now know that somehow they stole some girl's mobile and used the phone to set up a meeting with the eldest son."

"Yes, the girl is my friend's girlfriend, Jane Thornton. Did she know the son?" asked Paul.

"Not sure. Perhaps they attended university and mingled with them. It would certainly explain how the mobile phone was stolen. We're not so interested in how, but in what is going to happen now. Your involvement may help us."

Paul frowned. "Me? How? I just helped the lad."

"We retain our suspicions of these four thugs, apart from the fact that we now know them to be kidnappers. Sir Ernest and his team are in line for an unpleasant meeting with them, whatever their business in Afghanistan. You are our only link inside the circle, and you are a trained soldier, which is more than half the battle in this game, if you can excuse the pun."

"Where are they now?" asked Paul.

"Afghanistan. If you agree to work for us on this, you too must go there."

Paul's face was blank as he pondered his future. He had been affected by his tour of duty and had sought counseling from the Reverend James Dunkley, the parson who himself was a war veteran. He remembered that Reverend Dunkley had recommended a new therapy used on veterans—a computer program that simulated battle in virtual reality, where the soldier could face his nightmares and put right what needed to be put right. It had helped many soldiers. Here was a chance to do the same. It was better than virtual reality, *and* he was already involved.

"I hope the pay's good," blurted Paul.

"Then you'll do it?" asked Hanson.

"Depends on what *it* is," answered Paul dryly.

"Well, here's my card. A car will pick you up tomorrow morning for a full briefing. Be packed and ready to leave, because we might send you direct. I'm just waiting on the arrangements now."

The car ambled on as they neared Paul's home. After a while they neared Paul's house. It was now dark and his street was not well lit. The Jaguar pulled over in front of the house, and Paul remarked, "That's funny."

"What?" Hanson's face was stern.

"That car in my driveway. It's not mine."

Hanson reached for the gun in his glove box and whispered, "Let's hope it is nothing; but if it is, we have to be ready. "Hanson pulled something into his pocket from under the seat and said, "Give me your keys, and I will go in the front door. Are you able to cut the power and enter through a side window to cover me?"

"Yes. Here's my keys."

Hanson backed the Jaguar up so that the waiting attackers would see only one person approach the house. As Hanson left, he said, "On my signal, burst in and give it all you've got. Here, take this." Paul took Hanson's gun and left first to make a side entrance to the house, in readiness for Hanson entering through the front door.

The lights were out, so whoever was inside lay in waiting in the dark. Paul had no reason to lock his windows. In fact, he had left them open to air out the house that day after cleaning it. Pity the burglar who entered Paul's house. Keeping low, he crept to the side of the house, sizing up the window he had to crawl through. He grabbed a milk crate he used for his garden pots and emptied it to use a stool. He was soon opening the window and crawling in. He placed the gun ahead of him on his dressing table. As he crawled onto the dressing table it inexplicably started to topple, with Paul riding it onto the floor.

The lights went on, and Paul was staring at two masked men training handguns on him. They wore black balaclavas with eyeholes.

"Didn't you think we would be watching the street?" blurted one of them.

"Get outside!" barked the other, waving the gun at him.

Paul stared at his gun, lying on the floor near him.

"No ideas!" said the first gunman as he trod tightly on the gun. "Go on!" he shouted.

Paul got to his feet slowly and walked toward the door. As he did so, he felt a heavy blow to his lower back, and he coughed in pain.

"That's in return for last time!" scowled the second gunman, pushing Paul into the doorway. As Paul staggered to his living room, he saw another accomplice standing over Parson James Dunkley, who was gagged and tied to a chair. Paul's eyes met his, and they blinked to each other before Paul said, "Sorry they dragged you into this!"

"Shut your mouth and sit down!" a voice behind him thundered.

Paul sat next to the parson as two of his captors sat in front of him, with the third one standing. All had their guns ready, giving Paul limited scope for response, especially with the parson present.

*What happened to Hanson?* thought Paul.

Paul observed them. They wore black trousers, dark-colored shirts, and sneakers. One wore sandals. They appeared to have olive skin. Two spoke with English accents; a third captor's voice had a Middle East sound to it.

"Where is Everleigh's son?" the first captor said.

"How would I know?" replied Paul.

The speaker nodded to the one standing, who immediately punched the parson in the solar plexus, winding him badly. The parson folded in pain.

"Stop this, you bastards! Punish me, not him," shouted Paul.

The speaker continued, "I will ask again. Where is Everleigh's son, the one you rescued from us?"

Paul's mind whirred at what he could say to appease them to protect the parson. As he stared at the two captors seated in front of him, he noticed a slight movement in the open window behind them. He looked more closely and noticed Hanson pointing to the beeper to his Jaguar, and then he motioned downward with his hand horizontal. Paul readied himself for fireworks, giving a small nod, which he followed with the words, "I understand now. You're after the wrong man. The man I rescued was not Everleigh's son."

"This is no time for tricks," replied the speaker angrily.

"I'm telling you the truth, if you will just listen."

The speaker nodded again to the captor closest to the parson, who now placed a gun to the head of the parson. As this occurred, the alarm on Hanson's Jaguar went off like an air raid siren. Two of the captors ran to the window.

Paul lunged at the parson, tackling the parson and his chair in one movement. As they hurtled across the room, the speaker yelled his last breath as a bullet entered the back of his head and his body went limp. His weapon flopped on the couch beside him.

The two captors wheeled around in panic, not knowing from where the shooting was emanating, and responded by pointing their guns in the general direction of where Hanson had shot through the open window. The third captor swung his weapon toward the parson to regain control of the situation. As he did so, a second shot rang out, hitting him in the chest. The second captor leaped through the front window, rolled into the garden, and ran for his car. Paul got to his feet and opened the front door. He quickly reeled back as shots were fired toward the doorway by the fleeing captor. He heard Hanson's call: "Let him go Paul!"

Paul ran back to attend to the parson and quickly unbound him. Hanson soon appeared in the living room.

"Well, you arrived in good time, whoever you are," exclaimed the parson.

"Derek Hanson…. In fact, I was dropping Paul home, and we took some precautions."

"Thanks, Derek. Looks like we owe you our lives."

Paul asked, "Why did you let him go?"

"I put a bug under the car. I want to know where he goes, because this is only half the team."

Paul was still curious. "One thing: I thought I had your gun?"

"I didn't tell you about the one under my seat," quipped Hanson, smiling.

Paul laughed in relief. Soon police and ambulance men were swarming over his place.

# TEN

Yousef Rahmaan was waiting at the Hotspot Nightclub for the captors to return with the information he needed. He was on the FBI's Ten Most Wanted fugitive list for a history of criminal activities including smuggling and terrorism. He wore fancy dress: A black cloak and golden mask helped him blend into the crowd at the masquerade party that was taking place in the club that night.

As the lone escapee approached the nightclub, he picked up his mobile phone to ring Yousef, who answered quickly.

"Yousef! It's me, Amar," he said. Amar Kalim feared that his failure would anger his boss.

"Amar, what's wrong?" replied Yousef.

"I can't talk. I have to ditch my car. I see you in the club."

An unmarked MI5 car had pulled up in the side street where Amar had parked his car. Amar ran toward the club.

Hanson's phone rang.

"Sir, we see the target; he's entered the Hotspot Nightclub in Vine Street."

"Surround the place, but don't enter until I get there."

Back at Paul's house, a black Bell Ranger helicopter hovered above Paul's head, flooding the street with light.

Hanson shouted, "Paul, we've found their rendezvous point. Are you okay to come?"

"Yes," shouted Paul, as the helicopter blew refuse around them before landing.

Paul followed Hansen to the helicopter. After Hansen gave the pilot the thumbs-up, they were quickly airborne. The wind was a little gusty that night as they flew over twinkling lights. Paul's heart raced. The soft vibration and surreal cockpit reminded him of Afghanistan. The chopper soon dropped altitude, quickly popping Paul's ears, and landed in a small park a hundred meters from the nightclub. They sprinted up the street toward Hanson's operatives.

Hanson leaned into the car window "What's the update?"

Taylor and Hudspeth had watched Amar enter the nightclub. "He's inside and has not come out, sir," replied Taylor.

"We've put three men on the back door," added Hudspeth.

"Good. This is Paul Sanders…. I'll go inside, and Sanders will stay with you because the kidnapper knows his face."

"Sir, you'll need a mask, because it's a masquerade party. We've got balaclavas," smiled Taylor.

"Well, it can't hurt. In that case, Paul can come."

Hanson and Paul quickly made their way to the club.

"You lads are a bit scary. Where's ya' invites?" barked the bouncer.

"Right here" said Hanson, waving his MI5 ID card.

The bouncer pursed his lips and swung the door open, and Hanson and Paul entered the throng. A medieval kaleidoscope of color flashed across the dance floor against gyrating music and the pulse of strobe lights. Black capes, red silks, and glittering masks barred their pathway to the bar as they pushed through. A shiny green mermaid placed her arm over Paul, who stiffly lifted her by the waist and placed her behind him as he caught up with Hanson.

They arrived at the bar, which was bathed in deep blue light. The bar shone under beveled mirrors that cast the full spectrum of colors across the polished green marble bar. Yousef sat at the bar, still robed and masked, delaying contact with Amar to flush out any hidden threats. Amar had wandered the club, knowing Yousef's caution with such meetings, and now waited on the mezzanine level. Yousef was watching him periodically when Paul and Hanson arrived at the bar. Paul was surprised as he caught their reflection in the mirror: two balaclava-clad gents who on any other night would cause alarm to onlookers.

A girl in pink bunny suit with a large white pom-pom for a tail leaned across to Hanson and said, "Provocative!"

Hanson smiled behind his mask without replying, and looked away.

She persisted. "Why don't you provoke me?" She grabbed at Hanson's mask. He snatched her hand too tightly in the moment, causing her to cry with pain.

Yousef saw the gaffe and intervened. "That's no way to treat the lady," he cautioned.

Paul turned on Yousef, staring at his golden mask, into his jet black eyes. "Leave it, squire!"

Yousef stood eye to eye with Paul, aggressively, before Hanson grabbed Paul's arm and shouted against the music, "Not here."

Yousef returned to his drink and waited.

Paul scanned the crowd and his gaze fixed on Amar, who wore no costume, and appeared nervous. "Mezzanine level, three o'clock," Paul said loudly.

"Yes, I see him," replied Hanson.

Yousef noticed their interest in Amar. He reached for his phone and texted Amar, "Get out now!" But by the time Amar pulled his phone out of his pocket, it was too late.

He was flanked on both arms by Hanson and Paul, who began dragging him down the stairs. When they were halfway down, they saw Yousef standing at the bottom of the stairs, pointing a handgun at them. He fired two shots that hit Amar in the chest, causing him to collapse and tumble down the stairs onto others who were climbing. Paul jumped over the rail, landed hard, and dodged terrified partygoers as he ran after Yousef, who had rushed into the crowd. Paul looked left and right, staring hard, but Yousef had vanished.

# ELEVEN

The turbulence was gone as the jumbo jet soared over a desolate landscape.

"Are we over Afghanistan yet?" asked Jane from across the aisle.

"Didn't you hear the captain say that ten minutes ago?" replied John.

Jane shook her head and pointed at her earphones. The plane lost altitude as it approached Kabul, a low-rise city with an ancient Biblical character. Dusk was falling, and as the great plane approached, a city of arches and mud walls clustered with twinkling lights lay beneath, with its millions of inhabitants. Clay-colored undulating hills, with magic orange sunlight retreating, formed a backdrop to the city.

"This is your captain speaking. We are about to land in Kabul, where the temperature is twenty-eight degrees centigrade, or eighty-two degrees Fahrenheit, with a light wind from the southeast. I hope you have enjoyed your flight. Thank you for flying British Airways."

The engines increased power as the plane completed its landing sequence, touching down ten minutes later. A bus collected the passengers and drove them across the tarmac. Sir Ernest seemed bored, while Jane was curiously looking from side to side at the surroundings. John saw blocks of apartments against the hills on one side. Jane pointed at another side of the airport, where a suburb crisscrossed a hill as shadows fell across it.

"Yes, when I was here last time, the whole of that area was littered with wrecked aircraft," explained Sir Ernest.

John saw the Union Jack flying and added, "I feel better already, except I don't see our people."

Faulkner replied, "Does that make you feel better?" He pointed at a row of US Apache helicopters and armored carriers, which were flanked by a row of F-16 fighters. The bus approached the airport terminal, a flat-roofed white building with so many windows it resembled a large harmonica. John saw a large Russian Antonov aircraft sitting on the tarmac and exclaimed, "Look at that!"

Andrew Faulkner, the paleontologist travelling with the group, remarked, "Yes, Kabul can take those giants."

After the usual airport procedures they entered the arrivals lounge, where a man in Afghan garb carrying a sign labeled EVER-LEE stood. They piled into a Toyota four-wheel drive and sped away into the Kabul traffic.

"Can't stay in one spot for long," said their driver. He was a typical Afghan, with brown turban and gray tunic.

"Why is that?" asked Jane.

"You are Westerners! People here want to blow you up," he replied, dodging in and out of traffic as they passed low-lying walled buildings and vacant lots filled with rubble. The city was devastated. They passed rows of street vendors selling out of shanty town cubicles covered in dusty canvas. Soviet-style buildings abounded as they moved through the traffic.

"I'm amazed at the number of people here," said John.

"A few million and increasing, I believe," replied Faulkner.

Jane and Everleigh sat with glazed eyes. After a while they arrived in the suburb of Sherpur.

"These must be hotels," said Jane.

"No, madam, these are houses for VIPs," replied the driver.

"But they're so big," continued Jane.

They looked at streets filled with three- to four-story Russian Afghan architecture. Some of the houses resembled Oriental palaces, with ornate curved verandahs wrapped around spiral or roman pillars in pale blues and browns. Yet each was fenced like a fortress, with armed guards outside and barbed wire strung on first-floor verandahs. *Do they expect to beat off climbing intruders?* thought John.

"Who are these VIPs?" asked Sir Ernest.

"Don't ask," replied the taxi driver. "All we know is that they barged into Sherpur with tanks and the Americans by their side. You cannot argue with steel. Soon you may find out more, because you are staying at one of these houses, just around this corner."

They soon arrived at a mansionlike house. It was four stories high, with a large glass column held by roman pillars. At the top of the glass column was a triangular keystone with a motif of a horse rider against moon and stars. Guards dressed in green military-style uniforms with French Foreign Legion-style hats and carrying AK-47s surrounded their car with other attendants. The guards escorted them to the "house." A man in his forties with jet-black hair, white tunic, and baggy trousers, appeared.

"I am Hakeem Khan," said the man, extending his hand.

Sir Ernest shook hands and replied, "Sir Ernest Everleigh, Mr. Khan; and this is my entourage: Jane Thornton, Andrew Faulkner, and John Rowntree."

"Welcome to Kabul! Please make yourselves at home. Your rooms have been prepared."

They were led up a spiral staircase made of white marble with black and gold railing to their rooms, which had large white doors inlaid with floral patterns. John's room was large, with a desk, television, and double bed. John walked onto the balcony and looked over Sherpur, with its array of villas. John looked down and saw Sir Ernest chatting with Hakeem Khan. He swung his attention around to the house next door and saw a young boy, not more than twelve years old, putting his finger over his mouth as if to hush John. John smiled and nodded. The boy shook his head, pointed at John, and beckoned for him to go downstairs to the back of the house. John saw the boy disappear and thought nothing more of it. He walked downstairs to join Sir Ernest in the garden that surrounded the house.

"The Ministry of Culture and Kabul University have complained for years about the looting of our country, but nothing is done" complained Khan.

"Well, you know that's why our country has already returned tons of these looted antiquities. I think that Kabul needs to grow and strengthen its national collection," replied Sir Ernest.

"What do you mean by 'strengthen'?" asked John.

"I really mean 'increase security.'"

"I understand that you are meeting an official tomorrow from the Ministry of Culture to discuss the relic," said Khan.

"We just want to investigate the relic first. Then we can discuss where it should go. If it has historical importance, of course I will recommend it for the Kabul's national collection. If not, then we will see," replied Sir Ernest.

John saw the boy again flash across the garden toward the rear of the house.

"Do you mind if I explore the garden Mr. Khan?" asked John.

"Be my guest." replied Khan.

John strolled down the garden and saw the boy hiding behind a large pot.

John whispered, "Do you speak English?"

The boy shook his head and again put his finger over his mouth to hush John. He took John's hand and led him to a small garden shed. Just as they were about to enter, a shout was heard behind them, causing the boy to run and slip through a hole in the fence. John looked back and saw one of the guards chasing the boy. The guard could not make it through the bed of red roses like the boy could. The guard turned to John and smiled before putting his hand on John's shoulder to guide him back to the house.

Everyone had disappeared, so John took the stairs back to his room. As he approached his room, he saw a small balcony at the end of the corridor, which he guessed might overlook the small shed. His curiosity alive, he opened the balcony door. He realized that the balcony wrapped around the entire first floor of the house, and he peered over the railing. He saw two guards carrying a rolled-up carpet, which appeared to be very heavy, onto a wheelbarrow. They took the narrow side pathway on the darker side of the house. John followed this activity by walking around the verandah to the front of the house, where again he peered over to see the guards bundling the heavy carpet into the boot of the four-wheeled drive, which had backed into the driveway of the house.

To John's surprise, one of the guards emerged from the boot, with the carpet apparently lighter, before placing it in the wheelbarrow—this time rolled up more compactly. John went downstairs again and retraced his steps into the garden, but this time he stood just out of the line of sight of the garden shed. He craned his neck to see the two guards taking a second carpet from the shed. As soon as they were gone, John walked briskly to the shed and strode in. A bloodsoaked sheet lay unraveled. He started to feel nauseous as his eyes scanned the scene. Then he saw a Pakistani passport and a British passport. He picked them both up. Bloodstains covered the name HAKEEM KHAN on the first passport. He saw the photo. The face was not the one he had just met. He looked at the second passport and saw the name MARTIN CRAWFORD—the missing student.

His adrenaline was now pumping, and he thrust Hakeem's passport into his pocket and strolled out of the shed, trying to keep his cool. He looked behind him as he sped around the corner to just see the return of the wheelbarrow. He searched downstairs for Sir Ernest, but Sir Ernest was nowhere to be found. John climbed the stairs of the house and again returned to the balcony. One guard went into the shed while the other waited. After a couple of minutes, both guards were looking intensely at the ground, as if searching for something.

John knocked at Jane's door, and she emerged, sleepy.

"Look, Jane, something's wrong. Where's Sir Ernest?" asked John anxiously.

Jane could see the perspiration on his forehead and asked, "What on earth do you mean?"

"Hello, Jane! There's no time to explain; where is Sir Ernest?" pressed John.

Jane pointed across the hallway, and John took her hand and knocked on the door. Sir Ernest appeared. He was talking on his mobile phone. Jane stood in front of John and boldly said, "Hang up!"

Sir Ernest stopped talking, moved the phone away from his ear, and paused. A voice was heard from the phone: "Hello? Hello?"

"I'll ring you back!" barked Sir Ernest.

Jane and John came into his room and shut the door.

"Well, what?" asked Sir Ernest.

John pulled out the bloodied passport and threw it on the desk exclaiming: "I also saw Martin Crawford's passport!" Sir Ernest picked it up and glanced at it. Jane took it from him and studied it.

"You're not saying that our host is an imposter?" Jane looked scared.

"Worse than that. He's a murderer! I saw them loading the bodies in their car," John almost whispered.

"I'm going to ring the British embassy," said Sir Ernest. He rang on his mobile while John and Jane sat on the bed.

Minutes later, Sir Ernest was frustrated.

"What did they say?" asked Jane.

"They are liaising with the police and the military," said Sir Ernest. The phone rang, and after a further conversation, Sir Ernest was furious: "E-V-E-R-L-E-I-G-H, for the third time. Hey, doesn't anyone speak proper English?" Sir Ernest hung up and exclaimed, "It's bloody useless. I would get a damned bureaucrat…. I can't get anywhere. We should make a run for it."

"How do we do that? We've been told that it is dangerous for Westerners to walk the streets, so they would have to drive us, and that's probably what they have planned except we'll be kidnapped and probably ransomed," advised John.

"What about our own military police, or ISAF, or whatever they call them?" asked Jane.

"I've already asked about that. Apparently they have their hands full, today of all days. All I received were promises that everything that can be done is being done."

"Can that mobile ring internationally?" asked John.

"You want to ring Scotland Yard?" joked Sir Ernest.

"I have a friend who has served in the military in Afghanistan, and he may know what to do," suggested John.

"Be my guest," commented Sir Ernest as he handed over the phone.

John dialed the number that Paul had given him. Paul answered his mobile.

"Paul Sanders."

"Paul, it's John here, from Afghanistan. We've hit a spot of bother already."

"I'm listening," replied Paul curtly.

John explained the situation to Paul quickly.

"John, put Sir Ernest on the phone."

"He wants to speak to you," said John to Sir Ernest, handing him the phone.

"What was the arrangement with the money?" asked Paul.

"Well, we were to hand over half the money for a map, and they were to take us somewhere in the countryside," replied Sir Ernest.

"Have you the money with you?" asked Paul.

"No, a courier is arriving tomorrow morning, as the banks are closed today," replied Sir Ernest.

"Does Khan know this?"

"Khan is dead," replied Sir Ernest.

"Let's call him Khan," said Paul.

"When we arrived, it was the first thing Khan asked me. I thought it was a bit rude," replied Sir Ernest.

"We know why he has no manners," added John, listening intently to Sir Ernest's replies to Paul.

Paul asked for the phone to be handed back to John. The first thing Paul said was, "John, listen very carefully. When that courier arrives tomorrow..." Paul paused.

"We're dead," John finished Paul's sentence for him.

"I didn't want to put it as bluntly as that; but yes, you are in great danger," continued Paul.

"What should we do?" asked John.

"I think that it is too dangerous to try and leave. The slightest move out of the ordinary, and they will torture you to get the money, and hold you hostage anyway. No, you need to play this out to survive. You need to buy time. Somehow you have to stop the courier. Then you must get them to take you to the bank instead, where you will be safe, or at least safer than where you are. I should be able to arrange a welcome at the bank for them," explained Paul.

John turned to Sir Ernest and explained the plan. Sir Ernest replied, "I don't know how to contact the courier."

Paul said, "Sir Ernest needs to tell them that there's been a change in plan, and that you have to be at the bank when it opens. Then you all must leave for the bank first thing in the morning, to arrive at opening time. Pray that the courier does not arrive before you leave. Tell Sir Ernest he must do everything normally. He must ask for the map as proof, before he goes to the bank. He must carry on as a hardnosed businessman about to do a deal, so they do not get suspicious. Everyone must act normally."

"I've got it," replied John.

"John, there is something else I must tell you. I have been approached by MI5, in view of what happened to you, to help them," explained Paul.

"What on earth for?" exclaimed John.

"Your kidnapping was not a random act, but a case of mistaken identity. The kidnappers thought that you were Sir Ernest's son. I believe those kidnappers are connected to the people who have you now. I believe they are smugglers and extortionists. In fact, they broke into my home and even kidnapped Parson Dunkley."

"Whatever for?" asked John.

"They thought he might know where you were, and then they used him to make me talk, still thinking you were Sir Ernest's son. Look, I don't know what deal Sir Ernest has done to get this relic, but he's stirred up a hornet's nest. Its too late now to warn you to watch your back, but it seems that if they still think that you are Sir Ernest's son, you are in danger of kidnap again," replied Paul.

"When are you coming here?" asked John.

"MI5 have me on a private charter jet coming into Kabul tomorrow morning, early—certainly before banking hours. If this plan goes well, I can have people in place. I will get back to you on this phone with the name and address of the bank that Sir Ernest should take them to tomorrow morning, so that we can intercept you all safely at the bank. Even better, I will text the actual message to Sir Ernest's phone, and he can show the text message to Khan as proof of the change in arrangements. Well, good luck. I'd better go." Paul hung up.

# TWELVE

I t was now late afternoon, and Andrew Faulkner had joined them in
Sir Ernest's room, to be told the bad luck that had befallen them.
They were worried that the text message from Paul had not arrived,
when Sir Ernest's mobile phone rang.

"Everleigh. No, we have not heard from ISAF…" Sir Ernest was
heard to say.

"I would like you to listen very carefully," said a voice on the phone.
"MI5 are now in control of our situation, and I believe you will be hearing from them tonight. They are arriving tomorrow morning and have
advised that under no circumstances is anyone to do anything, unless it
is under their direction. Our lives could depend on it. Do I make myself
clear?" Sir Ernest hung up the phone.

"I didn't hear Paul say that," said John.

"He didn't, but it is obvious, isn't it? The first thing that would happen if the police turned up at the front door is that we would either be
held hostage or shot," said Sir Ernest.

"I don't know about that," replied John.

"Are you prepared to take the risk?" said Faulkner.

John was silent. Just then, Sir Ernest's phone made a sound as Paul's
text message arrived.

"Is that the text?" asked John.

"Yes, let me read it." Sir Ernest showed it to the others and said, "It's good. I had better go downstairs and show Khan."

"Aren't we due for dinner in an hour?" asked Jane.

"Yes, she's right. If we don't go, it may look suspicious," said John.

"I think we all should go to our rooms, rest, get ready for dinner, and go down as if nothing has happened," advised Sir Ernest.

They soon went down to dinner, where a large banquet had been prepared Afghan-style with many dishes. It was a large dining room with French doors leading onto a balcony, where arched windows revealed the last red glows of sunset. A large tapestry of warriors on chariots in battle, portrayed in royal blues and golds, hung on one wall. The wooden dining table looked antique, and it sat on a large Persian carpet.

John went onto the balcony and was soon accompanied by Khan. John pointed to a large billboard standing on top of the hill overlooking Sherpur. The billboard displayed a red mural of Massoud, the assassinated leader of the Northern Alliance, who had valiantly fought the Russian invasion some years ago.

"I believe he is seen as a national hero in Afghanistan," commented John.

"By some," replied Khan in a noncommittal manner. "Come, let us sit down to dinner."

As Khan entered the doorway, Sir Ernest blocked him momentarily before they passed each other. Sir Ernest joined John, who was still admiring the mural of Massoud.

"They called him the Lion of Panjshir. He came from the Pahjshir Valley, north of here. He was the most famous Mujaheddin that fought the Soviets, but he was killed in the name of God." Sir Ernest's voice seemed far away as he stood at the other end of the balcony.

"It's easy to kill in the name of God, but harder to justify it," replied John.

"Yes. If God exists, I do not believe He would lend ownership of His name so easily. Yet if He existed, surely He would defend the use of His name against the innocent," replied Sir Ernest.

"If the umpire intervened in the game of life, the rules would be broken," John responded.

"So a cynical umpire watches us 'play', " joked Sir Ernest.

John smiled, and they returned inside to dine. As they sat down, platters of barbequed lamb on skewers were served, still sizzling. Khan was dressed impeccably, in white from head to toe, looking more like an Indian rajah than the imposter he was.

"Greetings to our guests!" announced Khan, who added, "I trust you have recovered from your long journey."

"Why, thank you, Mr. Khan. We did not expect such hospitality," said Sir Ernest coolly.

Sir Ernest seated himself next to Khan while the others filed in down the table. Wine was poured, and platters of food eased the initial tensions.

"Sir Ernest," began Khan, "I believe you are an Oxford professor."

"Lecturer," replied Sir Ernest.

"Let's put your scholarly abilities to the test. This tapestry on the wall—what is it?" asked Khan.

Sir Ernest studied the chariots and soldiers. A map showing the Mediterranean to Afghanistan formed the background to the fighting. "I think it likely that this is the army of Genghis Khan, seeking control of the silk road. The network of pathways from Damascus on the Mediterranean through Afghanistan is probably the Silk Road," replied Sir Ernest.

"Very good," replied Khan. "And what is the great game?"

"It is the tug of war between the Russians and the British to seek control over Afghanistan. The game has been raging since the nineteenth century and continued into the twentieth and this century. In fact, in the 1700s, Afghanistan was ruled by someone with your name— Dost Mohammed Khan—who was known as an educated, just and pious man, just like you," smiled Sir Ernest. Khan smiled back. "However," continued Sir Ernest, "he fell victim to the great game, and after wooing the Russians, he provoked the British before being ousted as Amir."

"Fascinating, Sir Ernest," commented Jane. "It is a country of such history."

"There is a lot more, if you would like to hear it," said Sir Ernest.

After wine and more history, Sir Ernest produced his mobile and said, "Mr. Khan, there's been a change in plans. The bank has advised us that we will have to go there to settle your payment. They have decided it is not safe to send a courier with so much money."

"That's not what we agreed. You will have to ring your bank and get them to send the courier here. We have better security here," objected Khan.

Sir Ernest paused before improvising: "Maybe you are right; let me ring them." Sir Ernest dialed the phone, ringing Paul's number, which went to voice-mail. "Looks like I'm too late; they've gone home" explained Sir Ernest.

Khan looked frustrated.

"Anyway, it will give us some more time tomorrow morning," added Sir Ernest.

"What do you mean?" asked Khan.

"Well, the courier they were going to use would not arrive until late tomorrow, so I agreed to go to the bank as I thought you might not want to wait," replied Sir Ernest.

Khan grabbed his wine glass and was about to drink when he said, "What is the address of the bank?"

Sir Ernest showed the mobile phone text message to him with the address. "All right, we'll go to the bank," Khan pronounced indignantly. The awkward moment passed, and with some wine and stories from Khan, the tension seemed to ease, albeit with a surreal feeling.

"Tell me Mr. Khan," asked Sir Ernest, "What will come of Afghanistan?"

Khan smiled and sipped his French red wine before answering, "Afghanistan is famous for its Mujaheddin, ever since the Russians failed to conquer our people. Yes, the Americans helped us, but—how do I put it?—'misunderstandings' occurred, and they left us…until now. Now the country is a battleground, and our people are sick of it. For this reason they have come to Kabul, because the countryside is too dangerous for them. I don't know when it will end, but as with the Russian invasion, all things will end, and I know this: the Afghan people will not lose."

Sir Ernest nodded, knowing when to leave a subject alone, but John couldn't help himself.

"Why does the Afghan believe that foreign forces are really conducting a crusade?" asked John.

"Because they are. It started centuries ago. The British sent forces to the Holy Land in the name of God, or rather for Rome. We Muslims defended our lands in the name of God also. God must have laughed when He saw a war over how we should worship Him. Today it is more complicated, but it is a still a fight between Muslim and Christian," replied Khan.

"But Christians and Muslims can work together. In fact, they already do all over the world. Why can't they?" objected John.

"Give me an example" challenged Khan.

"El Cid," replied John

"El Cid?" queried Khan, whose confidence was now dented.

"You don't know?" asked John.

"I know. Of course I know!" exclaimed Khan.

"Well, I don't know," said Jane.

"Well, for your benefit, Jane, El Cid conquered Valencia in Spain with a combined Christian and Muslim army—Spaniards and Moors. They jointly administered the city," continued John.

Khan's face had changed, and he moved to change the subject: "Sir Ernest, tell me what is so important about this relic that you are paying a lot of money to get."

"For a discount I might share this with you," joked Sir Ernest.

"No, I am happy to be ignorant, but you cannot give us a clue?" replied Khan.

Sir Ernest had consumed enough wine to say, "Why not something? It is an object that tells a very interesting story." Sir Ernest immediately regretted saying this, as he remembered that Khan would not be joining him in recovering the relic. "Look, it's late, and it would be good to get to the bank early. We'll leave at 8:45 a.m. What time is breakfast?" asked Sir Ernest.

"Eight o'clock. But what about a nightcap, Sir Ernest?" asked Khan, who had enjoyed some of the lively discussion.

"I am a little tired," replied Sir Ernest, who was relieved that the dinner had ended.

"All right. Tomorrow's the day," exclaimed Khan with a smile on his face. They all stared awkwardly at Khan before smiling back and making their way to bed.


As Jane went to her room, John approached her and said, "Jane, whatever happens tomorrow, I want you to know that I don't hold you responsible for what happened to me in Oxford."

"What changed your mind?" smiled Jane.

"Your pure nature?" joked John. "Hey, maybe I was a little rash, and knowing what I know now…" John realized this as one of those topics when the less said the better. He started to go but turned back sharply and said, "One more thing…do you think Sir Ernest knows more than he is letting on?" Jane eyed John in silence. "You know more?" smiled John. "No!" exclaimed Jane. "What then?" pressed John. "Sir Ernest is a mysterious man but…" Jane paused. "But do you trust him?" John finished the sentence for her. "It's not a matter of trust, it's that you don't ask him more than you have to?" Jane explained. "Why not?" John realized he had hit a nerve. "He's kind of scary and demands your full loyalty to do things that you might not want to do" she replied. "Like what?" John probed. "I've said enough and I'm tired John." "Well, good night Jane." John nodded and Jane smiled back, before they both retired for the night.

# THIRTEEN

John could not sleep past about 6:00 a.m., and with dawn approaching, he crept down to the rose garden and broke off the most beautiful red rose he could find. He retreated to his room after leaving the rose at Jane's door. As John put the rose down, he noticed the door was ajar, and he heard Jane's voice. He could see that she had just had a shower and was sitting on the bed, with hair wet, in her dressing gown. He could just hear her talking:

"The way this is going, there will be no rendezvous!"

John listened with curiosity. *Who could she be talking to?* he thought. He heard her hang up the phone and saw her dialing someone else. As she did so, she reached into her brown backpack that was sitting on the bed beside her. John heard some soft words and could only make out the words "Got it." He almost pushed the door open, but he stopped himself. She was talking softly now, and so John edged back to his room, puzzled. He decided to say nothing.

It was to be a day of reckoning. John wondered if he would see this day out, and he pondered how the many armed forces presently serving in Afghanistan must feel on the morning of each of their battles. *When your number is up, your number is up*, thought John, but he didn't believe it. He was someone who believed that you always have a fighting chance, unless you never see it coming.

Two black Toyota four-wheel-drives stood with motors running in front of the mansion. The guards had opened the gates, and everyone was assembled in front of the vehicles.

"Sorry I could not join you for breakfast," said Khan, who was the last to emerge from the house. "Sir Ernest and Mr. Rowntree will come with me, and the lady and Mr. Faulkner will travel with Farouk in the second car," commanded Khan. With the nerves that were felt by all of them, no one was prepared to argue with him. Khan walked over to the remaining guards after the others were seated in the cars and said, "Wait here for Yousef. He is expected here this morning, but his flight must have been delayed. When he arrives, call me and I will tell you what we are doing. Did you get rid of the bodies?"

"Yes," said the first guard.

The second guard was about to talk about the lost passport, but the first guard stepped on his foot.

"What?" barked Khan.

"Nothing. I was going to tell you where we put them."

"Tell your mother, not me. What do I care?" Khan wheeled around and stepped into the driver's seat of the first car.

The first guard turned to the second guard and said, "Are you an idiot? We will be blamed for that passport. Probably that little rascal from next door took it to sell it in the markets."

"Yes, you're right. If I get my hands on that little one, I will give him a hiding."

They set off at a fast pace, quickly leaving Sherpur. Each of the late-model black Toyotas was brown from dust. Khan knew the streets well and drove deliberately without speaking, creating tension in the car. After a few minutes, the silence was broken as Khan sounded the horn as they passed the busy markets. They left the markets, and at the end of the street Khan saw a car parked across the street. The two-car convoy drove up to it, and Khan sounded the horn vigorously. A policeman in cobalt-blue uniform, black bulletproof vest over his uniform, and Charles de Gaulle cap appeared beside his window. He stared up at the Afghan, and after a few moments of intense thought, opened the window.

"Yes, officer?" Khan asked, speaking in Pashto.

"Sir, there is trouble against Westerners today. It is not safe to be driving today," warned the policeman.

"Oh, officer, we are just going to the bank," replied Khan.

"Sir, for caution, I will have to travel with you," ordered the policeman.

"Officer, we have a guard in the car behind us. He is well armed."

Khan was nervous. The policeman eyed the car behind, looked again at Khan and said, "Just the same, I will travel with you. Are you armed?"

"No," replied Khan as the officer hopped into the backseat. As he did, the officer waved at his other officers, and soon the car obstructing the street let them pass.

The policeman commented on the violence against Westerners and about the weather, but the others were quiet. They soon arrived at the bank, which was contained in the first floor of a three-story office building with shops on the ground floor. The building appeared to have been built in the sixties and was a normal shop block with concrete, aluminum, and glass construction. They parked in the car park near five other cars. The second car remained outside the car park.

"Why does he not park inside?" asked the policeman.

"Standard procedure: he watches us," said Khan as he turned to the others and said, "Please stay in the car, because it is not safe today."

"But you'll need me," said Sir Ernest.

Khan said nothing, and then the policeman and Khan got out of the car.

"Thank you, officer. I think we are safe now," said Khan.

"To make sure, I will accompany you into the bank. Are the Westerners coming with us?" replied the policeman.

Sir Ernest had also emerged from the car and said, "Mr. Khan, are we going into the bank now?" Khan stood for a moment in thought.

The standoff continued for about thirty seconds until the policeman said, "What is wrong, Mr. Khan? It is not safe to be standing out here with Westerners, as we are a target."

Paul emerged from the building, wearing a suit. He was about thirty meters away and was walking toward them. John had wound down his window and muttered to Sir Ernest, "That's Paul." Sir Ernest nodded. At the same time, the guard from the second Toyota left his vehicle and was walking toward Khan.

Khan turned to the policeman and said, "Excuse me, officer, there may be a security issue." Before Khan began walking, his phone rang. Yousef called him by his real name:

"Omar, I'm at the house The courier has arrived. You're in a trap—"

Khan dropped his phone in his pocket without hanging up and pulled a revolver, aimed it, and fired two rounds into the policeman's chest. The policeman slumped to the ground, writhing with the sudden pain. Paul was now running toward the car, and Khan fired at Paul, who dropped to the ground, returning his own fire as one of the bullets hit the side of the car. Khan reentered the vehicle's driver's seat. Sir Ernest had also returned to the car as bullets were flying all around them, fired by unknown gunmen.

"This is meant to be a rescue!" shouted Sir Ernest.

The guard had also returned to his car, and Paul had now run around the other cars and was coming sideways toward the second black car. The guard resumed his seat in the drivers seat, and as he did, Faulkner grabbed him around the neck and had him in a headlock. At the same time, Faulkner screamed to Jane, "Run!"

Jane quickly ran from the car, dashing first toward Paul, but other bullets were flying and she was forced toward Khan and the others. Khan engaged reverse gear and floored the accelerator, causing the back wheels to spin. Burnt rubber emanated as smoke from the back of the car. The car almost ran over Jane as John shouted, "Watch out Jane!" and John swung his door open with his arms outstretched. Jane ran for John, instinctively falling into John's arms as he collected her into the car. Paul jumped in the path of the reversing car with gun still drawn, but he quickly jumped out of the way as it reversed out of the car park. Meanwhile, Faulkner continued his struggle with the guard, and Paul turned his attention toward them. He ran toward them and dragged the guard by his jacket onto the ground before thrusting his gun past his face, knocking him out.

Faulkner had left the vehicle, shouting, "He's getting away!" He pointed at Khan, who was speeding away from the scene. Paul hopped into the vehicle with Faulkner and then roared the engine to life, spinning the car in a wild arc across the driveway and out onto the dusty road in pursuit of Khan and the others. Khan pointed his gun at Sir Ernest, telling him that they would follow the fate of the policeman if they made a wrong move. The quick events paralyzed them into submission.

The AH-64D Apache Longbow helicopter zoomed onto the scene and hovered over the car park, where police were swarming toward the body of their fallen comrade. The pilot, from the British Army Air Corps' ninth regiment, had been scrambled that morning after ISAF headquarters in Kabul received orders to cooperate with an MI5 operative—Paul Sanders, call sign "Red Fox"—who had spoken briefly by radio just before the shootout.

"Red Fox calling Blue Fox, over," came the call on the pilot's radio.

"Blue Fox here. What is your position? Over," called the pilot.

"I am in a black SUV, pursuing similar black SUV. Over."

"Shall I spoil their day? Over," asked the pilot.

"Warning shots only. They have hostages. Engage only to stop them," replied Paul.

The Apache swept over the two cars that were snaking their way through winding dusty roads. The pilot waited for a straight stretch of road, planned his strike, overshot, turned toward them, and began his descent in a direct line for Khan's vehicle. The Apache's powerful cannon began to fire in a line leading to the vehicle, throwing up huge plumes of dust that blinded Khan's front line of sight. Khan braked. The helicopter hovered above. Khan stopped the car, ran to the boot, and threw off a tarpaulin, revealing an RPG rocket. He quickly mounted it on his shoulders and aimed at the sky, but the houses in the street obscured his view. He listened intently for the pulsing blades, in readiness to fire.

Paul's car pulled up about twenty meters behind Khan. Paul saw the RPG he was holding, which Khan quickly swung to aim at Paul's vehicle.

Khan fired the RPG, and it zoomed toward the vehicle. Paul shouted for Faulkner to jump, and they both leapt clear and hit the ground as their vehicle exploded. Paul felt the sting of debris hitting his face. Smoke engulfed the street, blinding the Apache pilot's vision. Khan, realizing he was safe, sped off, taking some turns out of the line of vision of the Apache. Paul clutched his radio and called the pilot.

"Blue Fox, are you all right, over?"

"Yes, what was the explosion? Over," asked the pilot.

"RPG. He took our car out, over," replied Paul.

"What are your orders, Red Fox?" asked the pilot.

"Have you the coordinates of the Sherpur house? Over," asked Paul.

"Yes, over," replied the pilot.

"Proceed to the house and report. That's all that can be done, over," instructed Paul.

"Understood. Blue Fox out."

The Apache proceeded to the house at Sherpur and found it deserted. The pilot reported this to Paul and returned to base. Paul was bitterly disappointed. He had missed saving his friend.

# FOURTEEN

Yousef had arrived at the house in Sherpur to meet Khan or Omar, the name he knew him by. Upon hearing from the two guards that Omar had gone to the bank, Yousef waited until, to his surprise, a courier arrived in an old truck with three heavily armed guards travelling in the back under the canopy. One of them clutched a black briefcase containing a bank authority to pay one million dollars on sighting the relic. Upon the courier telling Yousef that he had instructions to settle a transaction only with the authority of Sir Ernest, Yousef had telephoned Omar to warn him of a possible trap. Yousef, knowing the courier held the money they were trying to steal, decided to play along with the arrangement and told the courier that there had been a change of venue for the settlement, and that Sir Ernest was to now meet them on the other side of town. The new venue was a house that served as a nest for smugglers allied to Yousef. They set off quickly in convoy and reached the house half an hour later. In the meantime, Omar and Sir Ernest arrived at the house.

The house was a simple adobe structure with five rooms, including a kitchen. The black Toyota arrived outside on the muddy street, and Sir Ernest and the others were herded inside.

"What is your real name?" sneered Sir Ernest.

"You can call me Omar. I didn't like 'Mr. Khan'" said Omar.

They were placed in the front room of the house and tied up.

"What are you going to do to us?" asked Jane.

"We know about your deception, so we will not be kind unless we get what we want," replied Omar.

"How do we do that?" asked John.

"The courier has been intercepted by our people and is on his way here. Sir Ernest will sign the paperwork and we will be on our way," replied Omar.

A woman, all in black with hajib, was let into the house through the front door. She was carrying bags of groceries from the local supermarket. They seemed to have large amounts of Indian bread, vegetables, mineral water, and other supplies. She made her way to the kitchen, took off her hijab, and unloaded her groceries. She brought some mineral water to each of the prisoners, which they held with their tied hands, gulping anxiously. Ten minutes passed, and a knock at the door preceded Yousef entering the house. Yousef and Omar embraced each other before Yousef took Omar by the arm into the next room, out of earshot of the others.

"Listen, Omar, I've got the courier outside. We need to deal with him," urged Yousef.

"Well, just take the money from him," responded Omar.

"They are heavily armed, and there are four of them. We'll have to negotiate," said Yousef.

"That means we need the Westerners to cooperate. How can we trust them not to give us up?" asked Omar.

Just put your knife on the girl's throat, and send out the old man. If there is any problem, we will have to kill them all," advised Yousef.

A few moments later they reentered the room and Yousef started talking.

"I would like to you to pay attention, Sir Ernest, John Everleigh, and Jane Thornton. If you do as you are told, you will come out of this alive. Do not make a sound." He pulled out an elaborate gold dagger with Arabic writing on it and moved close to Jane, who stared at him in fear.

"Don't touch her!" shouted John.

Yousef pushed John to the wall and put the dagger against his throat.

"I said 'quiet.' Your father is going to go outside with Omar, and if he makes one wrong move, or even the wrong word, I will kill you both," warned Yousef as he looked back and forth between John and Jane.

John's adrenaline was pumping so hard he ignored the references to him being Sir Ernest's son, especially after Paul's phone call to him yesterday warning him that he was kidnapped because they believed he was Sir Ernest's son.

"Well?" shouted Yousef, looking back and forth at both of them.

"Do as they say!" replied Jane. John nodded reluctantly.

"What do you want me to do?" asked Sir Ernest.

Yousef nodded to Omar, who spoke to Sir Ernest: "Your courier is outside. Here is your map, so you can show him that you have what you want."

Sir Ernest looked at the document briefly. It seemed to cover the entire Middle East, with smaller maps inset in it, but he had no time to study it.

"You will come with me and instruct them to give me the money and sign his papers. Do you understand?"

"I do, but first, you promise to let us all go unharmed?" asked Sir Ernest, thinking that his bargaining power was very limited.

"Omar, before you answer, I would like to know if our deal with Everleigh still stands," interrupted Yousef.

There was an awkward silence as Sir Ernest looked at Jane, whose intuition sparked immediately. "What? You already know this man?" she asked."

"Jane…er…I dealt with him as a voice on the phone to buy the relic. That is all. I didn't know about all this. I knew that Khan was a well-known dealer in antiquities. This man was Khan's partner," answered Sir Ernest, who turned to Yousef and asked, "What did happen to the real Khan?"

"He became greedy. Look, let's go! Our deal stands as long as you do your part. You will all be set free if we get our money," replied Yousef.

"How do we know that?" barked John.

"Do not insult us!" scoffed Yousef. Sir Ernest bit his tongue when he remembered that when Yousef had increased the price from one million to ten million dollars, Sir Ernest had persuaded him to accept a deferred royalty of nine million dollars, payable from his book royalties after he wrote about the relic. In any event, he could hardly pay this killer another nine million dollars.

Omar and Sir Ernest left the house and walked to the back of the truck, where Yousef had asked the courier and his men to wait. An old man in a kurta and robes pumped water from a well and ignored them. They all jumped up and sat on the two benches under the truck's canopy, facing each other. The courier, Hassan Sahib, was an educated Afghan man dressed in white kurta, black waistcoat, and jeans. His men wore dark kurtas and robes. They had sunburnt, scarred faces and carried AK-47 rifles. Omar commenced the conversation:

"Thank you for coming; my name is Hakeem Khan, and this is Sir Ernest Everleigh. I am sorry for the mix-up in venue today, but we had a security issue that made this location safer. We have provided the material to Sir Ernest. Sir Ernest, you might show what you have."

Sir Ernest pulled out the map, which he showed the courier before saying, "We are satisfied; where would you like me to sign?"

The courier pulled out a letter, which he handed to Sir Ernest. The letterhead bore the name GREATER BAXENDALE BANK and read:

*Hassan Sahib*
*Manager*
*State Bank of Afghanistan*
*45 Rose Street*
*Kabul*

Dear Sir

**Re: Settlement of purchase of rights to relic: Khan Partners to Everleigh**

We confirm that your bank will act as agent for our bank in respect of our client, the Antiquities Foundation, which is providing the sum of one million dollars to purchase rights to a relic, and information in relation thereto, presently situated in Afghanistan. Sir Ernest Everleigh has been authorized by the Foundation to settle the transaction and take custody of the relic. The settlement is to be completed as follows:

1. The relic is to be sighted by both Hassan Sahib and Sir Ernest Everleigh, who are to certify in writing the delivery to Sir Ernest Everleigh.

2. Sir Ernest must produce a certificate of authenticity of the relic from an agreed expert. In this regard, the Foundation has agreed that Mr. Andrew Faulkner must certify in writing the authenticity.

3. Safe passage by at least three security personnel must occur on settlement, and it is a condition that the three security personnel must have Sir Ernest and the relic in safe custody at the time the funds are handed over.

4. The chief security officer must certify that, in his belief, there is reasonable safe passage and means of safe passage available to them at the time of settlement, which must include protective housing for the relic to avoid damage in transit by storm or tempest or act of war or act of God.

5. A receipt signed by Hakeem Khan for the funds must be signed by him.

The sum of one million dollars will be wired to the Foundation's newly opened Kabul account today. This amount is to be withdrawn in cash on the day of the settlement. Bank charges and fees are payable by the arrangement agreed in our earlier correspondence.

*Yours faithfully*

*Martin De Jersey*
*Director*

Sir Ernest handed the letter to Omar, who read it and became angry before pocketing it. "This was not what was agreed!" objected Omar.

"It was not my understanding. Of course, you know the money is not coming from me, so I don't make the conditions," replied Sir Ernest.

"But you should have told me sooner, because this will have grave consequences. Surely this can be fixed?" asked Omar.

"I would have to make some phone calls," said Sir Ernest.

"So what is the problem?" asked the courier.

"I don't have the relic, let alone the certificates you want," replied Sir Ernest.

"When can you get them?" asked the courier.

"I would say it will take at least four days," replied Sir Ernest.

"In that case, I am going to cancel the settlement today. I am due elsewhere anyway," replied the courier.

"No, wait. He can make the phone calls," said Omar, speaking in Pashto with some intensity.

"Mr. Khan, I have some experience with these matters; it will not settle today, even if your friend makes phone calls. These people in London will not hand over their money without getting what they are paying for. There has been a misunderstanding." The courier then continued in English. "Gentlemen, I must go now. When you have the relic and the certificates, ring me and we can arrange settlement on short notice, now that everything else is arranged. I will leave the letter with you. It is only a copy, in any event. Here is my card with my telephone number."

The courier handed the map back to Sir Ernest, who hopped out of the truck, prompting Sir Ernest to do likewise, and shook his hand. Omar followed reluctantly and also shook the courier's hand. The truck's engines roared to life, and they were gone quickly, leaving Sir Ernest and Omar looking at each other.

Omar barked, "This is a big mistake. Give me that map!"

Sir Ernest quickly handed it to Omar, who pocketed it.

"Get inside!" Omar shouted, taking his anger out on Sir Ernest.

As they entered the room, Yousef was standing there, carrying an AK-47 rifle as they exchanged some heated words in Pashto.

"Well, where is the money?" asked Yousef.

"They want the relic," replied Omar.

"What! Are they still there?" shouted Yousef.

"They've gone" replied Omar.

"You let them go!" objected Yousef.

"Are you stupid!, We would have killed each other. Three men held guns as we spoke," replied Omar.

"What do we do now?" asked Yousef.

"We get the relic. The bank manager said he will settle with us once we have the relic," replied Omar.

"You *are* stupid! The deal is blown. They tried to kill us at the bank. They will tip off the manager. It was only luck that he wasn't tipped off. Look, they'll know any minute. We must leave immediately. They'll *pay*. We have hostages," said Yousef.

# FIFTEEN

They rolled around like three peas in a pod in the back of Omar's Toyota four-wheel-drive, with their hands tied and coarse hessian hoods covering their heads. They felt like they were suffocating. Fortunately the air conditioning kept them from serious discomfort, but the bumpy road left them bruised and battered. They had stopped many times, and the hustle and bustle of Kabul had long gone. After a while the windows of the car were wound down, and they heard the back of the vehicle open before the rug was pulled from them. Their hoods and hands were untied, but Yousef carried a dull gray revolver tucked into his belt and pointed to it twice.

When they were free, Yousef beckoned some roadside vendors who provided mineral water in plastic bottles, which they drank desperately. Yousef handed some US dollars to the vendors, which caused them to smile and walk back to their stall. John looked out the window to see that they were one of two vehicles that had stopped to get water. John saw that Omar was in the other vehicle, laughing loudly. The other vehicle was a black utility with a couple of men in the back and the others crowding around outside. The vehicle was covered in dust. Most of the passengers wore black turbans (some purple and white), black tunics, and black gowns known as *salwar kameez*. Some wore similar clothing with the more common pakol caps and shrouds over their shoulders, with RPGs slung loosely against the shrouds. Others carried AK-47 rifles.

"Taliban," said Omar, who was standing behind their vehicle as he drank his water. John felt the adrenaline flow after hearing this, while Sir Ernest and Jane looked remarkably calm. Did they know something he didn't, or was this a false sense of security?

"Here comes our guide," said Yousef.

One of the Taliban walked alongside Omar as he returned to their vehicle. They were all inside, and all were startled by sudden gunfire. Laughter erupted from the Afghans both inside and outside the vehicle. John felt some relief as he saw the Taliban shooting into the air as they sped off. Omar and their Taliban guide talked nonstop in their own language for the next half hour as Yousef drove. A welcome silence crept in. In the distance John could see snow-covered mountains topped with streaking clouds. Occasional clusters of mud houses could be seen, but people were scarce.

They drove between two mountains. The road was still quite good but bumpy, softened by the forgiving suspension of the late model four-wheel-drive. Soon they pulled over to the side of the road, and Yousef, Omar, and the guide got out and looked ahead. John craned his neck and could see nothing but more snow on the blue-gray mountains in the distance. He could see a flat-topped building still some way off. The ground was remarkably flat in the valley that lay between the two mountains.

John felt uneasy. There was no law here. What chance was there that they would escape with their lives? They were effectively hostages for ransom now. He just hoped that the guide would deliver the relic.

"Where is this relic?" asked John.

"Shut up! I thought you learned your lesson in the UK. We wait!" yelled Yousef.

John realized that Yousef had been one of his captors on the night he was kidnapped. Now he knew why. As the mistaken son of Sir Ernest, a great deal more money could be demanded—if John was the son. However, having seen the real Mr. Khan's house, it was clear that Mr.

Khan was a real collector of antiquities, unlike Yousef and Omar. Did Khan plan his kidnapping, or did Yousef work alone to feather his own nest? Perhaps they were Khan's henchmen; but then, they killed him. And Jane's involvement was puzzling. Who was she talking to? Maybe she was involved with his kidnapping? No, she was not with Yousef and Omar.

They had waited about half an hour when the roar of a jet was heard overhead. John feared they were about to be bombed by a NATO military aircraft, and flinched. Yousef and the others stood still. The aircraft banked and flew down the valley and turned back toward them. It was losing altitude quite noticeably as it came toward them, but it was still far away. Then John realized the aircraft was *landing*. A cloud of dust heralded what would have been a rough landing on an old runway. As the dust subsided, the plane emerged and taxied close to the road where their car was parked.

A white Challenger 300 corporate jet stood in front of them, covered in dust. It was now clear that this was an old Soviet airstrip. The door swung open and steps folded out before a number of sheikhs, dressed in traditional Saudi garb, stepped off the plane. They were led by a man in his thirties who had a black beard and wore white-and-black dress. His Arab headdress was bound by a golden cord. The others wore similar white clothes, mixed with expensive brown and black fabrics. One of them held a falcon in his leather bound hand. The leader outstretched his hand to Yousef, who was closest, while the others kept their hands hidden.

"Where is Hakeem Khan?" asked the sheikh.

"I am Hakeem Khan," replied Omar.

The leading sheikh approached Omar. "And who is Yousef?" the sheikh asked again.

"I am," replied Yousef. Yousef stepped forward while the guide kept his distance, his AK-47 pointing toward the ground.

"Who are these Westerners?" asked the sheikh.

"They are the clients who will pay for the relic," replied Omar.

The sheikh spoke in Arabic to his men. The man with the falcon then let it go, and it was soon soaring above the valley. Yousef walked over to the man and asked him, "Will he hunt here?"

"Of course, if anything is left alive," he smiled as he replied.

The sheikh pulled a handgun from under his gown and pointed it at Omar and Yousef. "Where is the relic?"

"What are you doing?" exclaimed Yousef.

"I said, where is the relic?" shouted the sheikh. His men stood behind Yousef and Omar with their guns pointing to their backs, with the Taliban guide strangely still.

"But I thought you were meeting us today to hand over the relic?" replied Yousef, whose forehead was wet from perspiration.

"No, you've got it wrong. We were to meet you!" objected the sheikh, who asked, "Wasn't there something about a map?"

Omar replied, "Yes! Yes! Here it is." He pulled the map out of his pocket and handed it to the sheikh.

"Thank you. Our business is concluded now. But before we go, I would like you to listen to something." The sheikh pulled out a tape recorder and said, "I received a call from a certain policeman in London about a stolen mobile phone, and he played a message from you, Yousef. And do you know what it said?"

Yousef's mouth was dry as he whispered, "No."

"I didn't hear you," replied the sheikh.

Yousef was silent.

"Let me play what you said: *"Omar, it is Yousef here. You must finish Khan tonight before the English arrive. Ring me."* The sheikh switched off the tape. "Do you know who Hakeem Khan was?" Omar and Yousef were both silent. "He was my brother."

At that they both dropped to the ground at his feet. Khan looked to the sky for a moment and leaned over, shooting each one in the head with a single bullet. They slumped to the ground.

The Taliban guide stood and watched. The sheikh turned to the stunned Sir Ernest, John, and Jane, and said, "Hakeem was my brother. I have avenged his death." He turned to the guide, said, "Thank you for doing justice today," and handed a small leather bag to him. He undid the leather lace and looked briefly in the bag and nodded. The men dragged the bodies to a nearby ditch.

Sir Ernest spoke to John. "What will they do with us?"

John shrugged, but added, "Somehow, I don't think they'll kill *us*."

Jane approached the sheikh and said, "Sir Ernest, John, I would like you to meet Abdul Khan." Sir Ernest and John were both speechless. "I think I owe both of you an explanation," explained Jane sheepishly as she watched Sir Ernest. "I had a friendship with Abdul prior to Brendan, and I knew that with Brendan being your son, it would have been uncomfortable for me to tell you that I was involved with Abdul before Brendan. However, Abdul asked his brother, the real Mr. Hakeem Khan, to telephone you in the first place, so that you could find the relic. That came about because I asked Abdul to see if he could help, but no one believed that Abdul's brother would be killed trying to do this. The whole thing is so horrible."

"Is that who you were talking to at Mr. Khan's house?" asked John.

"Yes," said Jane. "I couldn't tell anyone because I had promised Abdul to keep our friendship a secret if he was to help Sir Ernest. Abdul could not help us in Kabul anyway. I told him what you had discovered about his brother being murdered by these terrible people. So Abdul arranged for the bank manager to put a tracking device on their four-wheel-drive, which led them to us. It was the only sure way. The manager also arranged for the Taliban guide to meet us."

Sir Ernest turned to the sheikh and asked, "Excuse me, Mr. Khan, I am sorry about your brother, but since I am paying for all of this, can you tell me what this is all about?"

Abdul faced Sir Ernest, eyeing him carefully. After a short pause, he said, "As a sheikh who has recently lost most of my wealth through a family dispute, I believed I could make some money. My brother dealt in antiquities, and it is he who did the groundwork in finding the relic you seek."

"Who are *they*?" asked John, pointing at his fellow "sheikhs."

These men are my security men. We thought that presenting them as fellow sheikhs would put these imposters at ease." They laughed at hearing this and ripped their white robes off, revealing black shirts and trousers. Each man had a gun holster around his shoulders. One had a machine gun concealed beneath his gown. He slung the weapon over his shoulder. John then spoke:

"Mr. Khan, thank you for the explanation. Please answer one thing: I was kidnapped in the UK, but during the kidnapping, Jane's mobile phone was found. Can you explain that?"

"Yes. My brother sent Yousef to England to negotiate with Sir Ernest. He met Jane first, for some background on Sir Ernest. On the night of the kidnapping, which my brother knew nothing about, I called Jane, and Yousef answered the phone. During the conversation, Yousef told me he had borrowed the phone from Jane. Jane later told me he must have stolen the phone. I was already suspicious when the police officer rang me as a contact in her phone. I realized then that Yousef had deceived us."

John then moved forward and said, "What now?"

Abdul turned to John. "You can drive back to Kabul in your vehicle."

Sir Ernest said, "I too thought you were here to give us the relic, so we can return to Kabul to get the money."

"I would gladly accompany you to Kabul, as I am in need of money, Sir Ernest. But as I said earlier, I do not have the relic. These imposters did not realize that my brother was only halfway to getting the relic when they killed him. When Jane called me, it was the only way to rescue you."

"Okay, how do we get the relic?" asked Sir Ernest.

"Are you still willing to pay what my brother was promised?" asked Abdul. His jet-black eyes stared like glass into Sir Ernest's blue eyes.

Sir Ernest responded:, "I suppose. We have come this far."

"Good. Then, Sir Ernest, you can come with us."

With that, the falcon's graceful wings fluttered and folded gracefully as it swerved and darted down into the hands of his handler. A few fine specks of blood could be seen on its beak as his handler placed the leather blindfold on its eyes.

Abdul put his hand on Jane's shoulder and turned toward the aircraft.

"Jane, you are welcome to come too."

"What about John?" asked Jane.

"He has a car, and the guide can take him. The guide has been well paid."

Jane broke away from Abdul and walked to John, putting her arm around his shoulders.

Abdul smiled and said, "So be it." He turned to accompany Sir Ernest and the others into the aircraft. As he boarded, he waved and disappeared inside.

"So close!" exclaimed Jane.

"What do you mean?" asked John.

"We won't see them get the relic," replied Jane.


The jet gathered speed and took off as the engines roared. They all watched overhead as the plane disappeared. Jane turned toward the four-wheel-drive as the Taliban driver got in the driver's seat and started the engine.

"Wait!" shouted John. "They're coming back!"

They all jumped out and looked down the valley to see a jet coming in to land. It was soon taxiing toward them. Although the jet was similar in appearance, it was not the same jet. The small Learjet bore a golden insignia on its side. John's eyes widened in surprise.

# SIXTEEN

The aircraft bore the insignia of the Vatican, with the crossed keys and triple crown with cross. John recalled that the crossed keys represented the keys of St. Peter to heaven; and that the triple crown, or triregnum, represented the pope as supreme pastor, teacher, and priest. The cross adorning the crown symbolized the sovereignty of Jesus Christ. John thought, *Is the pope on board?*

Their guide raised his gun, but John beckoned for him to lower it. He and Jane approached the jet as its engines powered down. The door fell downward to form steps, and two black-clad commandos emerged, carrying Heckler and Koch machine guns. They pointed the guns at John and Jane, prompting their guide to raise his gun. A standoff ensued, but John walked between them with his hands in the air, and stood waiting for the other occupants of the aircraft to step out. To John's surprise, Paul jumped onto the tarmac, and seeing them exclaimed, "John!" John stepped forward and they embraced in relief. Three priests quickly followed and stood in front of them as Paul explained, "John these are our new friends, Father Ian Augustus, SJ; Father Joe Campbell, SJ; and Father Lombardo Fezzalo, SJ. They have offered their help to you."

They all smiled and nodded, but remained silent. "This is Jane," replied John, and Jane nodded. "I don't know his name, but he is our

Taliban driver," explained John, tilting his head subtly toward their guide, who had lowered his gun again, causing the two commandos to do the same.

"Taliban! What's going on?" asked Paul.

"Look, it's a long story. If you are planning to fly us out of here, it would be good if we could talk on the plane, as it is not safe here," advised John. He took Jane's hand and stood in front of the three priests, who smiled and turned quickly to reenter their aircraft. John waved at their guide, who nodded and stared at them entering the aircraft.

The pilot had remained in the aircraft, and now the engines roared again into action. The passengers occupied a row of eight brown leather seats that lined the long cabin. Coffee tables were placed between various seats. As John took his seat he saw that a couple of computer stations had been set up in the cabin for the commandos. John, Paul, and Jane sat close together. No sooner had John fastened his seatbelt that he felt the plane gathering speed on the runway. He felt the thrust of the jet motors push him back into his seat as they took off quickly, before banking steeply left to climb above the flanking mountain, leaving that valley of death.

The plane gained altitude while John recounted what had happened to them.

"So you were drawn into a smuggler's web by Sir Ernest?" Paul turned to Jane and said, "How did you get involved in all this?"

Jane looked tense "I was young."

"You still are!" joked John.

Jane continued, "I had run away from home, against my parent's wishes, with a rich Arab, Abdul. Well, he was rich then. It was so glamorous. I met his brother Hakeem, who was a real dealer in antiquities. About two years after we broke up, I contacted Abdul, asking if he could help Sir Ernest find a certain relic."

"What was it?" asked Paul.

"I never knew. I was just told it was priceless and would change history. I'm sure it's related to religion or theology or something like that, knowing Sir Ernest. Anyway, after I put the two in contact, Sir Ernest told me that things were progressing, and sooner or later he might take me on an expedition to the Middle East. He never came back to me directly, and it was only in the lecture theater with John that I volunteered to go."

"So you know as much as I do," said John. Jane nodded.

John turned to Paul and asked, "How did all this happen?" He threw his hands open.

"Well, you may remember the last time we spoke, I told you I was on a private charter jet arranged by MI5. They didn't tell me the full story, but this was the jet. These Jesuit priests are travelling with Italian military intelligence officers who are part of Interpol. Father Joe Campbell will explain." Paul waited until the plane had reached cruising altitude, unbuckled his seatbelt, and walked a few seats in front of them before returning with Joe Campbell, who sat in the vacant seat alongside them.

"Father—"

"Call me Joe," replied the priest.

"Joe, can you explain to us your interest in all this?"

Joe leaned over toward them and began:

"We are scientists from the Jesuit order of the Catholic Church based in England. Our expertise is in paleontology. We were at a scientific convention when Andrew Faulkner, the paleontologist, gave a speech questioning whether the God of the Bible was actually an ancient astronaut—a theme that we have heard before, of course. So unfolded his theory, with some analysis based on prior work of biblical scholars. He recounted the epic of Gilgamesh, which originated with the Sumerians. Gilgamesh was the ruler of Uruk and was supposed to be two-thirds God and one-third human. His father was mortal, and his mother was divine.

"One of his forefathers had survived the 'deluge'—apparently a great flood that has been postulated as the real biblical flood—by being taken to heaven with his spouse. Gilgamesh, therefore, wanted to find this place and find the secret to eternal life. He and his companion Enkidu set off for a distant place called the land of Tilmun, and soon came to a mountain area protected by guards of great strength. In the ancient writings, Gilgamesh dreams that night and is awoken three times. Once he is overcome with an unbearable glare. The final time he wakes, the writings record him saying that a flame shot up, it rained death, and the glow vanished in the clouds and ash fell. Today we would describe that as a rocket taking off.

"Gilgamesh apparently arrived at a site cut into the side of the Mountain of Mashu, where roving light beams were observed. He finally met his forefather, who we assume must have come down from heaven. He tells Gilgamesh that he is mortal but gives him a plant that will give Gilgamesh eternal life. Gilgamesh loses the plant on his way home."

John leaned back, commenting, "Just an ancient myth, then?"

"Not quite," said Joe Campbell. "Faulkner then states that the prophet Ezekiel in the Bible saw a 'whirlwind' as a great cloud with flashes around it. In fact, the NASA scientist Josef F. Blumrich is understood to have been inspired by this account. He designed the Mars Mariner spacecraft for NASA on the basis that a reference by Ezekiel to 'wheels within wheels' or a 'chariot' was, in fact, a helicopter. A reference at another time in ancient Sumerian writings is to the God Ninurta, who travelled in a 'divine black wind bird' between heaven and earth.

"This bird or helicopter, as Faulkner would have us believe, carried awesome weapons that emitted beams of light and death rays. He points to the fact that the Sumerian ruler Gudea built a temple to the Ninurta god to house the black bird—which, by the way, was based on plans and a brick mold given to him by the gods after he 'dreamed' of the temple. A Babylonian king later records the sacred enclosure as burned brick, consistent with the takeoffs of jet engines."

Jane's imagination was firing now, and she said, "So they are saying that the Bible just records visits by astronauts to earth? These are theories, but did he refer to any proof?"

"Yes, but you just need to hear the archaeological background and context to understand the significance of the evidence. To the south of Uruk, from where Gilgamesh came, another Sumerian city called Ur was built. This city is where Abraham of the Bible came from. Apparently there were a number of gods who ran the Sumerian cities, and after various battles and grievances, Ninurta—the supreme God—was dissatisfied with their handling of the various cities, which included Sodom. I assume this was the city of 'Sodom and Gomorrah' fame.

"This dissatisfaction led to Ninurta utilizing 'awesome weapons' hidden in an underground bunker. What followed was the annihilation of a number of sinning cities on the Sinai Peninsula, apparently evidenced today by a blackened landscape of usually white limestone mountains. The suggestion is that nuclear weapons were used. By the way, the Magash Mountain from Gilgamesh's epic tale, with its underground space bunkers, was also destroyed.

"In other words, Eveleigh and his cronies are trying to dismantle the religious authenticity of the Bible. Thus the Sumerian civilization, including the fabled Ur, was destroyed. In 1922 a British archaeologist by the name of Leonard Woolley came to Iraq to dig up ancient Sumer in Mesopotamia. By digging into a buried temple, it soon became clear that he was digging up the royal tombs of Ur. Faulkner then announced that a relic, which he believed was a recent discovery at Ur, would upstage the discovery of the Dead Sea Scrolls and prove beyond doubt that the Bible contains tales of ancient astronauts. This is a very dangerous and mischievous claim, which we are very concerned about."

Jane went to freshen up at the back of the plane, and Joe resumed his seat.

While she was gone, Paul leaned over and whispered to John, "I heard her story, but do *you* trust her?"

John tilted his head and whispered, "The jury is out."

Jane just returned to her seat. There was a long pause before John asked, "Where are we going now?"

"Ask Jane," Paul smiled.

Jane's face dropped. "Excuse me?"

Paul stood up, walked over to Jane, and picked up her brown backpack, which she had taken with her to the toilet. She tugged it away from Paul. John stood up and said "Paul, what are you doing?"

Paul stood back and said, "Ask her to show you the contents of her bag."

"That's personal!" protested Jane.

Just then one of the Italian commandos arrived. "Leo, can you explain the customs laws to Jane, please?"

Leo was well built, with a distinguished-looking moustache and black hair, and spoke in a heavy Italian accent. "Miss, we must inspect your bag. You are now under our jurisdiction."

"I thought this is Roman law?" replied Jane.

"Very good. This is our law. You will be travelling into Italian airspace when we return to Rome. Your move, señorita?"

Jane was at a loss for words. She looked at her backpack and then at John.

"Just show it to them, Jane. You've got nothing to hide," advised John.

"Oh, but I have!" admitted Jane softly as she pulled the zipper on the bag. She pulled out something hidden in the lining. It looked like a folded garment. She carefully undid it and placed it over the nearest coffee table. The fabric was extremely old, and it appeared to be a tapestry of ancient warriors and their activities.

"What is it?" asked John.

"It's the relic."

"But how? What about the others and the map?" John was almost yelling at Jane.

"Why don't you explain, Jane?" said Paul.

Again Jane was silent. Paul then started to explain:

"When our people searched Khan's house, they found the tapestry of warriors and chariots on the floor, with its insides pulled out. Khan had internal security cameras in the house to guard his valuable artifacts; and our people, being suspicious, decided to play back the footage. What they saw was Jane pulling something out of the lining of the tapestry. Obviously, Khan had the relic hidden in the tapestry, and was going to exchange the relic for the money with Sir Ernest at the house. But he was killed before the others realized where the relic was."

"Then why did Jane come with us?" asked John.

"Sir Ernest knew that Jane had the relic, and if she had gone with them and was found out, then most likely Sir Ernest and Jane would have met the same fate as Yousef and Omar."

"So that means Sir Ernest had no choice but to go with them."

They all peered at the relic and saw ancient warriors and many other things.

"It's astounding," said John.

"It looks like a NASA brochure, only it's thousands of years old," said Paul.

"What is it, Jane?" asked John.

Jane paused, shrugged, and replied, "It's the second standard of Ur."

"What does that mean?" asked Paul.

The voice of Joe Campbell answered from behind them:

"The first Standard of Ur, which is a solid object rather than a flag, was recovered from the Royal Tombs of Ur, and now sits in the British Museum. It depicted Sumerians drinking, eating, herding cattle, and generally going about normal life. This standard is more like a real flag and is very special because it depicts these same people meeting visitors in spaceships. There is no doubt when I look at it. The detail shown is too great. Look at the giant legs on the craft—it has metallic hydraulic legs with steps leading inside the craft. The beings are wearing specialized clothing. There is insignia on the body of the craft and lights up the side of it. See the other equipment: there is just too much detail for this to be myth. I can see that this is the Holy Grail of atheism—proof that Ur was host to ancient spacemen. I can just hear Sir Ernest claiming that Abraham met these spacemen."

Jane started to cry, and one of the commandos brought her a drink that she gulped down in desperation. As she did, she felt dizzy, and moments later she was out cold, slumped in her seat. John turned to the commandos and said, "What did you give her?" The commando just smiled.

Jane lay in a deep sleep as they all settled back in their seats, still talking about the day's events. John had an uneasy feeling about what they were doing to Jane. After a few hours, the plane lost altitude and prepared for landing.

"Where are we going?" asked John.

"We are about to land in Oman, and then change planes to take Jane back to London," replied Paul.

"What will happen to her?" asked John.

"Not sure; she's been a bad girl, hasn't she?"

John nodded and asked, "What do you want me to do?"

"Well, you are returning with me," replied Paul.

John paused and thought carefully before answering. "Look, Paul, now that I know what Sir Ernest is up to, I would like to pursue him."

"No. It could be dangerous, because those guys he is with have killed two people. Not only that, but this plane is continuing to Iraq. That's where they have gone," warned Paul.

"Paul, I'm with this lot, who appear to know what they're doing. I'll keep my distance," replied John.

Paul frowned. "All right, I'll have a word to the security people here, but stay close to them."

"Okay," promised John.

"Oh, John, if you see Sir Ernest, there's been some bad news. His youngest son—the disabled one—is gravely ill, and doctors give him no hope for surviving the night."

John nodded.

# SEVENTEEN

Ur is about 365 kilometers south of Baghdad, in the vicinity of the Euphrates River. This was near the fertile land between the Euphrates and Tigris Rivers, where civilization began seven thousand years ago, and where the Sumerians built the first cities in the world, including Ur (circa 3,500 BC). In the ancient Sumerian and Akkadian language, *Ur* means "a city"; it was the capital of Sumer. It contains the most famous ancient site in Iraq, which includes the Ziggurat, dedicated to the moon god Nanna. The Ziggurat is a monument resembling a fort in the desert.

Ur was the birthplace of the prophet Abraham. Ur-Nammu (2113–2095 BC) was the first king of the third dynasty of Ur, making Ur the wealthiest city in Mesopotamia, which included Sumer and Akkad. Ur-Nammu wrote the first law in history. His son King Shulgi built the Ziggurat of Nanna, which still stands today, four thousand years later, although it was upgraded in height by later members of the Babylonian royal family.

The white Challenger 300 jet was leaving Iranian airspace, passing into Iraq. Tallil Air Base had already made contact with the pilot. Sir Ernest had fallen asleep after Abdul had refused to discuss business until Sir Ernest was fully rested after his ordeal. As Sir Ernest awoke, one of the men brought him a cup of coffee and some fruit. Minutes later, Abdul came back to his seat and joined him, commenting, "We are in Iraq now."

"Where are we headed?"

"Iraq," replied Abdul.

"Why?" asked Sir Ernest.

"You want to find your relic, do you not?" responded Abdul.

"Yes," Sir Ernest said.

"Well, first, our deal. Do I receive the one million dollars that you promised my brother?" asked Abdul.

"Of course. I'm not worried about legal niceties. You're the man now, and I am sure you will look after his remaining family."

Abdul smiled and said, "Good, then let me tell you a story. My brother met an American soldier in Afghanistan who had served in Iraq. This soldier had worked at Tallil Air Base, where we are heading now. Tallil Air Base was a wreck after the Gulf War, and it had to be rebuilt. This soldier worked with the American military engineers who rebuilt it. While they were rebuilding the runway, they needed construction materials. After scouting the area, they found a source of some limestone, which they drilled and blasted for their works.

"Some time passed, the resulting quarry got deeper, and to their surprise, the tip of a Ziggurat was found. They uncovered an aperture that led to underground passageways. A series of tombs were found, including one prominent tomb. In that tomb were found many beautiful objects. In fact, the discovery was similar to the nearby discovery known as the Royal Tombs of Ur, where a similar Ziggurat was found.

"The soldier indicated that one night the tomb was looted and a scandal occurred, and the result was that the tomb was covered up and kept secret so that the looting would not cause people to lose their jobs. However, the soldier made a map of where the site was and sold it to my brother for ten thousand dollars."

Abdul pulled out the map that he had obtained from Yousef and said, "And this is the map."

"Executive Jet 837 Romeo Echo, this is Tallil Tower. Come in, over," called the air traffic controller from Tallil Air Base.

"Roger that, tower. We're low on fuel. Request landing clearance, over."

"Hold your position 837, over."

About half a minute passed, and the pilot called again. "Tower, are you still there?"

"Hold, 837…just a few moments. Okay, 837, you're cleared to land at Runway 2."

"Thank you tower. Can you direct us? Over."

"Roger, turn right twenty degrees and continue southbound toward the right of the tower. Park in the hangar to left of tower. Over."

"Wind check?"

"Wind three-three-zero at nine. Take it easy."

"Thank you, tower."

The Challenger quickly lost altitude and came in for a smooth landing on the hot, steaming tarmac. Soon after it taxied to the hangar as directed, and parked in the shade. Abdul and the rest of the passengers left the aircraft.


They soon stood on the tarmac and were met by two American soldiers and an Iraqi official. They were all clad in desert camouflage combat outfits and wearing sidearms. The soldiers pointed to a desk in a hangar, with a few seats strewn around it.

"Please take a seat," said one of the soldiers.

Sir Ernest and Abdul sat down, and his men stood.

"Passports, please?" said the Iraqi.

They all handed them over to the Iraqi, who examined them closely, writing down their names and details in his notebook. "I assume you will stay overnight in Nasiriya?"

"Yes," replied Abdul.

"How long will you stay?" asked the Iraqi.

"We heard of the famous Ur ruins here."

The Iraqi smiled and replied, "We have the beginning of civilization here, and I can recommend a good hotel."

"That would be good," replied Abdul.

The Iraqi handed over a business card and wrote his name—Ahmed—and a phone number on the back of the card. "Tell them

Ahmed sent you. I have also written the phone number of a taxi service that speaks English here," said Ahmed as he got up. "You had better get your things from the plane. Who is your pilot?"

"I am," said Abdul's pilot.

"Well, see that man over there? His name is Sayeed. You can see him about refueling and payment. I hope you can pay in US dollars."

"Yes, of course" replied Abdul.

After collecting their bags and arranging the refueling, Ahmed and the soldiers led them to a bland building near a car park. Before parting ways, Ahmed said, "You will find a phone in that building to call a cab."

They were soon speeding past the typical Iraqi blockhouses, with rubble scattered about the streets.

Nasiriyah is about 370 kilometers south east of Baghdad. It has seen a lot of fighting in recent years. In 1991 it was the farthest point of penetration for coalition forces, and in 2003 the Battle of Nasiriyah was one of the first major engagements during the invasion of Iraq. Americans were not popular here. The famous story of Private Jessica Lynch being rescued occurred from a hospital in Nasiriyah.

The taxi dropped them off at a dusty hotel in Nasiriyah, but Abdul said to Sir Ernest, "Don't stay here; someone else is picking us up."

While they waited, Sir Ernest was given the hotel's guest phone. Some fifteen minutes passed, and Sir Ernest was still on the phone when a new blue four-wheel-drive picked them up. Sir Ernest hung up and walked to the car with the others.

"Sir Ernest, this is Walid, my brother's archaeologist. He is the one that found the new ruins," explained Abdul.

"Nice to meet you," replied Sir Ernest.

Walid drove them back through the suburbs to his house on the outskirts of Nasiriya.

"It's very hot here," commented Sir Ernest.

"It's so hot I can cook my dinner on the roof of my car!" replied Walid. "But the heat is not as bad as the dust storms we get here. It is like hell on earth, with the red glow of the sun through the dust."

"That's an interesting image. Remember, man, that thou art dust, and unto dust thou shall return," quoted Sir Ernest.

"Jesus Christ doesn't carry much weight around here," interjected Abdul.

They finally arrived at Walid's mud-brick blockhouse, which was larger than other houses and had an outside wall that contained gardens and courtyards with some shade trees.

"Do you want to go inside or sit in the garden?" asked Walid, after letting them in the front gate.

"The garden is fine" answered Abdul.

Soon they met Walid's wife and son. As devout Muslims, neither was wearing shoes. Abdul and the others also took their shoes off. Some food on platters with some cool drinks were served.

"Well, tell me about the new discovery," asked Sir Ernest.

Walid put his drink down and began talking. "We all know the Royal Tombs of Ur—and, in fact, we will drive past them tomorrow. The Americans were making a quarry when they discovered a—"

"I told Sir Ernest about the soldiers," Abdul stopped him, and added, "Why don't you tell him what you found when you started to dig at the quarry?"

Walid continued: "After Mr. Khan gave me the map and I found the quarry, we started to dig for him. We soon began finding a system of royal tombs similar to what we already have. We found an elaborate system of burial chambers and evidence of burial of servants and ritual, and so on—again, similar to the first discovery. We found one special burial chamber. In my opinion, it is the burial chamber of a king, and it is in that chamber that we found what Mr. Khan called the "relic." As you know, it was a standard not really like the standard of Ur. The standard of Ur is an object rather than a real standard. That object presently sits in the British Museum. However, the standard we found  is most unusual in that it portrays space-age technology alongside ancient warriors.

"So that's what the fuss is about," said Abdul. "But something is not right. Why was so much importance placed on the map, when the relic had already been found?"

"I assume that your brother's killers did not know the site had been found, and confused the situation," replied Sir Ernest.

Abdul's face looked blank as he stared at Sir Ernest and then shrugged. "Perhaps you are right, but if we have the map, where is the relic, Walid?"

"I gave it to Mr. Khan," replied Walid.

"And it is no longer at the site?" asked Abdul. "Then why are you going to the site?"

Walid appeared nervous.

"Walid, what are you hiding?" exclaimed Abdul.

Walid sat down and said, "Look, your brother owed me ten thousand dollars, so when he asked for the results of our work, I gave him the relic and told him that I will send over my full report once he sent payment. He never paid, and so I still have my report."

"Walid, my brother is dead!" announced Abdul.

"What? How?" replied a surprised Walid.

"That's not important. What is important is that you give me everything now."

Walid was silent. Sir Ernest stood up and walked over to Walid and said, "Perhaps there is another way to resolve this."

"I know how to resolve this," Abdul interrupted, standing next to Sir Ernest, who gestured with his hand up to stop.

"If you show us the site tomorrow," said Sir Ernest, we would consider buying the report for ten thousand dollars. Would that resolve the matter?"

"It would," replied Walid.

"Abdul, we'll go to the site tomorrow."

# EIGHTEEN

$\mathbf{A}$ few hours had passed since Paul and the commando, Leo, had taken Jane from the plane. They were approaching Nasiriyah in preparation to land at the Tallil Air Base.

John asked Joe Campbell, "What's Nasiriyah like?"

"I can't say that I've been there, but you should know that the name is a sore point for Italians" replied Joe.

"Why?" John leaned closer to Joe as the aircraft engines had increased their roar as they lost altitude.

"In 2003, the local chamber of commerce was to become the Carabinieri headquarters. Insurgents attacked the Italian police checkpoint, breaking through and unleashing an explosive-laden fuel tanker truck, which they detonated near the chamber of commerce. Many Italians, including Carabinieri, and Iraqi citizens were killed," Joe explained.

"They must think it important to follow Sir Ernest here," replied John.

Joe nodded as the cockpit door swung open and one of the commandos emerged, speaking in Italian to the priests.

John looked out the window and saw Nasiriyah, its rectangular white buildings crisscrossed with dusty roads and rubble. Then something caught John's eye. A huge wall of swirling sand, like a swarm of bees, loomed ominously toward the town and threatened the aircraft. It was clear that the plane was going to be engulfed if they did not gain altitude quickly. The plane gained altitude, but the dust storm soon overtook them, and the sound of grit hitting the plane could be heard. John could see nothing but the sandstorm out of the windows. The plane's jet engines sucked in the storm, and soon a loud bang was heard in the starboard engine. John gulped as his adrenaline started pumping.

"Attenzione, attenzione…" came the voice of the pilot, followed by some words in Italian for which John needed no translation. The plane lost altitude quickly, with the pilot banking desperately with what control he had left to correct its approach. The pilot, now flying blind, was about to attempt an instrument landing.

John held his breath and waited, leaning forward in the brace position recommended on the commercial airlines, after noticing the priests doing the same. He could see one of them making the sign of the cross. John dropped his agnosticism for this landing. There was a very heavy thud, and the plane shook as though it had just dropped out the air. John felt winded in his stomach from the impact, and felt himself move forward, bumping his head on the seat in front of him with the force of the landing.

Soon the doors were open and someone was shouting in an American accent. Things were happening quickly, and they were shuffled out and bustled into a US military Humvee. John glanced sideways at the failed engine, which was blackened by the explosion in midair. Streaks of black had streamed onto the body of the aircraft from the flames.

"Is anyone hurt?" shouted the American, who was wearing camouflaged desert army fatigues. He had sergeant's stripes on his sleeve with the name TAYLOR stitched on his pocket.

Joe Campbell replied, "I think we're all right, except for the shock of it. We're lucky. Where are you taking us?"

"We're going to transfer you to another vehicle. We're suffering an attack of insurgents who are using the storm as their cover. It's not safe," replied Sergeant Taylor.

John's heart dropped. This was not what he expected. They bunched into the vehicle and drove off slowly into the howling sandstorm. They had driven some unknown distance when Sergeant Taylor proclaimed, "I've lost my bearings." No one answered.

They continued on until a shape emerged in front of them. It was a white four-wheel-drive. As they got closer, John could see that the windscreen was riddled with bullet holes and the driver was slumped over the steering wheel.

The sergeant abruptly pulled up his vehicle and jumped out and ran over to the vehicle. Just as he did, their vehicle was surrounded with armed men wearing black turbans and Arab dress. They pointed their AK-47 rifles at John and the commando and pulled them out of the vehicle. The commando struggled and a shot was fired above his head, causing him to freeze. At this the sergeant turned around and drew his firearm, but quickly the armed men returned fire, forcing him to stay behind the stricken four-wheel-drive, helpless to assist John and the others. John was beckoned to come with them at gunpoint, but the priests were left in the vehicle, apparently of no interest to them. John was now a captive for the second time on his visit to the Middle East.

**

Walid had driven Abdul, Sir Ernest, and the others to the ruins of the ancient city of Ur. Sir Ernest asked Walid to stop to look at the site. The world-famous pyramidlike Ziggurat of Ur rose above what looked like pure desert. Ur, founded in about 4,000 BC, was the principal center of worship of the Sumerian moon god Nanna.

As Sir Ernest walked around he saw that the "desert" floor was in fact a sea of broken artifacts including pots, jugs, building materials, old houses, and so on. "This is a treasure trove for archaeologists," proclaimed Sir Ernest.

"That's why I live and work here," answered Walid.

Sir Ernest picked up what appeared to be paving stone that was covered in hieroglyphics. He threw it away and they returned to the car.

"Abdul, we should go back. There is a sandstorm on its way here," Walid warned.

Abdul just shrugged. "You'd better hurry, then."

Walid's four-wheel-drive sped off quickly, and after ten minutes they left the track they were on and the car encountered much rougher ground. Soon they arrived at the site. It was perfectly flat, with little yellow flags everywhere. These flags were used by archaeologists to mark objects of interest. However, there was not the same preponderance of artifacts as there was at Ur. Walid had studied satellite images of the area that showed the geomorphology of the terrain, which in turn had showed a system of roads over a flat site indicating a large structure such as a temple. On his first site visit, the only clue of the temple's existence was a ramp. Walid's men excavated down the ramp into a passageway, and into the side of the buried temple.

"Are we still at Ur?" asked Sir Ernest.

"The outskirts," replied Walid. "They thought this area was an old quarry because of the unusual holes, but it turned out to be the contours of another Ziggurat below. We have found the main chamber," said Walid. "Well, let's go in. We haven't time to talk," barked Abdul.

They walked briskly down the incline into the royal tomb, and were soon in darkness except for Walid and Abdul shining their flashlights. They walked through one passageway, then another, until they entered a large room.

"This is the burial chamber," declared Walid.

"Whose burial chamber is it?" asked Sir Ernest.

There was a silence and then Walid gasped, "Gilgamesh," as if he was afraid to say it.

The archaeological significance was great. Some scholars believe Gilgamesh's sister was extracted by Sir Leonard Woolley in the 1920s and now rests in the British Museum.

Their flashlights now converged on the half-opened tomb in the center. The sarcophagus sat in the center of the rectangular stone tomb, which was adorned in gold helmet breastplate and other trinkets. Sir Ernest reached into his pocket for a pair of pliers and approached the sarcophagus.

"What are you doing?" asked Walid sharply.

"Shut up!" shouted Abdul.

Sir Ernest grabbed the finger of the skeleton and snipped off a small segment, placing it carefully in a plastic bag that he quickly sealed.

"I thought you just wanted the relic, the Second Standard of Ur," remarked Walid.

Sir Ernest smiled and replied, "Yes, I did, but this is the real relic I wanted."

"Have you got what you wanted? We need to go," said Abdul.

"There might be something else. I need more time," protested Sir Ernest, who reached into his pocket, producing a camera. He promptly took photos of the sides of the tomb.

"We must go now!" said Abdul.

They retreated quickly from the chamber and ran for the car, for they now saw the angry wall of sand approaching them. Walid drove as quickly as he could on the bumpy road, but the giant brown cloud engulfed them, causing Walid to slow down due to low visibility. A few minutes of this slow-motion driving had passed when a group of Arabs could just be seen blocking their way.

"Insurgents," shouted Walid.

Abdul's men jumped out and drew their weapons. Gunshots were fired around them, and some bullets hit the car. By this time they were all behind the car.

Walid nudged Sir Ernest. "We'd better run for it. They'll kill each other now."

Sir Ernest and Walid quickly ran back along the track, their heads wrapped in headdress to shield them from the storm. Sir Ernest held his hand over his eyes and could see vaguely where he was going. As they ran, more shots were fired, and this time Sir Ernest could hear bullets whizzing past his head. Walid groaned and fell to the ground. Sir Ernest waded through the pelting sand and leaned over him. He could see the blood oozing through the back of his tunic.

"Walid! Walid!" But he was dead.

Moments later, Sir Ernest felt a gun barrel thrust into his back, and he stood up to see the black turbans and Arab dress of the insurgents. He assumed they must have killed Abdul and his men to get past them.

# NINETEEN

S ir Ernest was marched back to the tomb, which the insurgents were now using as a hideout. A chamber closer to the entrance served as their headquarters. He had been thrown on the cold stone floor in pitch blackness. *So this is what it is like to be blind.* He used his hands to grope for something more comfortable, and found a rolled-up tent. He unfolded and sat on it. After a time, he dozed off and dreamt of his son lying in the hospital in London. He was very sick. After a while Sir Ernest awoke, feeling terribly uneasy. He felt a premonition regarding his son. He got up and reached out to touch the wall, and after stumbling over soft objects, found the wall and followed it out of the chamber. Remembering the direction of the entrance, he walked around the corner and saw the light peeping around another bend in the passage. He walked slowly and quietly. He stood halfway up the passage in the eerie light, and could see the entrance. A figure appeared. It was surreal.

There was complete silence. The figure was walking, but not getting closer. Sir Ernest reluctantly walked closer. The figure spoke to him:

"Dad, I'm free now. I have a message for you."

"Thomas!" exclaimed Sir Ernest.

"Dad!"

"Are you all right?"

"I'm free! I don't feel sick anymore!"

Sir Ernest approached the figure and saw the face of his son, but the disfigurement of his disease had gone. His face was beaming with a smile.

"I'm all right," said the figure.

"What is the message, Thomas?"

"Dad, it's the light."

"What about the light, son?"

"It's God's breath."

Sir Ernest was silent as the sandstorm worsened, causing the light to fail, and the figure was blacked out. Sir Ernest went to embrace the figure. Just before contact, John Rowntree's face appeared through his vision, ending it. Sir Ernest's outstretched arms went momentarily limp and then dropped to his side.

"Not pleased to see me, Sir Ernest?" joked John.

Sir Ernest muttered something, but it was inaudible.

"What have they done to you?" asked John, now frowning.

"Nothing, nothing. Just put me in complete darkness," replied Sir Ernest.

"Are you all right?" asked John.

"I saw my son!" insisted Sir Ernest.

"No, you're not all right. They must have drugged you with something."

"I don't know. Perhaps you're right. I don't remember," explained Sir Ernest.

"Look, Sir Ernest, I was given some bad news about your youngest son, the one in hospital." John lowered his eyes.

"Go on," said Sir Ernest, sadly.

"Well, he fell ill and was not expected to last the night."

Sir Ernest was stone-faced, and there was just silence.

After a while, John said, "Let's just sit here, in this passageway. At least there's some light. We can't go outside. There's a couple of them keeping guard," advised John. They sat down, and each related to the other the events leading up to their capture.

After about half an hour, footsteps were heard entering the passageway. John stood up, and a voice echoed, "Stay down!"

A man in black Arab dress but no turban approached them and sat on the opposite wall. He crossed his legs and placed his rifle across them.

"I know of you, Sir Ernest. But this young man, I do not know."

The man with jet-black hair and dark brown eyes was covered in sand from the storm. Fine sprays of blood could be seen on the white tunic he wore under his black gown. He spoke good English with a Middle Eastern accent.

"Why did you capture us? We are not military," said John.

"Who said we wanted military? We wanted Sir Ernest. We knew of the deal that he had done with Walid, but Walid did not get permission from us to excavate here. And now he has paid the price," replied the insurgent.

"I don't understand," replied Sir Ernest.

"Walid knows that works like this require a community contribution. He knew that, but I am sure he did not tell you about this," he replied.

"No, my deal was just to pay him," replied Sir Ernest.

"Well, now you must pay us what is due to us."

"And what is that?" asked Sir Ernest.

"We'll see what you are worth. First, I would like to hear the great Sir Ernest Everleigh's defense of your blasphemous teachings, and then we can decide these matters."

"I don't insult religion. I just don't believe in it," replied Sir Ernest.

"And what about you? What is your belief?" the insurgent pointed his rifle at John.

"I did believe, but now I don't know," replied John.

"A great pair in a Muslim land!"

"Oh, don't pair us. John and I have opposing views on everything!"

"Let me start with a question for Sir Ernest. How do you know that God does not exist?" asked the insurgent.

"I don't. I am just not persuaded by the evidence for God. I do not have faith," replied Sir Ernest.

"Haven't you felt there is a world beyond ours?" asked the insurgent.

Sir Ernest hesitated—the thoughts of his son were still with him—before answering, "I am quite open to the possibility that other worlds, other dimensions, or other realms do exist, but this would need to be proven by science for me to believe it."

"And to have faith, science would need to prove that God exists," added the insurgent. "Yes, that is right," replied Sir Ernest.

"You make the same mistake as the entire Western world: you are deifying science. Science is a false God. In Islam we are taught to keep God in focus, not worldly things. We are taught that God is almighty and all knowing. It is misguided to give up God for science and hope that it leads you back to God." The insurgent was becoming a little restless as he spoke.

John joined the debate: "But I believe science can lead you back to God. In fact, Islamic scientists in past times have made great contributions to science consistent with their religion."

Sir Ernest turned to John and said, "Well, why would God allow Islam, Christianity, Buddhism, and Judaism to all proliferate? Is that His plan?"

"A good question, Sir Ernest, which I will answer," interrupted the insurgent. "Islam is the one true religion. These other religions of which you speak all arose through Islam as the one true religion. It is the source stemming from Abraham. The others have good principles also. Christianity is based on Jesus, one of our greatest prophets. We just disagree that He was the son of God. Judaism also shares prophets with us. Buddhism is a philosophy. We have no issue with a philosophy. All these religions have lost their way, but with good intentions."

"But why a multiplicity of religions at all?" pressed Sir Ernest.

John interrupted the insurgent this time. "Let me speak. First, you may not know that the Catholic Church accepts all religions as consistent, and just a different way of worshipping God in each culture. Some refine this to mean that religion evolves to fit every evolutionary step in each culture."

Sir Ernest became bolder in the debate. "Very neat, sir, but the bigger question is, why did God in all His power allow evil in this world?"

The insurgent said, "That is simply answered. He has granted us free will and will reward us if we do good, and punish us if we do evil. What is wrong with that scheme of things? If we humans were created as robots, programmed only for good actions, how would we know they were good without the possibility for doing bad? And why should these good robots be rewarded for only doing what they must do? It would make no sense. But, Sir Ernest, let me ask you another question. If God did not create man, then how was man created?"

Sir Ernest responded with a smile. "That is a good question. Charles Darwin gave us half the answer, and science is just working out the rest of the answer. Some scientists believe that man was created in a drop of water in clay from tiny particles that formed over millions of years…"

The insurgent interrupted Sir Ernest, saying, "By accident."

"Well, yes. By a multiplicity of accidents," finished Sir Ernest.

"It is interesting you say that, Sir Ernest. Let me quote from the Koran on this issue: 'We created man from a quintessence of wet clay'. That is from chapter twenty-three, verses twelve through fourteen. And the Koran was written long before modern science. Does this not suggest that if it did occur in clay, then it was God using the earth's natural processes that He himself created, to do what you believe occurred by accident?"

"Who was the scientist who suggested clay was the first template for DNA formation?" asked John.

"Dr. Cairns-Smith. He was a molecular biologist and organic chemist. A brilliant thinker," replied Sir Ernest. "We should have this debate at Oxford sometime. But let me press you further, then. I see your point on good and evil, but let's go to suffering. Why are some innocent children burdened with great suffering? Why did the almighty God not perfect the world to avoid this?"

"I can answer that," said John.

The insurgent smiled and beckoned John to continue.

"God is almighty, and has created the best world He can within His power. And so it is that there is suffering in the world, even by children. But the world is evolving, and I believe that one day there will be no suffering."

The face of the insurgent changed. "Allah could have made the world any way He wanted. It is just that we do not understand His methods or purposes. We are *man*, and He is *God*, and so we cannot even communicate directly, let alone understand, the exercise of His awesome power. That is why He has sent angels as messengers of God."

John became more motivated. "But let me put my full case to you. It is a matter of simple logic that God is almighty but could not have made a world without suffering. He sent His prophet Jesus—in your terms—as a messenger of God. But why would He have allowed such suffering to befall His prophet by choice, unless He had no choice in the circumstances of the world? It was an extreme act for Him to teach and be tortured to bring the message to millions." There was an uneasy silence before the insurgent nodded and got up to go outside. John looked at Sir Ernest, who shrugged. The anxiety of danger prevented any more debate, so they sat in silence.

Hours passed. The sandstorm ceased, and night fell. The sounds of distant helicopters could be heard. An armed insurgent appeared regularly to check on them.

"Why don't you show me the relic?" asked John, not revealing that he knew Jane had taken it.

"It's too dark," replied Sir Ernest.

John smiled. "Did you get it today, when you came?"

Sir Ernest paused, and to John's surprise, he replied, "Yes, I did get part of it." "Well, show it to me. If I am going to die, at least I can see it," demanded John.

Sir Ernest fumbled in his pocket, and John saw the camera fall out with the plastic bag. Sir Ernest held up the plastic bag and said, "It is a fragment of bone from the sarcophagus of Gilgamesh."

"Why, that's a staggering discovery for archaeologists, isn't it?" commented John. "Yes, it is."

"What is its significance?" John was very curious now as the jigsaw puzzle took shape.

"In the grand scheme of things, the origin of life can only be explained in a few alternate ways. First, it could have been an accident in a pond. Second, the 'many worlds' hypothesis, where we are the only possible world—a world with life. Third, Panspermia, where an off-world biological agent reached earth. In fact, they have retrieved genetic building blocks from a comet's stardust. Nobel Laureate Francis Crick and another have postulated *directed* Panspermia—that the earth was deliberately seeded by an alien culture as a research project."

Sir Ernest paused as John spoke. "And you forgot the fourth way: God."

Sir Ernest smiled. "Of course, to explain the position I find myself in, Andrew Faulkner postulates *directed* Panspermia, where the alien intervention was genetic engineering, starting with Gilgamesh. He says everything fits. The Sumerian culture started here at Ur, their mathematics and technology was an inexplicable leap forward. The stories of gods mating with men, and Gilgamesh supposedly being part God and part man. If Faulkner is right, it will show in his DNA—in the relic that is in that plastic bag."

"And you believe this will disprove the existence of God?" asked John.

"I am not putting all my eggs in one basket. Faulkner's theory is but one, and I am backing two of the three—that life began in a pond, or Panspermia. I will prove one of them correct."

"What about the 'many worlds' hypothesis?" asked John.

"Too good to be true. Scientists cannot afford such unproveable luxuries," replied Sir Ernest as he wrapped up the relic.

"Can I see your photos, then?" asked John.

Sir Ernest nodded, and after priming the digital photos to be displayed, handed the camera to John, who flipped slowly through the photos before handing the camera back to Sir Ernest.

Some time passed before a number of explosions could be heard, and the sound of one or more helicopters. The noises were now very close. Shouting emanated from the surface. John ran to the entrance to see a number of black figures sliding down ropes at great speed, machine guns firing. One of the insurgents ran toward John, butting him on his shoulder to push him down the ramp toward Sir Ernest. John stumbled and fell toward Sir Ernest. As he hit the ground, his ears were deafened by a loud bang and a brilliant flash of light that blinded him. Shots whizzed above him, and the insurgent fell heavily on him. John felt someone pulling the insurgent off him, and two men in black gas masks were standing over him.

"Come with us!" they shouted as one of them rushed to help Sir Ernest.

"Who are you?" shouted Sir Ernest.

"British soldiers, sir. We're here to rescue you."

They were quickly hustled by the SAS commandos onto the Lynx AH7 helicopter and were airborne destined for nearby Tallil Air Base. They later transferred to a private jet, bound for London.

# TWENTY

J ane awoke in a luxury hotel room in London, sprawled on a bed.
A headache greeted her before she groaned and fell back to sleep.
Two hours later, she awoke again. This time she visited the bathroom
and reached into her handbag for some headache pills. She soon show-
ered, dressed, and switched on the television. She had no memory of the
Vatican plane trip. She felt anxiety upon realizing that her last memory
was of Afghanistan, rolling around in the back of a car in the desert. *I
must have been rescued to be here in this hotel room*, she thought.

Then she saw the relic laid out on the table near the bed, and she felt
a tingle go up her spine. She suddenly remembered that she had taken
it from Khan's house in Kabul. What was she to do with it? Sir Ernest
had told her to take it, and had given her instructions. She pulled out her
diary and flipped through the pages, hoping that something would jog
her memory. Who brought her to London?

A knock at the door interrupted her thoughts. She opened the door,
and standing in front of her was Brendan Everleigh.

"Well, do I get a 'hello'?" asked Brendan.

"Brendan? I didn't expect you!"

"Jane, dear, whatever are you talking about? We booked this room
together before you left for Afghanistan. You must be jet lagged or

something. What have you been taking? Anyway, aren't you going to let me in?"

Jane awkwardly moved backward and let Brendan in. He entered the room and promptly commented, "Wow! So this is the relic?" Jane nodded slowly. "Won't dad get a shock when you tell him that you've sold it for six million pounds!"

Jane appeared bemused and repeated, "Six million?"

"Get with it, Jane! We have to meet the art dealer in half an hour. Let's get going."

"What are we going to do with the six million?" asked Jane.

"Jane, you have really lost it. To buy the AMB shares, of course. Let's go!"

Jane, still groggy, was soon sharing a cab with Brendan through the bustling London traffic. She grasped her bag tightly, holding the relic. They hopped out of the cab and entered an impressive office block, and took the lift to the fifty-third floor. A circular reception desk of reclaimed oak lay behind the glass façade with the firm's name—FROST ARTEFACTS—embossed across the crimson fabric-adorned reception wall. There was no receptionist, so they rang the bell and waited. A woolly, white-haired man appeared and said, "Arthur Frost," and shook hands with the nervous couple before taking them to his office. The office was lined with crates full of straw with unusual artifacts protruding. Ancient Greek pottery and Egyptian hieroglyphics on a large stone tablet hung on one wall. Mr. Frost's desk was crowded with piles of documents and packages.

"Excuse the mess, but we have just received a shipment for a showing next month."

"No problem," answered Brendan.

After some more pleasantries, Frost asked, "Well, where is the relic?"

Jane lifted her bag onto her lap, pulled out the ancient tapestry, and laid it across Frost's desk. Frost stood over it, studying the pictures portrayed on it. "Marvelous! Most unusual," remarked Frost, who now had his magnifying glass over certain parts of the tapestry. "It's so well preserved for such an old tapestry. It should be falling to bits." Frost was now staring at Jane and Brendan as if to obtain a response, but they were silent.

"I suspect it might have been placed in some airtight container that prevented oxidation. You understand that I am under strict instructions from Count Nansen to test the relic," added Frost.

"Of course, go ahead," replied Jane, now more alert.

Frost carefully carried the tapestry to a corner table in his office and placed it under some type of microscope. After a few minutes of examination, he pronounced, "I am satisfied with its authenticity." He walked back to his desk and pulled out an envelope, which he handed to Jane. Jane handed it to Brendan, who opened it, revealing two bank checks. The first was for five million pounds, payable to Alsop McEwen Biomedical Ltd. The second check was for one million pounds, payable to the Antiquities Foundation.

"What will Count Nansen do with the relic?" asked Jane.

"I understand that after your father's book is published, the relic will become famous due to Sir Ernest's work, and this will allow Count Nansen to have a public exhibition."

Jane's memory was now returning fast as she replied, "But what is Sir Ernest getting from Count Nansen?"

"The prize, of course," replied Frost.

"What prize?" replied Jane.

Frost took a breath before saying, "I think I may have said too much. Anyway, I have another appointment out of the office."

Brendan quickly placed the checks in the envelope, pocketed it, and stood up. Jane followed, and they shook hands with Frost and left.

They quickly left the building and caught a taxi.

"Where are we going?" asked Jane.

"The stockbroker. Don't you remember? It's just as we planned."

"Ah, yes, I've got it. We are going to buy into a biotech company now," replied Jane.

"Good, you've come back to us, Jane" said Brendan.

"I wonder what Frost meant by 'the prize'?" said Jane.

"Oh, probably one of Dad's many activities. I can't keep track of half of what he does."

As the taxi pulled away from the building, a black BMW followed closely behind, with Paul behind the wheel. Sitting next to him was Leo, the Italian commando from the Vatican aircraft. The bug woven into the fabric of the relic was well hidden and had broadcast to Paul and Leo the purpose of Jane's hotel booking.

The stockbroker's office was only a few blocks away, and soon Jane and Brendan were scurrying up the steps into another glass tower. The door of the BMW swept open and Leo jumped out, racing up the steps to follow them. They had entered the foyer and were waiting for their lift just as Leo composed himself, standing just behind them. The lift arrived and they entered with two gray men in pinstripe suits who were in intense discussion, oblivious to the other occupants of the lift. Soon Jane, Brendan, and Leo exited the lift and were up against a locked glass door, behind which were rows and rows of workstations populated by ranks of stockbrokers.

A well-dressed lady came to the door. "Yes?" she said to the three of them. Jane and Brendan were eyeing Leo, but Jane did not recognize him as he was now wearing glasses and had shaved his moustache off.

Brendan replied, "Well, we are here to see Gunter Keller."

"That's a coincidence," exclaimed Leo, causing Jane and Brendan to look behind them. "I have an appointment to see Mr. Keller also."

The lady smiled and replied, "Looks like someone has double-booked."

Brendan replied, "In fairness, we didn't have an appointment. I'm sorry, sir, perhaps we are the culprits."

Leo replied in a heavy Italian accent, "Oh, I just remembered. I was going to bring in a couple of reports to show Mr. Keller, but I have forgotten to bring them. Why don't you go ahead, and I will contact his office to reschedule."

Brendan looked relieved and said, "Are you sure?"

"Yes, yes, you go ahead." Leo nodded to him and turned toward the lift, leaving Brendan and Jane to be let in to see Gunter Keller.

Gunter Keller had the corner office on the floor. Gunter, a senior stockbroker in funds management, had a drinking problem from years of the nail-biting stress of managing other people's money. He would lie awake at night worrying about whether he had put this or that client into the right shares, but one day the worrying stopped, courtesy of scotch or whatever else was available. It was no wonder that he met the mention of the other gentleman for the appointment with a blank stare.

"Come in, come in!" said Gunter, welcoming them into the plush red leather chairs in the back of his immense office.

He pulled open the mahogany drink cabinet and poured himself a drink, and offered drinks to Jane and Brendan, which they politely declined. Gunter was now in the habit of going into drunken rages, and when the phone rang, he picked up and was heard swearing before throwing the phone on the floor.

"I apologize for that, but some people cannot carry out a simple instruction."

They sat and chatted for about twenty minutes while Gunter put away three well-laden scotches before Brendan pulled out the checks and showed them to Gunter. Gunter grabbed them and looked at them.

"Five million pounds for AMB. What's this one million to the antiquities people? Sir Ernest didn't tell me about that!"

"Well, they're the ones that advanced the money to get the relic."

"What relic? You're talking gibberish, man!" barked Gunter.

Brendan appeared frustrated and replied, 'That's how we funded this purchase."

"Now you're talking in riddles. Get to the point," snarled Gunter.

"You know. We're buying the shares in Alsop McEwen Biomedical," shouted Brendan. Gunter twisted his head sideways and shook it before replying, "AMB! Of course. I thought you were talking about us investing in antiques, my boy."

Brendan opened his mouth to reply when Jane put her hand on his arm and interrupted. "Mr. Keller, we need to pay this money to purchase the shares in AMB today. Can you do that today?"

Gunter smiled and replied, "What a pretty girl you are. There's plenty of time for that." Brendan became annoyed. "Mr. Keller—Gunter—can't you understand that we have to settle this now?"

Gunter's face changed. He got up and headed toward his desk and sat down before picking up the phone. "Mary, can you come in here please?"

Shortly after that, an old lady entered the room.

"Mary's been with me for twenty-five years," Gunter announced.

"Too long," replied Mary.

"Oh, don't be like that, Mary."

Mary stood in front of him, staring at him, but remained silent.

"Oh, all right, Mary. Take these two checks and get them banked. They're bank checks, so you won't need a special clearance. But we have to be ready to draw on them right now, or at least within half an hour," said Gunter

"The funds won't be cleared that fast, Mr. Keller," replied Mary.

"That's all right, Mary. It will be a broker-to-broker settlement. Just bank them now."

After Mary left the room, Gunter turned to Jane and Brendan and said, "Well, where is Sir Ernest?"

"He's somewhere in Afghanistan," replied Brendan.

"How can I proceed without his authority?" asked Gunter.

"I have his authority," insisted Brendan.

Gunter stared at him for a few moments and then said, "Get him on the phone."

Jane said, "Brendan, I have a couple of phone numbers where we might get him, but he could be anywhere."

They started to make calls on Gunter's phone, as Gunter fixed another scotch for himself and retired to the couches.

They tried calling Sir Ernest for about twenty minutes, to no avail.

"When is the settlement due?" asked Jane.

"In about ten minutes" replied Brendan, as Gunter started to snore.

Ten minutes passed, and Jane advised, "You'd better wake him up, Brendan."

Gunter had gone silent, and just as Brendan approached him, he let out a huge snore as though he had been saving it for that moment. He quickly turned on the couch and maintained his deep slumber while broker's notes and other letters slipped onto the floor.

"Get Mary!" exclaimed Brendan.

Just as Jane went to the door to do so, the phone rang.

"Stay here!" shouted Brendan.

Jane leaned over to pick up the phone. "Mr. Keller's office. Who's calling?" Jane cupped the phone and whispered to Brendan, "It's Gunter's lawyer."

"Yes, you want authority to settle from Mr. Keller. Well, he's nodding to me that you can settle." At this point, Brendan was nodding and Gunter was napping. "All right, all right. I will put Mr. Keller on," conceded Jane as Brendan screwed his face up at her. Jane put the phone in Brendan's hands, winking at him. Brendan composed himself and spoke. "Hello," said Brendan, trying best to imitate Gunter's voice. "Yes. Settle it, old boy." After a few moments, Brendan hung up and hugged Jane. "We did it! We did it!" he said gleefully.

Outside the building, Leo and Paul saw Jane and Brendan leave the building. Paul commented, "It looks like Sir Ernest has bought himself five million pounds in AMB shares."

"What is AMB?" said Leo.

"I don't know, but we're going to find out."

A few days later, Paul saw off Leo at Heathrow as the latter left on a flight back to Italy. As he left the airport, Paul received a call on his mobile phone.

"Paul, it's Joe Campbell."

"Yes, Joe. I was worried when we didn't hear from you. What happened?"

"We ran into trouble. We almost crash-landed in a sandstorm, and then insurgents took John."

"What! Where is he now?" asked Paul.

"Paul, he's okay. The SAS picked him up very soon after he was captured, and I think he is  back in London now. What is surprising is that Sir Ernest was also rescued from the same insurgents, and he came back with John."

"Incredible. Those two have nine lives. I'll have to have a stern talk to that John" "If he'll listen," quipped Joe, who asked, "What did you and Leo turn up?"

"We've found out that Sir Ernest's son and Jane sold the Ur Standard for six million pounds, and that five million has been invested in AMB and one million was apparently repaid to the Antiquities Foundation. We had someone watch the AMB premises. To make a long story short, it seems that Sir Ernest and a fellow by the name of Ian Richardson are making a play for a joint project between AMB and themselves."

Joe  remarked, "If Sir Ernest is investing five million pounds of his money or the Antiquities Foundation's money, then something very big is afoot. Paul, you had better brief John on this."

"What are you going to do?" asked Paul.

"We have an ally who may know what to do here. We'll be in touch. Good-bye, Paul."

# TWENTY ONE

It was Monday morning, and the TV presenter at Channel 305 BusiStream opened the *Financial Times* newspaper to the second page, to one of the leading stories: ALSOP MCEWEN BIOMEDICAL IPO. The presenter, Catherine Tonkin, read that the float was due to close on Friday, but leading financial analysts Slooth suggested it had been a struggle for the underwriters to raise the funds in the volatile stock markets. The biomedical sector had also suffered from recent downturns, and investors were turning more to IT stocks, which were enjoying a resurgence.

"Catherine, your first interview is here," called a voice from behind the screen.

Catherine nodded and switched on her computer before leaving the set. She soon appeared behind the glass that separated the set from the waiting room.

"Catherine Tonkin." She extended her hand to the first of the two pinstripe-clad men in the waiting room.

"Of course. I feel as though I know you!" replied Jim Alsop.

"That's my occupational hazard, I'm afraid," replied Catherine as she shook hands with Ted McEwen. "Please come this way. We are on in five minutes."

They soon were sitting next to Catherine at the curved table bearing the BusiStream logo of stripes and dollar signs over a globe.

"Good evening to all our viewers. Thank you for joining another session of BusiStream. Tonight we have a number of guests, but first we are going to start with the two principals of a new biomedical float, Alsop McEwen Biomedical. With me are Jim Alsop and Ted McEwen, managing director and technical director of AMB. Ted, if I can start with you: aren't investors tired of another biomedical float?"

Ted's face was a little red and slightly irritated with the question. "We believe we are unique in that we not only have a biomedical business but have also already produced record-breaking medicines. Our corporate pro-file is starting to look like a major pharmaceutical company—" "Without the multibillion-dollar market capitalization," interrupted Catherine.

"Well, that's where investors can get a tremendous uplift. If we were a multibillion-dollar company, there could not be the potential for ten or twenty times of uplift on their investment," replied Ted.

Catherine turned to Jim Alsop and said, "And Jim, I believe you lost Professor Ian Cummins three years ago, yet genetics is very important to your business."

"Oh, Ian is more interested in the academic side of genetics. Look, he has some real talent, and indeed our time together bore great fruit, but in the end we had to commercialize ideas, not write academic papers. I think we and Ian have different philosophies, but our record of success with the number of products we have brought out, and our potential for large-scale licensing deals with pharmaceutical companies, proves that our technical ability is intact."

As Jim was talking, a red light on Ted's mobile phone was blinking, signifying a text message. Ted glanced at it while Catherine fired another question at Jim. The message read, "Ted, come to our office ASAP to discuss IPO," and was signed "Douglas." Douglas Cory-Smith was the executive director of their underwriter, a firm of stockbrokers called Heydon Capital Markets.

They went to a commercial break, and immediately Ted grabbed Jim's arm, beckoning him to leave. They smiled stiffly at Catherine and caught a taxi to Heydon's offices in Bishopsgate. After battling the traffic, the taxi arrived in St. Mary Axe, in London's financial district. The taxi let them out, and they entered 30 St. Mary Axe—one of London's best known buildings. It was known as the Gherkin, after its unique cigar shape.

Soon they were sitting in Heydon's plush boardroom around the antique oak table, which appeared out of place in the otherwise futuristic cable-and-steel boardroom that overlooked the ornate St. Helen's Place and beyond. Douglas Cory-Smith entered, and they nodded at each other while a well-dressed lady in white blouse and gray skirt appeared.

"Coffee anyone?"

"Later, Nadia."

She withdrew, and they were alone.

"What's up?" asked Ted.

"It's a case of what's *not* up, and it's not your IPO funding," replied Douglas. "Well, you're the underwriter. What are we to do?" replied Ted.

"What's the exact position?" asked Jim.

"Out of the twenty-five million pounds, we have about sixteen million," answered Douglas.

"Okay, we need nine million. What about the minimum subscription? We only have to get to twenty million," observed Ted.

"You get me the four million, then!" countered Douglas.

"Douglas! As I said, you're the underwriter. What do *you* suggest?" shouted Ted, now agitated.

"All right, let's all calm down. We're all in the same boat, so let's not score points," advised Jim.

Douglas paced around the room and stood looking out the window. A red London bus ambled up St. Mary Axe among the bustling traffic.

"What about those three institutions that passed up the mezzanine financing? They objected to the fact that we had no FDA approval for our latest medication. Now we have it. What about them?" asked Ted.

"What? Why didn't you suggest that before?" exclaimed Douglas.

"Douglas, just tell them we felt honor-bound to give them the mezzanine price," suggested Ted, who felt cornered by the situation because a failed float could ruin any future expansion plans once the London financial community had shunned them.

"We can't do that because we have a prospectus with a fixed price," replied Douglas. There was a silence for a few minutes before Ted spoke. "Okay," he said, "let's look at it from this angle: wasn't there a financial advisor who introduced all three institutions?"

"Yes. What of it? He's hungry for commission, that fellow," quipped Douglas.

"Okay, use it. Ring him and offer him triple the normal commission," said Ted.

"How about double? Triple starts to eat away our underwriting fees! Why don't we take it our of your shares!" laughed Douglas.

"You know that's not allowed during a prospectus, so it's over to you, Douglas. Offer him double, but you may have to give him what it takes." Ted leaned back in his chair as if he had given his final mandate. "Okay, you two may have to give a whirlwind presentation to them, though."

"Whatever, Douglas. Let's do it then."

Douglas left first, adding, "Excuse me, but can you please see yourselves out…and be on standby!"

Ted was just finishing breakfast the next morning, Tuesday, when his mobile phone rang "Ted, it's Douglas. You're on. Can you and Jim bring your stuff and get down to our office at 10:00 a.m.? We've got all three institutions coming. I don't know what the advisor told them, but they're hot for it."

"Okay, I'll get onto Jim. See you there."


At 10:00 a.m., Ted and Jim fired up the PowerPoint presentation on the screen, and Jim spoke the magical words about FDA approval and the wonderful profit potential of their latest products to the seven representatives from the three investment funds. In fact, they offered seven million pounds, which would cost Douglas almost two-thirds of his underwriting commission. Douglas and Ted stayed afterward to discuss an increase in commission and other matters, and Jim took a cab back to AMB headquarters. It was an hourlong cab ride through one of the new industrial parks of Greater London. Jim was soon walking up the stairs to his reception when a voice was heard behind him:

"Alsop McEwen & Company?"

Jim turned around in surprise and said, "Biomedical, you mean."

"Whatever, sir. I have to give this to the company," said the man, who appeared to be a courier of some sort, tendering a document to Jim.

"Well you can give it to me. I'm a director of the company. What is it?"

"It's a writ. You'd better show it to your lawyer. Good day to you. What's your name?"

"Alsop."

The man thrust the document at Jim and walked off. Jim read the writ. It was labeled IAN HAMILTON RICHARDSON, Plaintiff. He read a few parts of the claim, and saw at once that their former partner Ian Richardson was claiming one third of Jim's and Ted's shares in the company, plus damages. Jim felt sick to his stomach. He looked first at the office and then back at the car park, not knowing where he should go. Someone appeared from his office.

"Oh, Mr. Alsop, you have a call."

"Not now, Jenny. I've got to go back to the city."

"But Mr. Alsop, it's Ted. He wants you to go back to the city."

He didn't want the office staff to know, so he pocketed the document and walked up to take the call.

"Jim, it's Ted. Hey, we're having a bit of celebratory lunch." Jim was silent. "Jim, are you there?"

"Er…yes, but I've just got back. Do you want me to drive back now?"

"Hey! They've wired the funds already. We're oversubscribed. We can close the float as soon as you and I sign some legal papers that need to be signed off," insisted Ted.

"Oh, okay. I'm on my way."

For some reason, Jim couldn't bring himself to tell Ted about the writ.

An hour later, Jim was again in the Heydons boardroom. A document was sitting on the board table. "What's this?" asked Jim.

"Those investment funds said they just wanted us to warrant some basic things as a condition of them investing," replied Ted.

"Like what?"

"Oh, that we have got our FDA approval, our accounts are up to date, there's no litigation, et cetera."

*No litigation!* thought Jim, in a panic. *Should I tell Ted about the writ, and that it would be a lie for me to sign the warranty?* Jim's thoughts raced.

"Jim! What's the problem? Just sign it, next to my signature," urged Ted.

"Ted, I think we need to get our lawyer's clearance for this."

"Jim, you're joking, aren't you? We've got the money, *provided* you sign!"

Jim pushed the papers away from him.

"Okay, okay, let me ring Lester."

Ted grabbed his mobile phone and was soon talking to their lawyer: "And so you see, it's just a routine document, really.... Okay, Lester, I'll get it scanned and e-mail it to you. Speak to you after lunch, then."

Ted hung up, and just then, Douglas came in. Ted put his finger over his mouth to silence any comment by Jim. Douglas went over to pick up the document and noticed the blank unsigned line above JAMES ALSOP, DIRECTOR on the document.

"Why haven't you signed it, Jim?"

"Douglas, I am just getting my lawyer's clearance. Let's go to lunch, and we can sign after lunch."

They quickly retired upstairs to Level 39, where the Gherkin's restaurant operated, and ordered lunch. Jim ordered a double scotch, while the others ordered wine.

"Steady on, Jim! You have to be sober enough to sign that document after lunch!" joked Douglas.

Jim smiled and was more relaxed now that the alcohol had tranquilized him. Just after the main course, Douglas got up and excused himself.

"Sorry chaps, another urgent deal to complete. Ted, make sure Jim signs, will you? In spite of his condition." They all burst out laughing.

Just as Douglas left, a well-tanned man appeared in tweed jacket and open-neck shirt. Ted looked up at him, and it took a moment to recognize him as Sir Ernest.

"Oh, hello, Mr. Everleigh," said Ted.

"Hello, gentlemen. I just got back from the Middle East and read about your float in the newspaper. Thought you might want some help."

"Whatever do you mean, Everleigh?" slurred Jim.

"Looks like your celebration is premature, because your float is in trouble and you're closing on Friday. At least that is what the newspapers say."

"Don't believe the newspaper. We're okay, thank you," responded Ted firmly.

"Look, if it's the price, I may lift it a bit, but I still need your facilities," offered Sir Ernest. "No thanks," answered Ted.

"Oh, also, is there anything in the rumor that your old partner Ian Cummings is suing you?"

"What did you say?" blurted Ted.

"You heard me."

"Why, that's preposterous! I hope you're not spreading that scuttlebutt," grumbled Ted.

Sir Ernest lifted his hands as if to repel the scorn. "Okay, here's my card if you change your mind."

As Sir Ernest disappeared from the restaurant, Ted started ranting about how he despised the man. Jim cut in and said, "It's true, Ted."

Ted looked at Jim and said, "What do you mean, it is true? I think you've drunk too much. No one is suing us. I would know about it, and so would you!"

At that, Jim reached into his pocket and threw the writ at Ted. Ted picked it up, read it, and then screwed it up tightly with one hand and gasped, "Bastard!"

There was a lull in the restaurant chatter as Ted realized he had almost shouted the word. Then the chatter resumed.

"Why didn't you tell me, Jim?"

"I tried to, but I couldn't. That's why I couldn't sign the papers," replied Jim.

"Well, that's obvious. We will have to tell Douglas."

"Ted, no! That will scuttle the float. Look, I'll just go down and sign the papers, and the float will go through."

Ted gulped down the rest of his glass of wine before answering, "And we will be bankrupted by the lawsuits that would follow. Next idea, Jim."

"No, Ted, listen We' ll sign the document, and then once we have the money, we can settle with Ian. We'll do a deal on the shares or something, and then the writ will be withdrawn. We can say we didn't know—you didn't know—when you signed."

Ted smiled. "Jim, I can tell you the law works a little better than that, but maybe you're right. Let's use our lawyer to delay the signing. I'll talk to Lester to request some amendments. We can swear about Lester in front of Douglas, and delay the signing until Friday. In the meantime, we can negotiate with Ian."

# TWENTY TWO

Jim and Ted returned to Heydon's boardroom and made the call to their lawyer, Lester Cruickshank, indicating they wished to delay things "while they negotiated with another investor." Lester soon e-mailed some proposed amendments through for Douglas to put to the three institutions.

Douglas burst into the boardroom, furious.

"What the hell is your lawyer doing? Does he want to derail the float?"

"Douglas, you know what lawyers are like. We can't control them."

Douglas was about to reply when Nadia entered the room. "Mr. Cory-Smith, James Barden is here."

James Barden was the key partner of the large law firm advising Heydons on the AMB float. "He's my lawyer" Douglas explained to Ted and Jim. "Please show him in, Nadia"

A few moments later, James Barden entered the room and announced, "I've received a request for a meeting from the stock exchange. We'll have to go now, in view of the urgency of closing the float tomorrow."

"What on earth is that about, James?" asked Douglas.

"They wouldn't say," replied James.

They quickly left the building. As they walked beneath the white-framed glass archways of the building's foyer, Sir Ernest could be seen, mobile phone in his ear, pacing the floor. Jim muttered to Ted, "Everleigh! What shall we do?"

"Keep your cool Jim. Just ignore him."

The group caught Sir Ernest's eye, and he quickly wheeled around and followed them. "We'd better catch a cab," said Ted nervously.

"No. My car's in the car park just down the road. We can walk it," replied James. They began to walk, but not quickly enough for Ted and Jim, who saw Everleigh catching up to them. They had not walked far when Sir Ernest's voice was heard:

"Oh, gentlemen, I forgot to tell you something important!"

The group stopped and turned to Sir Ernest, with Ted and Jim's faces showing aggravation. "This is Sir Ernest Everleigh, Douglas. He had expressed some interest in mezzanine funding," explained Ted.

"Nice to meet you," replied Douglas, "but we are in a dreadful hurry. Can we have a discussion later?"

"It's really quite important," insisted Sir Ernest.

Ted turned to Douglas and James and said, "Look, you walk ahead, I will meet you in front of the car park. It won't take a moment."

Douglas and James walked ahead, while Ted and Jim walked more slowly with Sir Ernest. "What is it, then?" asked Ted indignantly.

"You'll remember our last meeting," replied Sir Ernest.

"Yes, get on with it!" said Ted.

"Well, I have a sample of DNA from a human being dating back about six thousand years from a tomb in Iraq. This will form the basis for my project, but I have a parallel project to give you as well. It's called my Origin of Life project."

"What's that about?" asked Jim.

"If we cooperate, I'll be able to reveal full details on both. Gentlemen, you'll be pleased to hear that your old friend Ian Richardson will be working on these projects in your lab."

Ted's face went red with anger at this, and he exclaimed, "This is blackmail!" "Blackmail? It's just a business proposition." Sir Ernest stopped as Jim and Ted stopped also. "Yes, you know the deal. Let me know if you want to do something before it's too late." "Meaning?" replied Ted.

Sir Ernest just smiled and walked off, leaving Ted and Jim staring at each other in disbelief.

James' Mercedes was sitting in front of the car park with the engine running as Jim and Ted got in. Shortly afterward, James dropped them in front of the stock exchange, where they were met by one of his junior clerks, who drove the car back to James' office. The entrance to the London Stock Exchange in Paternoster Square was gray, made mostly of glass and with only a coat of arms as a feature. It felt even more somber to Ted and Jim, who had lost all hint of celebration on that dark day.

They made their way to the stock exchange manager's floor and were quickly shown to his office.

"Robert Prasad, you must be James Barden. We spoke on the phone." The manager shook hands with James and motioned for them to sit down.

"Well, let's cut to the chase, shall we?" suggested Douglas.

Prasad looked a little uncomfortable and then said, "Is there anything that we should know?"

Ted stepped on Jim's toe in case he spoke up.

"Like what?" asked James.

"Okay, we have had a letter dropped to us today, and I suppose I ought to show it to you to get your response." Prasad tabled a thick, stapled letter. James picked it up and read it, flipping through the pages.

"Well?" queried Douglas.

"It's from a firm of lawyers—Thistlewaite & Hazelhurst—acting for a Mr. Ian Richardson. It claims title to some of AMB's technology, and claims equity to a third of the major shareholders' shares."

"That's outrageous!" exclaimed Ted.

"Absolutely outrageous!" repeated Jim.

Douglas eyed them both and asked, "Did you two know about this?"

"We've heard scuttlebutt, but this is news to us," replied Ted.

"How should we proceed?" asked Douglas.

"You'll have to ask your lawyer, but at the very least, an amendment to the prospectus will be required, and all investors notified."

"They'll just pull out!" objected Douglas.

"That may be, but you must comply with stock exchange regulations and company law, which I am sure you want to do," replied Prasad.

Douglas leaned back in his chair and turned to James. "Can we injunct them?"

"Injunct them from what?" asked James.

Douglas was silent.

"The problem is that by the time the matter is resolved by the courts, even if you are successful, the float will have failed due to the expected stampede of investors. Investors don't like uncertainty, especially while you are floating on the stock exchange," said James.

"I know that! I'm looking for solutions."

Prasad turned to Jim and Ted and suggested, "If you and Mr. Richardson were to settle out of court, then your lawyer might advise you that no amendment to the prospectus is required, but that is a matter entirely for your own lawyers."

"Thank you for that," replied Jim.

"Look, I have another meeting downstairs, but why don't you use the conference room? My assistant will show you there. Thank you for coming. I hope you can resolve the matter. I assume I'll be hearing from you, Mr. Barden."

James nodded.

Minutes later they were sitting in one of the stock exchange conference rooms, arguing over what to do. Ted rang his lawyer, and after explaining the writ, said, "Lester, get on the phone to their lawyers and see what they want. Get back to me or Jim once you get something."

"Ted, can I see you outside?" asked Jim.

Douglas sat staring out the window as Ted and Jim left the conference room and stood near the lifts.

"Why don't we ring Everleigh and see if we can sound out a deal with him?" suggested Jim.

"Jim, don't be stupid. If we can settle with Richardson, we may not lose any investors." "Ted, I think we need him as a fallback. I can smell blood here. *Our* blood. We haven't got the luxury of choosing anymore."

"I suppose I can talk about what deal he wants. Let me ring him. You go back inside and see if there is any outcome from James talking to Ian's lawyers."

Jim returned to the meeting, while Ted rang Everleigh on his mobile.

"Everleigh, it's Ted McEwen here."

"You can call me Sir Ernest, if you wish."

"Look, maybe I was little rash today. You caught us at a bad time."

"Oh?"

"On a separate matter, if we did want to do something, are you willing to invest the five million pounds in the company?"

"Yes, providing my terms are agreed to," replied Sir Ernest.

"As we have a prospectus out, we can only issue shares at the same price as everyone else."

"That's all right, but we would have to sign a cooperation agreement along the lines we discussed for my two projects. What about Ian Richardson?"

"Our relationship with Ian is a separate matter and is confidential. I can only say that I will have to come back to you on that issue. In the meantime, can you put something in writing to our bankers, Heydon Capital Markets, committing to buy the shares? You can put the terms of our agreement to me, so that I can settle it with our lawyers."

"Done. I'm looking forward to working with AMB."

Ted bit his tongue, hung up, and returned to the conference room. Jim stood up and approached Ted as he entered the room.

"We may have a deal, Ted."

"How can we have a deal? James has just rung up."

"No, he put them on conference call, and I agreed to it."

"Well, you can't move without me," objected Ted.

"Listen, they will settle for one third of our shares only, and will wipe any damages or costs."

"We don't even have legal advice as to whether they would win!" said Ted.

"Ted, you are forgetting what you told me three months ago: that if Ian ever sued, he would win. Don't you remember that?"

Ted smiled. "That's a fair cop. What else are we up for?"

"Ian knows about the Everleigh projects—no surprise there—and part of the deal is that he gets a directorship and a position on these projects."

"No directorship. He can be project director on Everleigh's project. That's all." "Ted, I agreed to it already!"

Ted's face went red. "I wish you had waited."


Following meetings on Wednesday and Thursday, their respective lawyers settled the deed of settlement and cooperation agreement required to formalize the arrangements with Ian Richardson and Sir Ernest. However, an amended prospectus was required due to the change in shareholding. The prospectus was circulated to all investors who had already invested in AMB shares.

Jim and Ted arrived at their lawyer's office, Townsend Ward, in Fenchurch Street, London. The firm was housed in an old building, but was soon to move to a new one due to the growth of work experienced by the ambitious younger partners such as Lester Cruickshank, who was just thirty-two years old. His sandy hair and freckled complexion contrasted with his dark blue shirt and matching polka-dot tie. Lester showed them through the rabbit warren of workstations to his roomy corner office, where John Hazelhurst and Sir Ernest sat smugly.

"John Hazelhurst, solicitor. You must be Ted McEwen, and you must be Jim Alsop."

"Yes. Pleased to meet you. You're Ian's lawyer, I take it," replied Ted. "Yes."


They all sat down, and Lester tabled some documents.

"Here are the counterparts for the deed of settlement and the cooperation agreement between Ian Richardson and AMB. I have also taken the liberty of preparing some minutes of AMB, approving the transactions and Ian Richardson's appointment to the board as a director and also as project director."

"That's fine. We held the meeting yesterday, as you instructed," replied Ted glumly.

"Here is the project description for each of the projects," said Sir Ernest as he handed two thick spiral-bound booklets to Jim, who flipped through the pages briefly before laying them in his lap.

Lester then turned to Sir Ernest. "Did you bring the bank check?"

Sir Ernest reached into his pocket and retrieved an envelope with a watermark of the Antiquities Foundation and handed it to Lester, who opened it and remarked, "Five million pounds, as agreed. Here is your share certificate. You will get a computerized statement following the float."

Lester then opened the documents at the signing pages and said, "Gentlemen, if you could start signing where indicated by the signing markers. You will note that Ian Richardson has already signed."

"Why isn't he here?" asked Jim.

"He didn't want to gloat," replied John Hazelhurst.

"Stop it," smiled Sir Ernest "He's joking, of course. We want this to work, you know." They all began to sign where indicated.


Douglas was back in his office at Heydon's when the phone rang.

"Douglas, it's Ted. We've just signed the documents, and Jim and I are leaving Lester's office. Any news on which investors will pull out?"

"Okay, we've had the three institutions pull out, which lost us seven million, but with the five million from Sir Ernest, we have made that up. We also have a surprise investor."

"Go on."

"A major Italian media conglomerate, Zelacorp, rang and will take the rest of the oversubscription, namely four million. I even had a call from the chairman and major shareholder, Frederico Cesare. You might have heard of him?"

"Yes, I have read about him. He's quite flamboyant. That's great news," replied Ted.

"Yes. He offered to invest ten million. I said we could only take four million, and he could buy on market if he wants more." Douglas was jubilant.

"Okay, we are finishing a little better. When's the listing?" replied Ted.

"Late next week."

Ted thanked Douglas and hung up with mixed feelings. The approach by Cesare felt strange, on top of what he already had on his plate. Ted walked back into Lester's office, where Jim was chatting with Lester, and said, "Jim, I've got some good news for you. We've made it."

**

Ted was in his office at AMB's lab facilities when the phone rang. "Ted, its Douglas. You'll be pleased to know that our share price has moved up 20 percent since the disappointing listing debut last week."

"That's great. It must have been that announcement we put out yesterday about the AMB-Everleigh joint project," replied Ted.

"No. Actually, we know who it is. You remember that Italian company that took up the large block of shares at the last minute?"

"Yes."

"Well, they have been buying on market. You should have received the trading reports. They've already doubled their shareholding in one week!" Douglas sounded excited.

"That's good, but what does it mean? What do they want?" asked Ted.

"Probably a strategic shareholding."

"No. I can't see any synergy between media and biomed, unless they see some opportunity for media rights from Everleigh," said Ted, his mind deep at work.

# TWENTY THREE

A war has been going on between creationists—namely, between those who believed God created man per the Bible account, and evolutionists who believed that Darwin's natural selection explained the creation of man all the way back to a single cell or even a chemical accident occurring in a mud puddle. No better battleground has there been for the war between creationists and evolutionists than the missing link between man and ape. Darwin created the first watershed event for the creationists when he postulated that man had evolved from the animals by the process of natural selection. However, the creationists fought back by postulating that God had merely used Darwin's natural selection as a tool to create man. Some have argued that Darwin's theory has gaps and that God's intervention was needed to make natural selection work properly. The term "God of the gaps" was even coined, and this controversy has not been helped by the controversies in the scientific world, such as the rivalry between paleoanthropologists and molecular biologists. Paleoanthropologists and paleontologists such as Andrew Faulkner used the fossil record—empirical evidence won from getting their hands dirty in a dig from analyzing the direct evidence (the morphology of whatever fossil they are examining). From this work they theorized that man and ape split from a common ancestor fifteen or twenty million years ago, depending on which school of thought applied.

Enter the molecular biologists, who used mitochondrial DNA (the little changing DNA in the energy-producing part of a cell) instead of the nucleic DNA (the more changing DNA in the chromosomes in the nucleus of the cell). From this analysis they were able to calibrate time periods by the mutational changes in the mitochondria. For example, a change of 2 percent could mean a million years had passed. Thus they concluded that the missing link—the common ancestor of man and the apes—was only five to seven million years old. This conflicted with other views of the paleoanthropologists, who asked why the molecular biologists' views should prevail over theirs. Gradually the DNA evidence was accepted as decisive.

DNA is similar to a gigantic computer program, where the order of the key DNA molecules—call them T, A, G, and C—contain a code that, when acted upon by support mechanisms called RNA and ribosomes, manufacture proteins. These proteins then fold beautifully into all the shapes and sizes for all the parts of the human body.

Genes are sequences of DNA that translate (through the protein manufacture process) into a person's features such as brown eyes or black hair. Just as a computer uses zeroes and ones in order to do a task, so too with DNA: the order of the Ts, As, Gs, and Cs contain a code to do a task. Mutations are unexpected changes (or errors) in DNA, and this explains why Darwin's natural selection works. Some of these changes produce improvements, which make the offspring with the new DNA stronger than his or her parents. This leads to that offspring surviving more often than not—"survival of the fittest," under Darwin's theory. This was not known to Darwin when he postulated his theory, and so the discovery of DNA was a startling confirmation of it—perhaps on par with the confirmation by astronomers that Einstein's general relativity theory (which predicted the curvature of space) could be proven by observing the bending of light during an eclipse.

*Genome* refers to the total DNA blueprint of the living thing in question. It was found that the genomes of humans and chimpanzees were more than 98 percent identical, suggesting that the chimpanzee was the last common ancestor between man and the apes. A number of discoveries by paleoanthropologists and associated scientists in the field added to our knowledge. These discoveries included Neanderthal man, Cro-Magnon man, Australopithecus, Homo erectus, Homo habilis, and others, leading to Homo sapiens (man). What was fascinating was that the mitochondrial DNA analysis had suggested a common ancestor, colloquially referred to as "Eve," as man's common ancestor from three hundred thousand years ago. Eve was traced to Africa due to the fact that the female of the species maintained substantially the same mitochondrial DNA.

And so it was that Andrew Faulkner crossed the line from using the Gilgamesh fossil's morphology and paleoanthropology to using DNA analysis to infer his findings. Martin Crawford had sent him a sample of Gilgamesh before he went missing. Preliminary DNA testing was encouraging as an indicator that his theory was right; but he needed demonstrable proof, and this would only occur with full DNA analysis and computer modeling on a grand scale. His model would draw on the enormous database already generated from the human genome project, where the entire human genetic code was mapped and converted into data on a computer available for researchers, medical practitioners, scientists, and others around the world. The comparison between Gilgamesh's genome and the human genome would provide a startling theory, which Faulkner had promised to deliver to Sir Ernest. He and Sir Ernest would publish in the scientific journals and then be in the running for the Nobel Prize.

Andrew Faulkner walked with Jim Alsop around the new lab facility at AMB. The lab had an entire floor dedicated to the "Missing Link Project."

"I'm not so used to labs. I'm more used to four-wheel-drives and camels," said Faulkner. "Jim, can you take me through what is happening here?"

"Well, we have prepared the samples you have given us, and you will see here that we have a low-speed centrifuge to get the gunk away from the sample," replied Jim.

"We did try and dig inside the bone to get the best sample, so I don't think there will be much embalming contamination, but it is good to be safe, I suppose," explained Faulkner. "Then we will do a high-speed spin on it, put in some dyes, ultraviolet light, and show up the DNA."

"What is this machine here?"

"Okay, that's the moment of truth. We put the DNA into gel and run an electric current through it. The gel has holes in it, and believe it or not, the DNA worms its way through the tubes. The negative charge on the DNA makes the DNA strands line up from smallest to largest, allowing us to compare like with like. We use a laser to recognize the As, Gs, Ts, and so on."

"Oh, that's electrophoresis?" said Faulkner.

Jim said, "You've got it. Anyway, we then feed it into the computer. Actually, that's been the time-consuming part for us, because of the format you want the data in," explained Jim.

"Well, we have developed a set of algorithms that will provide the inferred genome of Gilgamesh and convert it back into compatible data for comparison with the human genome, where we will use another algorithm for the comparison—"

Faulkner was interrupted by the sight of Sir Ernest coming up behind him.

"Andrew, good morning. Sorry, Jim, I need him for something."

Sir Ernest and Faulkner walked out to the reception area.

"Listen, how long is it going to take before your final report?" asked Sir Ernest.

"About three weeks, I believe. Why?" answered Faulkner.

"It's the timing, I have got this member of the Nobel jury, Count Nansen, on my back. He wants to see the final paper we are going to submit to *Landmarks in Science* magazine. And on my Origin of Life project, I've got my mathematician tearing his hair out because he hasn't got the workings of the algorithms your guy gave him," complained Sir Ernest.

Faulkner rolled his eyes and replied, "You know what mathematicians are like. They're in another world, and my guy has been overloaded working with Jim on formatting the DNA results. In fact, Jim was just explaining the work they're doing on this. Ernest, you still haven't explained to me how your other project—this Origin of Life project—fits in with our Missing Link project?"

Sir Ernest looked irritated. "Well it doesn't, and I never said that it did. Our project is *standalone*. The Origin of Life project is something for a book I'm doing with Alistair Thornton." "Who's he?"

"He's the ex-vicar of Morgrove. He's got a bit of an axe to grind with his church." "You'd like that" chided Faulkner.

Sir Ernest turned to walk away and added, "Just get the workings to my mathematician."

**

Frederico Cesare had flown in on his private jet to Heathrow, and by helicopter to the nearest helipad in the City of London, before being escorted by an array of advisors to Heydons' offices. He and his advisors sat in the boardroom. John Rowntree had been invited after receiving a call from one of Cesare's advisors in London, and so he knew why they had invited him. Jim Alsop and Ted McEwen entered the boardroom with Douglas and quickly curbed their conversation.

"Thank you for coming, gentlemen," announced Douglas. They all shook hands and exchanged business cards. John felt a little inadequate, having no business card.

"How is Italy?" asked Ted.

"Warmer than here, but I am sure you know that!" replied Cesare. The pleasantries continued for a few minutes before Cesare said, "Well, now that I am your largest shareholder, you might tell me something about the company."

Jim Alsop nodded and then circulated a PowerPoint presentation of AMB's affairs. He then flicked on the overhead projector and proceeded to do the presentation on the projection screen. After it was over, Douglas said, "Frederico, you said that you had one other matter to discuss with us."

"Why, yes. I wish some board representation. Having such a large investment in the company, it is only fair; and I am sure your shareholders are happy with the share price since we started buying."

"Who did you have in mind, Frederico?" asked Ted.

"Okay, the young man is present with us now. He is John Rowntree. He comes highly recommended to us." Frederico was smiling as he trained his brilliant blue eyes on Ted for his reaction.

"I'm sorry. Do I know him?"

"That's me" said John.

"Aren't you a little young to be a public company director?" asked Ted. "You might give me your background, John. A directorship is not for the fainthearted."

"I'm a teacher by profession, but I'm currently at Oxford. I wish to pursue law now," replied John.

"More lawyers!" joked Ted.

Douglas stood up at this and said, "Gentlemen, can you excuse us for a minute while we discuss this outside?"

Jim, Ted, and Douglas left the room, retired into Douglas's office, and shut the door. With the three of them still standing, a heated argument ensued.

"Douglas, did you know about this?" asked Jim.

"No, I did not!" exclaimed Douglas defensively.

"This is crazy. Why are they putting a young boy on the board?" asked Ted.

"He's not a young boy. He's a teacher-cum-lawyer," answered Jim.

Douglas then paced to the window and advised, "Look, I did receive a strange call prior to the meeting, from their London stockbroker. He asked me that if we wanted to offload our shares, could we place them? And I said, why would they do that, because they just bought in? He replied that his client could be capricious. I suppose it's just a precautionary conversation—that my client wants to be fully satisfied with his investment."

"Okay, it's pretty clear, then if we don't appoint his nominee, then they may dump the shares," concluded Ted.

"Why would they do that? They would lose money from that," said Douglas.

"I don't know, but I don't think it is worth the risk. They're just putting this young chap on as a spy. They are probably suspicious types who believe a public company veteran may not give them an objective view. Perhaps that's how they do business. I don't know what they do in Italy in such matters," added Ted solemnly.

"By the way, where is Ian Richardson? He's a director, and so he must be consulted." Jim nodded and quickly phoned him for his approval. "Thanks, Ian. We'll discuss it all later." Jim hung up.

"Hey, just do it," advised Douglas. They all nodded and returned to the boardroom.

"Well, now! John Rowntree, welcome to the board," announced Ted.

John rose and shook hands with Ted and Jim. He then turned to Cesare and said, "Thank you for this opportunity, Mr. Cesare."

Cesare nodded.

# TWENTY FOUR

S ir Ernest was furious and had telephoned John on his mobile.
"Rowntree, what game are you playing?"

"I have no idea what you are talking about, Sir Ernest."

"Don't be coy with me."

"Look, we were rescued in Afghanistan by some people who turn out to be friends of Frederico."

"What friends?" asked Sir Ernest.

"They wish to remain private, but all I can tell you is that since AMB is undertaking projects based on your work, they see me as one of the best people to monitor what is going on." "Well, you're not to interfere. This is serious business, there are public company funds at stake, and so my projects must succeed."

"I'll do my job," replied John."

Sir Ernest hung up abruptly.

The weeks rolled by, and John was instructed by Cesare to get involved in the Missing Link project and the Origin of Life project, both current at AMB. His presence at the lab was resented, and he received follow-up calls from Sir Ernest asking why he needed to get involved to that extent.

Soon a board meeting of AMB directors was called. Jim, Ted, Ian Richardson, Douglas, and John were present, with Sir Ernest and Andrew Faulkner invited to attend as observers. Their company secretary was the last to arrive in the frosted-glass-lined boardroom. She was carrying a number of folders. Curious AMB staff watched as she closed the door. Ian whispered in the ear of Jim Alsop, and the two went outside to the corridor.

"Jim, I just want you to know that I am not coming here to blame anyone. I am wiping the slate clean as to what has occurred. We are both scientists, and I know our work comes first. Ted, I know, is more bitter; and I could be bitter against him also, but you can tell him I will let bygones be bygones."

"Ian, I was never happy with what occurred. One thing led to another. We all fell out, as it were, so I agree with you. Let's try and move ahead to make AMB a great company."

They shook hands and reentered the boardroom.


The meeting started with the usual formalities of past minutes, board papers, and the reelection of Ted as the chairman. The meeting soon moved onto some important topics.

"The next item on the agenda is the tabling of the report of the Missing Link Project, and I believe Andrew Faulkner has the floor on this one," announced Ted in his role as chairman.


"Thank you, Mr. Chairman. I would like to hand out to you the final report from the work that has taken place in the past few months."

Faulkner then distributed a spiral-bound, thick booklet entitled *Missing Link Project.* The booklet bore AMB's corporate logo and name.


"Mr. Chairman, can you please explain to us the commercial benefit of the Missing Link Project to AMB?" asked John.

"I think that is a question for Andrew Faulkner, as he has promoted this project to us in company with Sir Ernest Everleigh," said Ted.

"The software we have used has wide uses for DNA profiling and databasing. It will provide new ways to process DNA, to find links to diseases, and so on. The traditional way of storing data from the human genome is to merely categorize the genes by name, but our software can categorize by other criteria, giving a more functional database. AMB can license this out, and perhaps develop its own interactive DNA database using these new criteria," answered Faulkner.

"For the record, Andrew, the same would go for our Origin of Life project. Is that correct?" asked Jim, concerned by John's question.

"Yes. They are using some of our algorithms for that also."

"Andrew, can we please get on with it? We've been waiting for this report for weeks!" complained Sir Ernest.

"All right. As a paleontologist, I would much rather pick up a bone in a cave than click a mouse on a computer to solve the mystery of man's evolution, but paleoanthropologists have conceded that the pure DNA analysis of different fossils from different races of people can allow us to extrapolate back to a common ancestor. This has already been done, and a female—dubbed Eve—has been postulated. In our case, we have Gilgamesh as our subject—the long lost part-God, part-Human Sumerian—who is linked to tales of spaceships and spacemen."

"Just myth and speculation?" interrupted Jim Alsop.

"I agree that it is speculation, but what is not speculation is Gilgamesh's genome, which we have now analyzed, and what we now believe has shown us the missing link between man and chimpanzee." Faulkner walked to the projector and turned it on, displaying the first slide in a presentation. A slide with a long strand of DNA was shown.

"Here you will see that there are the active parts of the DNA and there are the so called 'junk parts' of DNA." Faulkner clicked to the next slide. "As you can now see, we have marked various parts of this section of the genome, and magnified the junk sections. However, we have not found them to be junk. By applying one of our algorithms, we have been able to trace on the Gilgamesh genome a number of phases. We have seen about eleven phases over a period of six million years at about the same times apart—not exactly, but good enough—where a major leap occurred. What we call a major leap is determined by how close the chimpanzee is to a human. So that, say, six million years ago, we start with a chimp having 100 percent of its normal genome; and then, four million years ago, our chimp or man chimp has 99.5 percent of the human genome and three million years ago it has 99 percent, and so on. In other words, this junk DNA has given us a history of development from chimp to man." Jim Alsop then interrupted. "Andrew, why is it that normal human-specimen DNA does not show this information up?"

"Jim, this is where it gets strange. It appears the reason why we know this on this DNA is that the whole genome has had recombinant genetic technology applied to it. Each of the changes that we found in the junk sections was transplanted there, because they were out of sequence compared to a normal human genome. This allowed us to pinpoint them in the first place because they were anomalous." Faulkner clicked to the next slide before another question intervened.

"You don't mean there has been genetic engineering?" asked Jim

"Well, that's how it looks. In fact, the theory we have come up with is that the very last phase was a substantial one, which involved an accelerated genetic push. Our theory is that these junk areas are not really junk areas, and that they do have functions that we just don't understand yet. However, whoever performed the genetic engineering did understand, and genetically advanced ancient man by inserting a 'super code.' This overhauled many segments of the genome, including the junk areas. For some reason this pinpointed the most differentiating genetic features on the human genome. It seems that Gilgamesh's super-genetic boost imbued in the Sumerians their advanced mathematics, law, society, and so on, compared to other societies."

"So you are postulating the myth that a super race from who knows where performed the genetic engineering?" objected Ted.

I am just giving you the scientific results and the natural inference from them," replied Faulkner.

"No, you are speculating in a very nebulous area," replied Ted.

Faulkner, now red-faced and rattled from Ted's rebuke, clicked clumsily through some other pictorial presentations and added some more background before turning the lights back on.

"I do find it astounding. Absolutely astounding," commented Jim.

Sir Ernest, who had been silent for the entire presentation, stood up and said, "Andrew, can I see you outside?"

Faulkner left with Sir Ernest, while the others spoke with excitement on the findings.

"What is this?" barked Sir Ernest.

"What do you mean?" asked Faulkner.

"You told me that your report would conclude that humans were conclusively created by natural means on earth, and not by supernatural means. Not only does your report make no finding or comment on this, but also the gist of your presentation is that perhaps God came down and genetically engineered Gilgamesh. People may even claim that Gilgamesh was Abraham, as they both were at Ur in Sumer. I think you have misled me!"

"Now wait a minute. I've kept you informed of this project all along the way. Didn't you read the reports I gave you?"

"You mean the occasional e-mail? That's not the same, and you know it."

Faulkner looked upset and replied, "You knew about the myths, and I agree: I did believe the genetic development arose more from the mathematical behavior of DNA molecules, but our work now shows more genetic engineering. How could I foresee that?"

"I expected a lot more than this," objected Sir Ernest.

"What about the money you have made from this venture?" responded Faulkner sharply. "You mean the money made by the Antiquities Foundation?" answered Sir Ernest.

"Come on, Sir Ernest. You *are* the foundation. They bankroll your projects. Anyway, what do you want to do now?"

"Well, we have to honor our deal with AMB," said Sir Ernest.

"What about submitting our paper to *Landmarks in Science*?"

"I don't know, I'll have to think about it," said Sir Ernest.

"You'll do no such thing. You and I have a contract, and it states that we will jointly submit our paper to *Landmarks in Science*," argued Faulkner indignantly.

"All right, go ahead and do it."

Sir Ernest returned to the board meeting.


"Sir Ernest, since we're paying a bloody fortune for these projects, why don't *you* give us a briefing on this Origin of Life project?" urged Ted.

Sir Ernest cleared his throat and stood up. "I don't have a presentation, but I can take you through the main principles of it." Sir Ernest approached the whiteboard in the corner of the boardroom and drew a series of boxes and arrows. "It is clear that Darwin's principle of natural selection relies on the DNA molecule, which is a complex machine made up of complex molecules binding together in complex ways. The question arises as to how the DNA molecule itself evolved. I say *evolved* not in the Darwinian sense, but in the sense of the considerable body of scientific evidence that is now being built up in an effort to demonstrate where the DNA molecule came from.

"It is better known as 'chemical evolution.' That is, if you have a rock puddle—call it 'prebiotic soup'—could it become biotic, i.e., containing life? The first clue to its origin came from the Miller-Urey experiment in 1952. Scientists Miller and Urey passed electric sparks through a mixture of methane, ammonia, and hydrogen to simulate earth's early atmosphere. They produced five amino acids. Later experiments produced twenty-two amino acids. Amino acids are the basic building blocks for proteins, and proteins make up our bodies.

"As for the building blocks of the DNA molecule itself, which is responsible for arranging the amino acids into proteins, sparking experiments have also produced one of the key DNA molecules: Adenine, of the T, A, G, C fame. Chemical evolution would thus see evolution from nonliving materials such as amino acids, into living material. Call it a very simple organism. From this simple organism to an organism with DNA and beyond, we call that biological evolution. From DNA to now, we call it Darwinian evolution."

John raised his hand to ask a question.

"John, you're not in one of my lectures. Just ask."

"Wasn't there an issue about this experiment because the gases they used didn't fit the current model of the early atmosphere?"

"Yes, but we have moved on from the fifties. One scientist postulated that these building blocks of life could have been started in comets that later rained down on the earth. In a stunning demonstration of the scientific method, NASA sent a rocket into space in 1999 to collect dust off the tail of a comet, and the rocket returned with a vast array of organic chemicals including proteins, carbohydrates, amino acids, and other hydrocarbons, proving the theory correct. The theory proposed also that the comet would be bombarded with cosmic and gamma rays when it passed close to the sun, giving good scope for chaotic chemistry akin to the sparking experiments conducted by Miller and Urey.

"What was exciting was that comets contain clay, and where you have clay, you have water, which is needed for life. This is also fascinating. Molecular biologist and organic chemist Dr. A.G. Cairns-Smith, who has published on this topic and whose description of the origin of life problem must be praised for being second to none, has postulated that clay would form an excellent template for self-assembly of the building blocks of life, leading to creation of DNA."

"Where do you come in, Sir Ernest? It sounds as though they have it beaten," said Ted.

Jim then intervened: "Mr. Chairman, I have read Dr. Cairns-Smith's book Seven Clues to the Origin of Life, which Sir Ernest has been kind enough to leave with me, and I would like to quote you some of it. From page thirty-seven: 'I grant that the path of chemical evolution seems sensible and in the right direction…but there is a promise of an easy walk up to the foothills of the mountain…. It is a promise unfulfilled…. The trouble with this path is that it leads toward…a near-vertical cliff face. Suddenly in our thinking we are faced with the seemingly unequivocal need for a fully working machine of incredible complexity'—and that fully working machine is the DNA mechanism, is it not, Sir Ernest?"

"Dr. Cairns-Smith believes in chemical evolution as the origin of life, and proposes a good solution for the self-assembly problem. As I have said, he has outlined the daunting nature of the problem; and thus, for those who solve it, the rewards will be great. This is where we can accomplish a significant milestone," said Sir Ernest.

"Jim and I had a discussion about Dr. Cairns-Smith last week, and it seems the greatest stumbling block was that it was implausible for nucleotides or prevital nucleic acids (i.e., the building blocks of DNA) to generate spontaneously. In fact, he states that experiments such as the Miller-Urey experiment demonstrate why prevital nucleic acids are implausible, and actually lists in great scientific detail nineteen reasons why he believes they cannot spontaneously form," said John.

"And yet this is the same scientist who goes on to postulate they could possibly form in clay?" countered Sir Ernest.

"What was the outcome of the clay theory?" asked John.

"The obstacle they found was that organic compounds became stuck to the clay, making further chemical reactions difficult," answered Jim.

"I'm lost," said Ted.

"Let me recap," replied John, who continued:

"We understand that Darwinian evolution only commenced when DNA was created, not before. Before that, chemical evolution is postulated, posing the question of how DNA chemically evolved. All life is created by DNA. DNA is a molecule made up of chemical bits and pieces, which, on their own are lifeless. So how did all these bits and pieces get together to form life? These bits and pieces do not know how to form themselves into DNA, as they have no brain. They are lifeless. They were just bits and pieces in a mud pool or a comet.

"But scientists have shown that a lightning strike on a mud pool, or cosmic rays on a comet, produces the right bits and pieces to create life. In other words, we have the building blocks of life. The big problem is how the building blocks came to be put together into a working DNA mechanism—or, more precisely, how did they self-assemble themselves to become the elegant double-helix DNA molecule, with its machinelike capability of making life presumably with no plan? Put another way, how did DNA know how to make a living thing?"

"That's sufficient. Thank you, Mr. Rowntree. Our Origin of Life project will answer this question," replied Sir Ernest, who then quickly left the meeting.

# TWENTY FIVE

S ir Ernest took the lift, which opened at the top floor. He walked to a glass door bearing the letters ORIGIN OF LIFE PROJECT below a large logo consisting of an hourglass. The upper part of the hourglass showed sand with a bolt of lightning hitting the sand, while the lower part of the hourglass contained the double-helix DNA strands.

He opened the glass door to reveal long lines of computer workstations with staff busy at their screens. He walked to the end of the workstation area, toward an enormous bank of computer servers housed in a glass-lined room where large ventilation fans could be seen cooling the servers. Next to the server room was an executive office with the name ARUN KUMAR, PROJECT MANAGER on the door.

Arun was soon at the doorway as he saw Sir Ernest approach. Arun was a professional mathematician with a degree in biology, and so he was very excited about the project.

"Sir Ernest, it is so good to see you. I thought there was a board meeting today?"

"Yes, there was, but my attention span for some of the drudgery only goes so far. So tell me, how far are you away from completing the project?"

Kumar beckoned for Sir Ernest to sit down with him on the plush red leather couch at the back of his office.

"As instructed by you, we have prepared algorithms to model a number of prebiotic soup situations. We are modeling whether other forms of energy, such as those from chemical reactions, could have caused a biotic system to arise. In terms of our phases, we have modeled the RNA phase. You will remember the body of work called *RNA World* we discussed last week? Well, we believe we have advanced beyond that to show that RNA would produce an enzyme that catalyzes the formation of another information-storing system, which would get us to the beginning of Darwinian evolution," explained Arun.

"That's good. Any stumbling blocks?"

"Yes. The problem we are trying to overcome is this old issue of nucleotides. This hypothetical RNA in our modeling assumes the existence of nucleotides, and I have no studies showing them spontaneously occurring."

"What about that work you showed me the other day, Arun?"

"No, they were synthesizing them in the laboratory, but the conditions were not natural."

Sir Ernest looked irritated. "I don't want to hear that! You had better work up a model for the spontaneous creation of nucleotides, haven't you!"

"But Sir Ernest, what about Dr. Cairns-Smith's nineteen reasons for spontaneous nucleotide production being implausible?"

"Look, that upstart John Rowntree has just rubbed that in my face. Don't you do the same!"

Arun's face changed, and there was an awkward silence as Sir Ernest got up.

"Arun, we must have the project finished within three weeks, because I have some severe time pressures. My window of opportunity for this work is only open now, and we must snatch the moment!"

Arun walked out with him to the lift and added, "I have not received the workings from Andrew Faulkner yet either."

"Leave Faulkner to me," said Ernest, who smiled and got in the lift.

The next day, John received a call on his mobile.

"Mr. Rowntree?"

"Yes," replied John.

"Oxford University here. It has come to our attention that you have not been attending lectures for some weeks."

"Ah…yes. I have been on leave. Didn't you get the letter I left at your administration office?"

"No, we did not."

"Okay, I had better come in and sort this out," remarked John.

"Really, the main thing is for you to approach each of your lecturers or tutors and explain your position. It will then be up to them. Oh, I should tell you that Sir Ernest Everleigh will take the last lecture in philosophy tomorrow, and so it might be a good time to approach him, as he has been hard to contact in recent weeks."

"Tomorrow? Yes, I can make that lecture. I'm surprised he is doing that, because he has a lot on," said John.

"Oh?"

"Thank you for your call, then." John hung up and returned to Oriel College, where he had arranged to meet Paul at a nearby coffee shop.


Paul arrived at John's table just as the waitress was cleaning up.

"Paul! Great to see you. Please sit down."

"Yeah, John, sorry I had to mend a few fences and have only now got my head above water. Can't wait for you to tell me what has gone on since you got back," remarked Paul. "Cappuccino?" asked John.

Paul nodded before John caught the eye of the waitress: "Two cappuccinos, please?" John then related the events that had occurred at AMB. "So, Sir Ernest seems set for great things. The guy is a good operator. He's mobilized two projects, and the word is, he's in line for the Nobel Prize."

"You're joking! How can he pull that off?" asked Paul.

"He's about to submit a scientific paper to *Landmarks in Science* magazine; and once he does that, he's in the running for the Nobel Prize, along with the coauthors of the study he is producing," explained John.

"How do you know all this?" asked Paul.

"You heard that I was appointed a director of AMB?" said John.

"The biomed public company?" asked Paul.

"Yes, that's right. Well, I can see why the Italians put me there, because it gave me access to what's going on," replied John.

"Okay, then how can we stop him? He's a zealot, and he's out to steamroll anyone that gets in his way. John, I hope you don't forget you lost your job because of him," urged Paul.

"I haven't forgotten, but I'm looking at the big picture too. He's trying to convince the world that God does not exist, and I am starting to believe that he's on the wrong side." John smiled as he looked at Paul and added, "I know I am preaching to the converted here, but I am not a creationist, nor am I a proponent of intelligent design. I am trying to see the whole issue using the scientific method. The first problem I have is that scientists are really breaking Occam's razor." "What's that?" asked Paul.

"If you have competing theories, the simplest theory is to be preferred. Scientists exclude the simplest theory—namely, the existence of God—from the scope of scientific study. Why? I can understand why there has been upset when good scientific theories like Darwin have been under attack from creationists on a flimsy basis, but this is no reason to throw the baby out with the bathwater. It all boils down to this: there are gigantic questions for scientists that they are choosing to ignore. They seem to be saying that because Darwin has a good theory, then other theories as good as Darwin will solve these big questions. That's why Sir Ernest believes he can win the Nobel Prize by solving them."

"John, this is all very well, but you can't stop him. The momentum Sir Ernest has is enormous. Nothing can be done to stop him."

"Frederico Cesare is a powerful man. I am sure he has something in mind to stop him, otherwise he wouldn't have invested the eight or nine million pounds into AMB," argued John. "What can he do?" countered Paul. "His money can't change public opinion. *Landmarks in Science* is one of the best journals in the world. Nobel laureates have written articles in it. Money can't stop that."

John looked dejected as Paul's words echoed in his mind. "So Paul, we have come this far to just watch him march into success?"

Paul shrugged.

The following morning, John walked into the lecture theater to hear Sir Ernest's last lecture of the term. There was a full house, and it seemed that there were many students who were not taking the philosophy course. An air of excitement permeated the theater. John could not find a seat and sat in the back of the auditorium on the top step. Others were already taking many of the other steps to sit and listen to the "oracle." Jane was sitting a few rows down and was looking around, and suddenly her eyes caught John's eyes and she looked away. Moments later, she got up from her seat and stepped around the other students camped on the steps and stood over John. "John, I've been wanting to call you. I'm so sorry for how things worked out."

John looked upward bitterly and then stared hard back at her and said, "Are you referring to us or the project?"

Other students' ears pricked up as they sensed the tension between the two.

"The project," replied Jane.

"I don't know what you mean. I thought the project succeeded?" asked John.

"You know what I mean," replied Jane gingerly.

"Well, it looks as if you people got what you wanted," responded John.

"John, I didn't get anything out of it. I was just doing it for the cause," replied Jane. "You got Brendan," said John sharply.

Jane blushed and returned slowly to her seat.

Sir Ernest entered the auditorium to a standing ovation of cheers and clapping. He seemed quite surprised at the jubilation that his students and outsiders were expressing. A television crew could be seen filming his appearance. It seemed that the righteous cause of atheism was enjoying a groundswell of support. Sir Ernest raised his arms and beckoned for the applause to stop. Gradually the noise died down and he opened his lecture:

"My dear students, I see we have some new friends here today. We are on the verge of a great victory, a great vindication. It is times like these that only words from Julius Caesar appear appropriate: 'I came, I saw, I conquered.'"

The crowded theater went wild. Gradually the applause faded away, and heads turned to someone hopping down the steps toward the podium. It was John.

"Oh, Mr. Rowntree, I didn't think we would be honored with your presence. Did you wish to say something?"

John, who had been on his way out in disgust, walked over to the microphone and said, "Beware the ides of March!"

There was some jeering heard as John nodded at Sir Ernest, whose smile turned to a grimace. John turned and walked out.

Once outside, John took the pathway away from the Harris lecture theater but stopped as Jane's voice behind him echoed:

"John, why are you doing all this? You're an agnostic!"

John turned and smiled. "Jane, I need to know if God exists."

"Well, I don't need to know!" replied Jane.

"And why not? What about your soul? What if God is true? Don't you have any worries about the afterlife?" posed John.

"I was brought up with all that. I know about the soul. If it exists, I prefer to think of heaven on earth, so I can keep my soul healthy here, thank you. I live for the *here and now!*" snapped Jane.

"Interesting. Heaven on earth—wasn't that the singer Bob Marley's dream?" observed John.

"What of it?"

"He was a Christian."

Jane paused and became more conciliatory. "Okay, assume my soul exists. What would I need to do to save my soul? Go to church?"

"I think I rebelled against that myself," replied John.

"Then what?" pressed Jane.

"For what it's worth, I believe it all boils down to five principles: love God, love each other, follow your conscience, and look after your spiritual development." John turned to go.

"That's only four," exclaimed Jane.

"Oh yes. Fun is okay," smiled John.

Jane smiled back and pondered what John meant by that, but then she blocked John's path as he walked on and said, "John, forget about debates. Prove to me that I have a soul!"

John took Jane's arm and led her off the path onto the grass. "NDEs," answered John. "Near death experiences!" exclaimed Jane.

"Yes. They have lasted as long as five minutes or more, and during them the patient is clinically dead. There is no oxygen going to the brain, meaning the person is not only unconscious but also that he can't dream. Yet they have these lucid experiences that are sharper than dreams, and afterward they remember it better than a dream. But there are no brain-waves as with a dream. From medical science's viewpoint, there is no mechanism for them to remember, because the brain was inactive," explained John.

"I've been through this with Sir Ernest. There are drugs such as ketamine that can induce an NDE—an out-of-body experience," said Jane.

"Wrong, Jane. Ketamine does not produce a number of the key elements of an NDE. Let me give you some of the medical facts. Within six and a half seconds after a cardiac arrest, an EEG will show that all electrical activity in the brain has ceased, because the lack of blood flow cuts off oxygen to the brain. There is certainly no brain activity consistent with the NDE, whereas with a drug the brain has activity. The next few minutes are when the patient experiences the vision, because when they are revived, they recall it."

"John, between you and me, Sir Ernest has looked into NDEs because his own son had one."

John bit his tongue, knowing he could not reveal that he had overheard Sir Ernest with his son's doctor that day at the hospital. "Jane, I can't speak about that case, but there are documented instances where the patient has seen details of the operating theater that could not have been known by the patient," John explained.

"Such as?" snapped Jane.

"The BBC program *The Day I Died* featured the NDE of Pamela Reynolds. Her eyes were taped shut during her brain operation, and three clinical tests showed her to be *brain dead* during the NDE. She had an 'out of body experience' rising above the surgeons, could hear what they were saying, and saw the instruments used. For example, during the operation the surgeons were making an incision , and one surgeon said, 'We have a problem,' and the other said, 'Try the other side.' She related this conversation and the type of instrument used.

"John, this might indicate some superhuman ability or subconscious telepathy between human beings. Where is the spiritual side to all this?" asked Jane.

"Jane, there is more to it than the out-of-body experience in the operating theater. She also described a *Wizard of Oz* experience of rising fast in a tornado like elevator before seeing relatives, and an intense white light that was described by them as the 'breath of God.' "

Jane interrupted: "She could have subconsciously heard the conversation, and perhaps she saw instruments like these for other operations."

John continued, "The surgeon who was interviewed said the detail she related could not be explained, because she was unconscious. Remember, she had her eyes taped shut. Look, Jane, you are missing the main point with NDEs. First, there are hundreds of NDEs documented by clinical studies in the United Kingdom, United States, and the Netherlands. Secondly, substantial percentages of patients display key indicators such as the tunnel, out-of-body experience, and positive experience during the NDE. Third, patients have lucid and logical thought while their brain was inactive and 'dead.' The Dutch study was featured in the prestigious *Lancet* journal. The study concluded that the NDE experience during clinical death indicates that consciousness is not located exclusively in the brain. Finally, unlike dreams and drugs, most people have positive and profound changes from NDEs, including strong purpose in life and self image, compassion, and belief in the afterlife."

Jane stood aside to let John pass with the parting words, "John, will our souls ever be together?"

John smiled and replied, "I think I'd be near death for that to happen!"

Later that day, John telephoned Cesare in Italy.

"Mr. Cesare, I'm returning your call."

"Call me Frederico. John, tell me what is going on at AMB."

John related the events of the past few weeks, and the jubilant mood of Sir Ernest and his followers.

"Ah, Sir Ernest has excellent taste in the classics. My company is named after Zela, where Ceasar is reported to have said the famous words, 'I came, I saw, I conquered.' I think that Sir Ernest will not achieve the swift victory that Caesar did at Zela."

"But how do we stop him?"

"I have an idea. Give me a couple of weeks, and I will tell you whether it has worked." Cesare hung up.

# Twenty Six

S ir Ernest was sitting in the wood-paneled study of his country mansion in Oxfordshire, busily finalizing the last chapter of the book he was writing with Alistair Thornton. He was smiling at the heading of the last chapter—"The Origin of Life"—when the phone rang.

"Ernest?"

"Yes."

"It's Andrew, and I'm terribly upset."

"Whatever about?" asked Sir Ernest.

"I've just found out that you had submitted two papers to *Landmarks in Science:* our Missing Link paper and your Origin of Life paper! Are you trying to sabotage our paper?"

"Andrew, Andrew, calm down. I was going to talk to you about this, but the process is still in progress."

"What process? What are you talking about?"

"You know, the magazine had appointed a referee to peer review the paper, and there's a problem."

"Problem? What problem?"

"It appears the referee is alleging you fudged the figures on the genetic coding to fit them to what you wanted them to be, and his conclusion is that the results are inconclusive."

There was silence as the shock hit Faulkner, who then asked, "Who is the referee?"

"Well, I'm afraid it is our Ian Richardson."

"Oh my God. This can't be possible!"

"Once I knew there was a problem, I had to submit my second paper as a backup." "There's something awfully wrong here," said Faulkner.

"What do you mean?" asked Sir Ernest.

"Well, it smells. The whole thing smells."

"Andrew, you're not suggesting that I put Ian up to this, are you? Ian's integrity as a scientist rises above his personal relations with me. I'm surprised you would even think such a nasty allegation," said Sir Ernest.

"Ah, I see now. You only retrieved the relic for the money. Well, we're finished, Ernest!" Sir Ernest began to speak, but the click of the phone in his ear stopped him. He then picked up the phone to ring Ian Richardson to warn him of Faulkner's allegation, and repeated the conversation to him.

**

The following month's issue of *Landmarks in Science* had a cover image of Sir Ernest with DNA bubbling out of a hot soupy liquid, with the headline A NEW MODEL FOR THE ORIGIN OF LIFE. TV and newspaper reporters thronged Sir Ernest's front lawn in Oxfordshire, waiting to get a comment from him.

Sir Ernest, oblivious to the excitement outside, spoke calmly to Count Nansen:

"Surely, as secretary of the Nobel committee, you can hurry up my nomination." "Sir Ernest, let me impress on you that this has been an independent process by the Nobel jury members, and I cannot interfere in their deliberations. In fact, it was only coincidence that we met earlier on the related topic of evolution. You will remember I warned you that anyone seeking a Nobel prize must fit within one of the categories of physics, chemistry, physiology, or medicine, literature and peace but your first project involving the Missing Link problem did not come easily within these categories," explained Count Nansen.

"All right, but December is not far off now, and it would be good if I could be considered as soon as the honorable jury members are able to do so."

"Sir Ernest, the matter is going through an independent process. That is all I can say. Now, good day to you."

Sir Ernest put the phone down and stared out the window to see the reporters that had arrived. He went to the front door and opened it.

"Sir Ernest, Sir Ernest! Does this mean you are in the running to get the Nobel Prize?" said one keen young female reporter.

"No, that's a premature speculation. They often choose people who are completely unaware of being nominated."

Another reporter asked, "Does this vindicate the Everleigh committee's decision to ban religion in English schools?"

"I am in no doubt that the decision was right, and this vindicates the decision. Education in England has improved as a result of the committee's findings."

The questions poured out, and Sir Ernest basked in the limelight of the excitement for over half an hour before holding his hands up and bidding them all farewell.

**

John was watching the six o'clock news in his room when he saw Sir Ernest's question-and-answer session. Someone knocked at the door, and John turned the television off. To his surprise it was Andrew Faulkner.

"Mr. Faulkner" said John formally.

"John, sorry about turning up here, but I could only get voicemail on your mobile." "That's okay," said John, who made a gesture for him to sit down.

Faulkner sat down and said, "I know you must have mixed feelings about this whole thing, and I wanted to talk to you. I think I have made a colossal mistake in trusting Sir Ernest, and indeed it was he who persuaded me to vote as I did on the Everleigh committee. I now know that you lost your job as a result of that decision. Funny how you don't realize the consequences of decisions like that. I suppose we sit in a sort of ivory tower, sometimes."

"Go on," urged John.

"Well, I know you and your group—Frederico's group, I suppose—are not happy with Sir Ernest steamrolling his way to success on a topic you might not agree with."

John smiled. "That's an understatement!"

Faulkner smiled also "Quite. Look, I can help you. The Origin of Life study is flawed." John's mouth dropped, and he then asked, "How?"

Faulkner found it hard to continue talking but forced himself to reveal it. "You remember the greatest issue with chemical evolution is how did complex molecules—that is, nucleotides—self-assemble? The problem is that there seems to be an unknown path to their self-assembly. Well, I've got my own spy in the Origin of Life lab, and he tells me that the simulation for the nucleotide phase is based on false or at best wild assumptions not supported by any empirical evidence. The most they relied on was some reverse extrapolation of known lab synthesis of nucleotides, which is hardly representative of prebiotic soup scenarios."

"Are you prepared to back that up with a proper critique?" asked John.

"Now, I don't want to get sued. Sir Ernest is a powerful man." Faulkner got up to go. "Thanks for listening, John. I hope that you can use this."

"Wait," said John. "What is your view on the banning of religion being taught in schools?" Faulkner said, "I won't repeat this, but I've changed my mind…in many ways." He left quickly, leaving John's mind whirring.


John soon phoned Cesare:

"Frederico, something interesting has just happened." John recounted his conversation with Faulkner.

"Your timing is good, because that idea I spoke of has paid off," said Cesare.

"What was that?" asked John.

"I had a feeling that Everleigh had been talking to the Nobel committee, and I was right. He has been in contact with the secretary, Count

Nansen, for some time. I have found out that they are considering Everleigh for the Nobel Prize in chemistry."

"Why, that is bizarre. He's not even a chemist."

"We believe it is more a political move by the Royal Swedish Academy of Scientists to shut out any possibility of God's existence from the realm of science, which they see as supernatural, not natural."

"What can you do?" asked John.

"I'm due to ring tonight. Do you think you are able to e-mail me a summary of Faulkner's critique? Enough for me to show it to them?"

"Of course. Give me a couple of hours. I might need to check some things, but I can do it. Frederico, Faulkner is scared of being sued. What about me?"

"I'll guarantee your safety on this. I'll make a call to my lawyer, and you'll have a document e-mailed to you tonight."

Cesare reached Count Nansen about three hours later and read to him the key parts of the e-mail that John had sent him. Count Nansen thanked him for the information. Cesare then placed the bait.

"Count, I don't think this issue has been properly aired, and I am sure the Nobel committee wants it properly aired as well…"

"What have you got in mind?" asked Nansen.

Cesare outlined a proposal that would come as a complete surprise to John.

"John?"

"Yes."

"It's Frederico."

"How did it go?"

"John, how are you at public speaking?"

"Why?" asked John.

"Well, because you have been nominated to debate Sir Ernest at a special Nobel symposium, to be held in the Stockholm Concert Hall where the Nobel Prizes are awarded." This took John's breath away.

"John? Are you still there?"

"Yes…but on prize night?"

"No, No, it will be a separate event, long before December's prize night. In fact, it will probably decide who gets the Nobel Prize."

# TWENTY SEVEN

Four, three, two, one, go!

"This is Sally Wong from OBNC News. I am standing in front of the Stockholm Concert Hall, Sweden, in what will be an enthralling night. This is traditionally the place where the Nobel Prize ceremony is held, but tonight a debate is being held between two British men on the science vs. God issue, in a David-and-Goliath struggle. Sir Ernest Everleigh, author, Oxford don, and civil service boss, is debating the little-known former teacher John Rowntree. The Nobel Foundation does arrange the occasional symposium, but this bout is unusual, as informed sources say it will be decisive for whether or not Sir Ernest receives the Nobel Prize for his work in chemical evolution.

"This would be quite remarkable, because Sir Ernest is not a chemist, but he has headed a major biochemical project known as the Origin of Life project. Tonight there will be an orchestra playing, followed by a couple of speeches from world authorities in the area, and this will then be followed by the great debate. The judges will be members of the Nobel jury who will be judging who is to receive this year's prize in chemistry. In many ways, this is like a real Nobel Prize ceremony, but with a lot more tension."

Inside the Stockholm Concert Hall, the orchestra had finished playing and the lights remained dimmed, highlighting the gray-blue podium. A royal-blue-and-yellow coat of arms sat upon a wide balcony adorned with red, yellow, and green stripes. The letter "N," with a gold ring around it, was embroidered on the carpet. The members of the Nobel jury sat in formal black tie on the Podium in blue chairs, with light gold patterns behind where Count Nansen now stood at the lectern. A sea of faces sat in the darkness, overlooking the podium. At the rear of the podium, against a stone wall, there were two giant photos of Sir Ernest and John.

John was in an adjacent room with his team, preparing for the debate, while Sir Ernest likewise was in another room with his team. John strolled out to stretch his legs after hours of preparation, and as he did, he saw Jane down the corridor staring at him. She nodded, and John nodded back. He then saw Brendan come out behind her, and the two returned to the room where Sir Ernest was in preparation.

Professor Simons, Arthur Briggs, Paul, and John's father sat around the table, which was covered in notes and books. John returned to the room and felt the adrenaline building up now as the time for the debate approached.

"John, take some of these pills, will you? You're not a politician, so this is all foreign to you," advised John's father.

"Dad, I want to keep a clear mind. Sir Ernest has a razor-sharp mind"

Professor Simons closed a book and pushed it forward and said, "I don't think we can take it any further. John, if you can repeat 80 percent of what we've got here, you will be doing well. Just do your best. You have the advantage on him because he has already shown his hand. We have read the Origin of Life study, and he is yet to hear your complete argument."

"What about the nucleotide issue?" asked Arthur.

"Well, we know that part of the report is ill-founded, but you cannot demonstrate the modeling is true or false on the stage. We can merely address it from first principles, and I think that's what the Committee wants. John, you know what to say. We have been over it already," answered Professor Simons.

A knock was then heard at the door.

"Come in!"

Frederico appeared at the door.

"Frederico, I didn't know you were here!" said John.

"Wouldn't want to miss it. Look, I just wanted to wish you and your team the best of luck. John, the pressure on you must be enormous. Take a deep breath and allow sixty seconds for the nerves to calm down," advised Frederico.

"Thanks Frederico. I'll try."

In Sir Ernest's camp, the mood was more businesslike, as Sir Ernest sat with a glass of scotch in front of him. Brendan, Jane, Ian Richardson, Ted McEwen, and Jim Alsop all sat around the table.

"Brendan, did you ask them whether they will consider reversing the order of speakers? How can it be fair for him to present first, when it is my project?"

"Dad, I spoke to them. They see that you have already released your study, and it is for the challengers to outline their challenge first, and for them to then defend it."

"Yes, but that gives John the right of reply—the last word," complained Sir Ernest.

Count Nansen then stuck his head in through the door, which had been left open by Brendan and Jane when they entered.

"Ladies and gentlemen, could you make your way to the podium?"

The Count then did likewise to John's team.

The respective teams sat in rows of chairs in front of the audience, facing the podium, while Sir Ernest rose to give his opening address in the debate.

Count Nansen went to the lectern and announced, "Ladies and gentlemen, I now open what must be one of the most significant debates of our time. The debate is being televised to over sixty countries. It is a debate as to whether the life can be explained by science alone, or did it have a supernatural origin? I would also like to make it clear tonight, so there are no misunderstandings, that Mr. John Rowntree's position is not that of the creationist nor the intelligent design movements. Let me explain. Creationists insist that the Bible is able to coexist with science. They have done this by adapting to new discoveries in science and explaining how the Bible might still be consistent with science. The Bible is still an interesting topic for discussion with scientists. For example, how did the author of the book of Genesis know the correct sequence of evolution before the conventional scientific theory of evolution was known?

"Neither is John Rowntree an advocate for the intelligent design movement. The intelligent design movement accepts Darwin's evolution, but seeks to qualify it by stating that the complexity of organisms is irreducibly complex for evolution alone to have produced such exquisite complex organisms without outside divine help. John Rowntree has agreed to accept, for the purpose of this debate tonight, that Darwin's evolution could have occurred unaided—although he says he would like to debate this issue on another day.

"In contrast to intelligent design, John Rowntree is going to argue that the origin of life before evolution could only have occurred by a supernatural origin. On the other hand, Sir Ernest Everleigh's position is that the origin of life can be explained by science alone. Sir Ernest also has conceded, for the purposes of tonight's debate, that Darwin's evolution alone is insufficient to explain the origin of life, because the process of natural selection and gene mutation that drives evolution relies on the DNA molecule.

"Therefore, the key question is, can science alone explain the origin of the DNA molecule? Sir Ernest has already released a paper postulating that science can explain this origin by a process of chemical evolution, and he will defend that position tonight. As Sir Ernest has already released his paper on chemical evolution, Mr. John Rowntree will first present his critique of the theory. Sir Ernest will then have the right to defend the chemical evolution position. Mr. Rowntree will then have a right of reply."

"Ladies and gentlemen, Mr. John Rowntree." The crowd gave a round of excited applause. John waited for the awkward silence to launch his address.

"Thank you, Count Nansen, ladies, and gentlemen. The topic of tonight's debate is profound, and I believe it is for this reason that the Nobel Foundation has lent its support to this important debate. I thank it from the bottom of my heart for this opportunity."

"Scientists say that a nonnatural cause for life is outside the realm of science, but never before has science known so much of the mechanism of life. The more scientists have learned, the more inexplicable the origin of life has become. My own view is that it is perfect science to state that the scientific evidence points to a nonnatural cause, perhaps applied from another dimension. I believe it does.

"Let me begin with a startling fact: Every single organism on earth is based on DNA. Another startling fact for you: No one has ever seen life spontaneously create. A third startling fact: No one has found a fossil that can be said to be the predecessor to the DNA-based organism. These three startling facts give us an immediate insight. Creation of DNA before life was not a common occurrence. In fact, scientists are saying it only happened once.

"I should say that my opponents postulate that this one occasion was the last of a series of evolutionary events, which they call chemical evolution. The importance of this cannot be understated. To demonstrate this importance, let me give you an analogy. We know that a diamond is a crystal consisting of carbon atoms. It forms deep in the earth's crust, inside certain types of minerals under pressure, and is then carried up a kimberlite pipe in a volcano. It is made up of geometric arrangements of carbon atoms known as tetrahedrons.

"So, in a sense, the minerals it was born in are like a mold, and the forces between the atoms act like an invisible cookie cutter to assemble the rows of carbon atoms nicely into a diamond. We know there are carbon atoms and other atoms in a DNA molecule, and so to speculate wildly, perhaps because life begins in water, let's assume that one of the beautiful snow crystals may be a cookie cutter for DNA. You spin them, and DNA is created. If this wild theory were true, it would explain where DNA came from, but it would not explain how the universe was structured to act like a cookie cutter and be 'bio-friendly.'

"Have we in fact found a mold or cookie cutter for DNA? The answer is no. So, unlike diamonds, which have self assembled in a…let's call them' kimberlite pipes molds,' DNA has no obvious mold. So scientists believe that because DNA only formed once, they must rely on chance or a series of accidents to explain DNA's existence. To rely on finding a cookie cutter for DNA is to say the universe is naturally bio-friendly and that rocks and minerals are not the only naturally occurring products of the universe. There is no evidence, as yet, for the universe being bio-friendly enough to allow self-assembly of DNA in the same way a diamond would form.

Let us be absolutely clear about chemical evolution. The DNA-based evolution accepted as Darwin's evolution does not begin without DNA as the evolution mechanism. Darwin's evolution is based on sound theory and evidence. However, I will show that chemical evolution is not based on evidence, and to postulate that such evidence may emerge is wishful thinking. There is no known mechanism to drive chemical evolution the way DNA drives Darwin's evolution.

So let us examine the likelihood of DNA coming together by accident. To look at this, we have to have some idea of what we are talking about. Let's not take an animal, but take one of the simplest living things, as our example: a bacterium called E. coli. You might have heard of it contaminating our waterways. It has been well studied, and so we know a lot about it. E. coli is made up of organic molecules, and each molecule consists of carbon and hydrogen atoms. "Each organic molecule has over sixty billion different ways of being arranged, and these molecules must be precisely arranged to be the type of organic molecule used by the E. coli, otherwise they will not function. If one were to prepare a model of an E. coli by using colored beads, then organic chemist Dr. Cairns-Smith—a proponent for a natural origin of life—has stated that such a model would take one thousand staff thirty years to complete, and would need a cathedral to house it. This is complexity on a grand scale. He also says that what is remarkable is that the organism itself can do this in half an hour. It can do this because within the millions of molecules it has, there is a hidden code embedded in its DNA that instructs the organism how to make the proteins that make up its cellular structure, and how to reproduce.

"So how did this vast machine, with its myriad of working parts, arise? By a series of accidents? Note I have mentioned that Darwin's evolution is not available here, because it relies on the DNA molecule. Here we want to know how the DNA molecule evolved or arose. My colleague Sir Ernest Everleigh will postulate chemical evolution, and will point toward possibilities that, to me, need proper scientific theories and explanation backed by evidence before even qualifying as sustainable scientific theories.

"But let me give Sir Ernest and chemical evolutionists the benefit of the doubt. Let's say that a bacterium did arrive through comet dust hitting the earth and then simmering in a hot pond, and one thing led to another, and an organic bunch of molecules came together, and the DNA molecule itself formed. Or, to be softer on Sir Ernest, a predecessor such as RNA arrived, and the As, the Gs and Ts, and the Cs joined together in the wonderful life-making DNA machine. What then? Well, the big question then is how were they jumbled together to form the correct code to make the complex protein structures, including enzymes, to make cells, arrange them, form into tissues, complex shapes, sustain them, and so forth. Was it like a lotto night, where the As the Gs the Ts and the Cs fell in the right order, to become the life machine? I don't think so.

"Now remember, biologists will tell you there is not much room for error. Tiny errors are permitted; but without precise order, the organism simply will not work. Furthermore, if errors accumulate, the organism is doomed. It's like saying, 'Hey, we have the computer now. It came out of our soup factory, so now we want the software to come out of the soup also.' But an accident on top of an accident is not compelling in the slightest. The same accidents that produced the DNA molecule would not produce the code, would they? Again, accident or error accumulation would kill the organism. How was this error accumulation fixed in DNA? You really can't rely on more errors. "Some scientists may challenge this and insist there were a series of accidents where jumbling of the letters occurred frequently during the accidents in the soup, and gradually life was formed. Sorry, but the science has really ruled that out. Let me quote from an eminent scientist, J.D. Bernal, a former professor of crystallography at the University of London, from his book *The Origin of Life*: 'One outstanding fact has now been verified: that the code for proteins and nucleic acids is nearly uniform over the whole of the existing species of life. The implication is that it must have been established at a very early stage in the genesis of life.... In other words, the existence of the code is one of the most important evidences for the genesis of life on earth.'

"Thus, not only is DNA in every living thing on the planet, but also the same code is shared, which makes it more than three billion years old. This has grave consequences for the chemical evolutionist, because he must now argue that in the primordial soup there emerged a working organic life form with the code already in it. Perhaps some brilliant chemical evolutionist will think of a way that this might have happened, such as the mysterious DNA cookie cutter that I postulated earlier?.

"After a century of science, the more we know, the more it is difficult to join the dots on the chemical evolution idea. In fact, the dots are so wide, if chemical evolution were a normal scientific theory, it would have been dumped long ago. Let alone the fact that there are at least ten different soup theories that are clever but inconsistent.

"If that is not enough to convince you, there is a third accident that occurred, which needs explanation. How did our first organism acquire the ability to reproduce? Already it needs its DNA material to make proteins to make its cell walls, shapes, and so forth: our first accident. Then it needs its code to make sure the machine can work to make the proteins and enzymes that sustain life in great complexity: our second accident. Then it needs the code to be able to reproduce itself, including the DNA molecule codes proteins and all: our third accident.

"Just to underscore the hurdle—no, the cliff face—that Sir Ernest must overcome: Not only is there the reproduction, but also the ability to regenerate, to regulate, for the whole organism to have attained its morphology, and the final mystery of consciousness. Of course, following full DNA capability, Darwinian evolution might commence to explain the intricacy of living things (which I agreed not to rely on for tonight's debate). But how did the DNA mechanism attain the capability to create such extraordinary complexity—by a multitude of extraordinary accidents—and 'know' how to create a highly organized being?

"This is enough to rest my case against Sir Ernest's chemical evolution. However, let me point to another striking fact, and this relates to the DNA code. This is not just any code like two plus two equals four, or three times nine equals twenty-seven. One scientist estimates that one gram of DNA can hold the equivalent amount of data that one trillion CDs can hold. A teaspoon full of DNA can hold all the books that have ever been written. The storage capacity of the DNA molecule is staggering. The genetic code for the human body is so complex that scientists took years to complete it; and not only that, it cost over three billion dollars. Thus, to record the order of those As, Gs, Ts, and Cs cost over three billion dollars. Now, I said earlier that tiny errors with DNA are permissible, but any other errors are not. A good example is sickle cell anemia.

"A red blood cell is made from DNA code and forms into chains of molecules containing hundreds of amino acids. Yet a single change from an A to T among the DNA code can cause one of these amino acids in the blood cell proteins to be wrong, making the blood cell defective, meaning it cannot carry oxygen properly. But the most important aspect of DNA is that it has the ability to perform Darwinian evolution, with the mutations and natural selection. If this is responsible for the human race, what a remarkable code the DNA is! In other words, not only is it very intricate and precise, it was formed from day one with the Darwinian mechanism that was capable of producing such wonderful human organs as the eye and the brain. Not bad for a series of accidents.

"No, ladies and gentlemen, Sir Ernest. It was no accident, and we can only turn to the inevitable conclusion that a supernatural entity delivered the seed of all evolution—the DNA molecule (or its predecessor) to earth—to grow into the giant it has become today: our garden of Eden. Thank you."

The audience commenced to clap, which increased until the audience stood up and the clapping became intense. John nodded and smiled as he walked back to his team to resume his seat.

After the audience had sat down and the applause had stopped, Count Nansen approached the lectern and announced, "Thank you, Mr. Rowntree. I now ask Sir Ernest Everleigh to give his address." Count Nansen then resumed his seat.

"Thank you, Count Nansen, the Royal Swedish Academy of Scientists, the Nobel Committee, ladies and gentlemen. I am glad my colleague John Rowntree and I agreed on the common ground of Darwin's evolution, because I noticed he came dangerously close to breaching that concession."

The audience laughed.

"In any event, there are millions of organic molecules that are possible, yet all of life is only based on two hundred organic molecules such as amino acids, nucleotides, proteins—the key building blocks of life. My friend says that if the DNA molecule cannot have arrived by pure chance—even with his slim concession that we say a series of accidents must have occurred—he says that chemical evolution is simply not possible. We don't postulate chemical evolution as a series of accidents. Yes, chance came into it, but what we do say is that the environment shaped chemical evolution, and in fact I like John Rowntree's analogy of the invisible cookie cutter.

"In fact, the first cookie cutter has been found, and this was the act of lightning upon methane, ammonia, and hydrogen to form amino acids. Yes, one of the building blocks of life. Later it was objected by some that methane, ammonia, and hydrogen did not represent earth's early atmosphere, but it does not matter. It is an astounding fact that amino acids were found this way, and perhaps these gases did occur at the right time. Even if that is wrong, a more startling theory arose. We now have evidence that the building blocks of life have been found on a comet. Not only amino acids but also the As, the Ts, Gs, and Cs that Mr. Rowntree keeps mentioning, and sugars. The theory now is that comets can pass through various types of radiation or ultraviolet light. Who knows what will happen to these building blocks of light in this new cookie-cutter environment?

"Now this has been proven. NASA sent up a craft that sampled the material from the comet, and the building blocks of life have been found on it. And, in fact, the scientist who postulated this theory did so before it was proven. What good science!

"Thus, by a process of chemical evolution, a soup of these organic molecules mixed with each other over millions or billions of years, and it was then just a matter of time before the right mix self-assembled and commenced to function as a very simple organism. Yes, we don't know what that was, but it's quite feasible it will be discovered, or maybe it has been washed away in the sands of time. Remember, it only happened once, or the series of events occurred once, and so we do concede that there would not have been many of these fossils around.

"This simple organism, having a few of these As, Gs, Ts, and Cs to play with, started to produce the odd protein, and gradually more accidents occurred. The organism evolved to get a little better. Yes, we don't know the exact process. Perhaps As and Gs were swapped by accident. We know that happens today; it is called transversion. Perhaps it just so happened that the As, Gs, Ts, and Cs could swap easily on this very simple organism, almost like the rotating dials on a poker machine, and one day the jackpot was reached and the organism could suddenly make a protein. Then it continued with its dials going, and it could reproduce.

"Note, therefore, that the combinations of what we call monomers became polymers. This is what I call Stage 1, the emergence from the primordial soup. Stage 2 of chemical evolution was this simple organism that emerged from the soup. Here we believe that an energy source such as lightning, cosmic rays, or even energy from an iron reaction in a volcanic vent could convert an information-storing system such as a raw RNA molecule into another information storage system such as DNA, to produce the complex organic polymers that we know make up a living cell. Thus, in Stage 3 we have a merging from the chemical to the biological evolution, where the simplest organisms can function—eat, make proteins, make energy, and reproduce. Then Darwinian evolution can begin from Stage 3, and this brings us up to the human race. Yes, the DNA code is complex today, but I postulate it began very simply from a few As, Gs, Ts, and Cs, and gradually got longer and longer and more complex as more functions were added. This explains its arrival. I do concede that we have no fossil of this intermediate phase between, say, the Stage 1 and, say, a simple bacterium like the E. coli my friend has outlined. But there are certain signposts that we can point to.

"It has been shown that amino acids can spontaneously form small peptide chains, and these peptide chains can form membranes to form a cell wall. Thus we have our container for DNA, proteins, and all the baggage it needs to make life. Our modeling shows nucleic acids and proteins forming. Other theories support ours, namely the RNA world theory, proposing that the pre DNA stage was led by the RNA molecule as a predecessor for DNA in that it is simpler than DNA and can perform similar functions to DNA. The fact that RNA can self–replicate, is made of nucleotides and is still part of the DNA mechanism as the protein making ribosome is good evidence for the RNA world theory. This gives you the ability for cell reproduction. This, in turn, might have given you the first ribosome. DNA uses ribosomes to make proteins. Our modeling has used mathematical analysis to process the tricoding of nucleotides and amino acids. We have used an algorithm to analyze these chains down into shorter chains and then to single nucleotides, which are the basic building blocks of DNA.

"We have then used chaos theory to show that these building blocks can self-assemble over long periods of time. We have then worked backward to extrapolate back to the prebiotic soup, and modeled forward to show the evolution of nucleotides to DNA molecules to proteins and enzymes, and then to the creation of a first simple organism. We have run a number of scenarios and found two or three of them could work. We have used analogies from chemistry to show self-assembly of organic molecules, such as the self-assembly of crystals in our modeling—very like the example that John Rowntree gave you, with the formation of diamonds that self-assemble under the right conditions. So too, we say DNA, RNA, or perhaps a crude predecessor could have self-assembled under the right conditions. Whether this happened in a mud pool on earth or in the tail of a comet, it matters not. The fact is that we believe it happened.

Therefore, we submit that the origin of life in a prebiotic soup is the best scientific theory available today, and there is no evidence for the intervention of some invisible supernatural origin from another dimension. I might add that resorting to a supernatural origin would see the scientist giving up; and although the challenge is great, I believe a solution will be ultimately found, just as Darwin's evolution became the accepted solution as to how modern human beings evolved. Thank you."

Sir Ernest packed his papers together and left the stage. The audience clapped loudly, and it seemed that there was a polarization in the audience where those who supported John Rowntree were not clapping as loudly as those who supported Sir Ernest. Some sought to rise from their seats, but the applause fell short of a standing ovation.

"Thank you," said Count Nansen. "I now invite John Rowntree to give his reply."

John rose slowly and walked to the podium. "Thank you again," said John, facing Count Nansen, who retired to his seat.

"Sounds like a leap of faith for atheism!" John smiled at Sir Ernest as he resumed. "I am glad I was able to assist Sir Ernest in some parts of his lecture, and indeed I would like to revisit this concept of the cookie cutter. But before doing so, let me address the main thrust of his argument. He postulates chemical evolution in stages from the prebiotic soup hosting the creation of a DNA organism, based on modeling he has done on computers and using biochemistry. As we all know, computers are only as good as what you put into them, and modeling is the same. With modeling, the key is the assumptions you make, because these make up the variables that go into the mathematical formulae or algorithms that are used.

"We cannot have a blow-by-blow contest between Sir Ernest and me about the modeling. That would require a detailed review taking many weeks. But I can point to one key assumption that Sir Ernest has used in his modeling, and this is the assumption that nucleotides are available for mixing with the other building blocks of life so that, accidentally, our life form could come together. Nucleotides are the key building blocks needed to make DNA, and thus their existence will be the key step before a DNA molecule can be shown to have formed. I'm leaving aside the question of the code within it. Organic chemist Dr. Cairns-Smith has referred to experiments such as those where amino acids were created from electric sparks to simulate lightning, and states that accidental formation of nucleotides is not only implausible, but also that there are nineteen scientifically based reasons why they cannot spontaneously form. I would submit, therefore, that Sir Ernest's modeling is, at the very least, speculative and based on this fatal flaw: his modeling is misconceived.

"Returning to our cookie cutter analogy, you will recall my earlier fictitious example of a snow crystal being a cookie cutter for DNA. Let's now assume instead, for tonight, that a new discovery was made by science. A new element in the periodical table is found. Let's call it the CC element; and when it is dropped in a flask of water with our building blocks of life, little DNA molecules start to form. Would we quietly amend the periodic table and say, 'This explains it! The universe is bio-friendly'? No, we would feel that something is very strange here. How could something with this much creative machinery form from lifeless elements? Diamonds form, but they do not have the life-creating machinery of a DNA molecule because they don't do anything. They have no long-term blueprint within them for a life-making and life-improvement machine. Would it not then look as though someone had been tinkering with matter to make cookie cutters that can manufacture DNA?

"Actually, a similar comment was made by astronomer Fred Hoyle about carbon atoms, which are critical for life, because they are made in the center of stars by the collision of three high-speed helium nuclei and need intricate quantum resonances for their creation, which happen to occur inside large stars. He labeled this as a lucky fluke. Or perhaps let's assume that the famous mathematician Mandelbrot stumbles upon a cookie cutter by discovering a new fractal. Fractals are the simple mathematical formulae that, when applied, produce complex images defining anything from a human heartbeat to organic growth. Indeed, fractals have been called the 'thumbprint of God.'

"If a 'cookie cutter' fractal were found that defined DNA, would this be the lucky fluke embedded in a bio-friendly universe that science would say 'explains' everything? No, it would seem that there are just too many lucky flukes here to make good scientific theory. If there were a cookie cutter for DNA found—a set of resonances at the quantum level, or a new element, or even a new fractal—whatever it is, that would be the first fluke (or series of flukes). The second fluke would be, how did the code get there? The third fluke: How did it become capable of reproduction? All these flukes are needed before Darwin's natural selection can begin—that is, before chance can take over. I have also mentioned other flukes such as consciousness. The thousands of evolving mutating working parts in an organism needed to be like thousands of poker machines, all of which not only hit the jackpot but did so in the right ways, at the right times and places, over evolutionary history. In Sir Ernest's lab there is an image of an hourglass. Imagine that in the top half of the hourglass there is dust, and in the bottom there are DNA molecules. What is the major process dominating the tube between the top and bottom flasks? Assume scientists have already found DNA building-block cookie cutters in our imaginary tube? They have found amino acids made from lightning —a biblical image if there was one.

"What if they find more building blocks made from other cookie cutters—perhaps ultraviolet light cutting the ice on a tail of a comet, or even more wondrous processes? Throw a fractal in as well. Will the tube prove to be honeycombed with our tiny cookie cutters? What if it does? The more cookie cutters that are found, the less scientific theory relies on chance or chaos for the creation of life. The more it relies on the fabric of a bio-friendly world to manufacture DNA, which is not really science's preferred position, because a bio-friendly world really points to supernatural origin, not just a bubbling rocky soup operating on chaos.

"The existence of DNA works too well—and at such a superb level of efficiency, intricacy, and complexity—for it to be forged by a series of accidents made from our lifeless periodic table and physical laws. Yet we search for that cookie-cutter fabric. Why does science not then grasp the clear inference from the scientific facts that the best model of all the scientific models is that the world has been seeded or shaped through its fabric with DNA from a supernatural origin? Chaos is a poor competitor to this origin. The evidence for this is that DNA (and the DNA code) is not only at the center of every living thing on earth. Not only that it has never been seen to spontaneously form; not only that we know of no process where it would naturally form. That we know of no process that would implant the life code within it. Not only that it has taught itself to reproduce. But the fact that the code itself is so good, so robust, so skilled at creating the myriad and complexity of life as we know it in a masterpiece of creation towering above no other."

John walked from the podium as his team ran over to shake his hand. His father greeted him first.

"John, a truly remarkable performance. I think you have outdone Everleigh tonight." The crowd responded again with a standing ovation, and John stood to face them and nodded. Then Sir Ernest caught his eye. He could see a look of submission creeping into it, and Sir Ernest nodded to John in a moment of graciousness.

# TWENTY EIGHT

A few minutes passed before Count Nansen approached the microphone and announced that the judges had provided him with their decision.

"John Rowntree is the clear winner."

The crowd again applauded with a standing ovation, and Count Nansen beckoned for John to approach the podium. John stood at the microphone and spoke:

"I would like to thank my team for the valiant effort they put in to back me in this debate. The depth of the problem we have debated tonight has taken an extraordinary range of talents from not only science but also mathematics, and we must not forget philosophy. My father told me that people used to laugh at the subject 'philosophy of science' at university, but I think it has been sadly neglected because many scientists are so involved at their work level that the overview of their work from the philosophical point of view can be missed. I would like to thank, again, the Swedish Academy, the Nobel Committee, and this great audience tonight. Finally, I congratulate Sir Ernest for his gallant debate tonight. I think if he was not such a formidable opponent, our team would not have been so motivated to win this. Thank you all again."

John walked from the stage again, to a round of great applause from the crowd.

**

Some weeks later, John was back in his room using the meditation techniques he had learned in Tibet when a knock at the door came. He rose from his lotus position and opened the door. It was Jane.

"John, can I come in?" asked Jane sheepishly.

"Do you think that's a good idea, after what you have done?"

"I suppose you have recovered from the publicity now," said Jane, avoiding the question.

There was an awkward silence before John replied, "I'll try and enjoy it while it lasts." John stared at Jane, pondering his feelings. "Look, it's strange you came at this time…"

John saw she was still standing and beckoned for her to sit on the bed.

"Well," sighed John.

"John, I was manipulated by Brendan and his father. By the time that I saw what was happening, it was too late," explained Jane.

"Well, you're a big girl. Why didn't you pull out?"

Jane looked upset and seemed to have difficulty talking. "Because I was scared of them. They were dealing with dangerous people. I didn't know what they were capable of. Sir Ernest was a driven man. He was driven so much by hatred for religion that he became fanatical. I believed in his ideology and all that, but after seeing the viciousness of it all, I started to have doubts." John smiled. "The lapsed Christian usually does that! What do you want now? Reconciliation?"

"I want answers, John."

"What are the questions, then?"

"For one, why do bad things happen? I've listened to Sir Ernest and I've listened to you on everything, but there must be more. What you are saying, now, it's quite surprising. It's not the tired old religious line. It's something new, and I don't really know what it means."

John looked at Jane intensely, pondering her intentions. He walked to the window and looked down to the quadrangle below. "Jane, it means that there is a God, but not the God with the white beard on the throne. It is a God acting within the framework of science as we know it, but in a timeless dimension outside of our time and space, and not human—not a personal God. A God who acts within certain laws of logic, mathematics, and science. Once you accept that, all the doubts you have disappear."

Jane tilted her head and said, "Well, I won't ask you about existence. You have convinced me of that during the debate. But why doesn't God intervene to prevent evil and suffering?"

"I have Professor Simons to thank for that. He came in one night and explained that it was a mathematical impossibility to have effective intervention on the thousands of evil events, because such interventions would cause event trees that increase exponentially in size to infinity with potential paradoxes from event tree conflicts. If you ran such an event tree on a supercomputer, tracking the ripple effects of the interventions—let alone actual interventions—the computer would crash because the ripple effects expand infinitely.

"So universal intervention is impossible. This means the ultimate results of the interventions in the future are unknowable in this world. And, by the way, therefore God's omniscience cannot extend to infinite event possibilities. Remember, you can never get to infinity. The key point is that once you encounter exponential growth of events, you get what Professor Simons calls event turbulence, and mathematicians know there are infinite unknown solutions to defining the behavior of events when this occurs—that is, it is unpredictable. This event turbulence is a 'showstopper' for intervention or any action you want to consider." John related the full discussion he had held that night with Professor Simons to Jane.

"All right, multiplicity of religions. Surely God could have done a better job than that. How confusing," said Jane.

"Jane, it is a similar explanation to intervention. The diversity of peoples and cultures is vast. Again, as with universal intervention, systematic universal religious intervention will give you infinite event turbulence also. Assuming the religious leaders the world has seen are authentic, this would suggest that limited 'intervention' has occurred, despite their turbulent past. However, I believe religions are evolving for the greater good." John waited for the next question.

"Nice" said Jane. "This is starting to make sense. But I have the best one for last for you: During the debate at Oxford, you applied strict logic to deduce that an all powerful God could not have made a perfect world. He made the best world He could have created, but surely an all-powerful God could have made the perfect human being?"

"Jane, let me clarify a vital point first. When you say 'all-powerful,' are you referring to the power to dominate or create, or are you speaking generally or technically? We can certainly say a king is all powerful in his land, and we probably accept that because we know what that 'all powerful' means. But with God it will mean different things to different people."

Jane clarified her question: " You may remember that during the debate you used the reasonable definition of 'all powerful' to mean the power to do what is logically possible and not absurd. That is the sense I would use."

Jane felt she had thrown down the gauntlet. John was now standing in front of Jane, as excited by the question as she was, and began, "The famous writer Arthur Koestler stated that man has a design defect. I will retrace God's footsteps as to whether this could have happened. I recall that you know something about mathematics."

Jane smiled. "You remembered. I am a little rusty, but go on."

"This is an implied challenge to the 'God is all powerful' proposition, because it implies that God created man defectively or that God does not exist. Molecular scientists make synthetic DNA using trial-and-error techniques. A mathematical formula defining the genetic code has not been found. However, like a pin code unlocking a computer, we know the code integrates with organic molecules to create life. Thus, it is now possible to make life-making DNA. However, let us assume that God, at the beginning of the universe (or at least at the right time after the big bang) started to make plans to create the correct DNA for the perfect human. Could He make a synthetic DNA that is perfect? Here I am using 'perfect' to mean 'more than faultless'—namely, to create a DNA molecule that would create the perfect human being. (Note that molecular scientists creating synthetic DNA already know the DNA code, so the problem presented to God here is infinitely more difficult.)

"Is it mathematically possible to create the perfect human being? To consider the question, you must formulate the correct context to answer it. The human body is an extraordinary biological machine. It is not a shape such as a star that you could cut out of a piece of paper. A star can be planned perfectly, without outside data. If it were a paper star, you could define the plans for its creation with some simple formulas, equations, and drawings (call this theoretical design). However, if you planned to build a paper plane, you not only need formulas and drawings, but you also need to test it in the air. And so you need outside data. Call this 'real-world' data—empirical data.

"Take an airplane. You may find you have hundreds or thousands of equations that are known to design it, but you also need empirical data to have complete formulas with solutions. A designer can work out the equations to get solutions and blueprints for the design of the airplane with empirical data. The designer would have used trial-and-error processes for designing the airplane, such as wind-tunnel testing for dynamics, or stress testing of metal, or inductive processes to give an empirically aided design solution (call this empirical design).

"It is fair to say that the human body is a more complex machine than an airplane, and thus would require many more equations, solutions, blueprints, and testing for its design. Engineers refer to equations that cannot be solved without empirical data as indeterminate (which can only be solved by empirical design). Intuition tells us that most of the equations that may make up a mathematical definition of a living organism are also indeterminate. An engineer refers to the number of unknown variables to describe the degree of indeterminacy—for example, three unknown variables means an equation has a third degree of indeterminacy. This is useful to apply to biology. The higher the complexity, the higher the degree of indeterminacy or insolubility. If you compare machines to organisms, the degree of indeterminacy or insolubility is vastly higher for an organism, meaning, intuitively, there is no hope to solve each equation without empirical design. Each variable in an indeterminate equation has an infinite number of solutions, and thus is insoluble, unless done with empirical design.

"The question then arises: Is it possible for God? Scientists tell us that the universe was created in the big bang, say, thirteen billion years ago, and outside the universe there is no space or time as we know it. The entire fabric of space and time was created in that instant, and expanded to create the universe as one system. Our model of God is that He stands outside the universe in another dimension, as a timeless God looking into a time-streamed world.

"Let's assume God is working on a DNA molecule on a drawing board in this other dimension to create a perfect human being. Here we are merely speculating a plausible design scenario—i.e., we are not specifying beyond doubt or proving God's precise design methodology, but answering the atheist's toughest questions, such as, "What possible reason could there be for the birth of abnormal children?" God cannot use testing, empirical data, or trial and error like the molecular biologists or an airplane designer, because He is outside of this world. Simulation is also impossible, as only design work in our world is possible based on assumed empirical data using iterative 'what if' techniques, i.e., trial and error. In other words, empirical design is not available to God in God's world unless He created an identical world as His 'divine wind tunnel,' i.e., as a simulator that creates the same problems anyway. God must create the DNA using theoretical design only. The first problem is that in God's realm our intuition on the number of equations needed to design a human being have a degree of indeterminacy so high that mathematical analysis alone cannot provide a methodology to solve the high number of variables—that is, finding a finite solution against infinite values."

"Wait!" Jane interrupted. "Just because you have equations with infinity popping up, does not mean they cannot be solved. Calculus does that." Jane smiled and added, "See, I do remember my mathematics."

"You've just reminded me of a splendid example: Gabriel's Horn."

"You've got me on that one," replied Jane.

"No, it comes from the Angel Gabriel blowing the horn on judgment day, and it highlights the divine, the infinite, and the finite. Imagine a horn of infinite length. Mathematics shows that you can calculate a finite volume of the horn, but the surface area of the horn is infinite—a startling situation. How many organs in the human body also exhibit infinite vs. finite values for the equations that govern them?   Look, I do not have to prove that there are numerous formulas needed to design a human body with infinite solutions or that are unsolvable. Remember, I am just answering the atheist's toughest questions, such as, 'What possible reason could there be for the birth of abnormal children?' And so I am saying that in any human body there are probably unsolvable equations, even if there are solvable ones. In fact, my intuition strongly tells me that there are a myriad of unsolvable equations, and that is enough to explain why a perfect human being has not been made in this world or why there are deformities and so on."

"Well, sorry to interrupt. Go on with your explanation," said Jane.

John continued: "Put another way, the problem with infinity is that you never get there. *That is, the design cannot be known without empirical design.* Assume a design of a human being could be found. There is a further problem. How would God know that this was a perfect human being? To know this, God must simulate all interactions—not only between the DNA and its execution of code to produce a human being, but also of the execution of the formation, growth, and living phases of that human being and its interactions with the world. Again, *the design cannot be known without empirical design.* This is a startling fact.

"The reason is that for the design to be known, simulations must be run of the execution phases and all interactions, to test whether the human being will be perfect. Assume that the following simple formula is one of the (less complex) total set of equations required to design a perfect human being—i.e., a linear equation, say, $A + B + C = Z$. Assume you only know the value of $C$ and $Z$, and so variables $A$ and $B$ can be an infinite number of values.

"Again, the problem is that you can never get to infinity to get to the solution—i.e., to the perfect human being. When this occurs in real life— for example, in designing an airplane—the missing variables can only be obtained by experiment, perhaps in a wind tunnel, i.e., empirical design. Einstein once said "God does not care about our mathematical difficulties. He integrates empirically."

"Now consider the vast number of formulas that would be encountered in designing a human being, where you cannot apply trial and error or you run out of inductive reasoning techniques. The lack of a world (call it the 'divine wind tunnel') in which to run the simulation would be a showstopper for designing the perfect human being. In biology they prefer using nonlinear equations to describe biological processes, but the principle is the same with whatever equations biologists could use, due to these infinite unknown variables. Thus, the design cannot be known without interaction with the world—the divine wind tunnel—to enable a trial-and-error process to proceed. (Biologists also refer to a feedback loop between DNA and the environment where empirical data is fed back and forth into the 'DNA design process.') Intuitively, this probably applies to any human being, not just our theoretical perfect human being. Thus, a God would need our world as His divine wind tunnel to introduce the DNA molecule to interact with the world, using empirical design. For example, the trial-and-error process needed to fill in the missing variables in each and every equation required to make any human being.

"Thus it is now clear why the world and evolution is necessary. The process is still continuing today as the 'perfection process' progresses. Biologists have stated that the chaos or 'noise' of the world is needed to provide the cycling back-and-forth interaction (the feedback loop via gene mutations) with this design process by inputting the missing variables into the ultimate human design. God's drawing board needs the world as His wind tunnel to enable design of the human being. Now the meaning of the universe is clear: to eventually overcome the misfortune befalling humankind by allowing life to evolve toward an omega point of perfection. This point is without evil, pain, or suffering, in an evolving worldly arena of human transactions and achievements for the universal good—and thus allows happiness as this omega point joins with God—becomes God."

Jane's eyes widened "Now I see . What you are saying is that the reason bad things happen is that there is a divine limit to everything from human design,  event flow and the meaning of life bounded and defined by infinity but set in motion by God to evolve towards perfection."

The phone rang.

"John?"

"Yes."

"It's your father. The Nobel committee have released the names of the Nobel laureates."

"Yes? Don't give me heart failure."

"Sir Ernest is not among them," replied his father.

"Oh…"

"Well, you did it. Have you no comment, John?"

"Only that I feel no pleasure from another's misfortune," replied John.

"You're more stoic than I thought, John. After what Sir Ernest had done, I thought you would be entitled to feel vindicated."

"Dad, you know the night of the Nobel debate? I looked at Sir Ernest, and he nodded to me that he knew I had won. He was gracious in defeat, and so I am gracious in victory."

"John, John, switch on your television. Faulkner's on now! I'll hang up."

John scanned through the channels and immediately saw Faulkner's face and his speech underway.

"I have reconvened the Everleigh committee into the banning of religious education in all English schools, and the committee has conducted a review of its findings. We have come to the conclusion that our decision was based on certain studies that have now been found wanting. What we have found is that, managed properly, the study of religion and science can be taught so that one does not weaken the other, providing that the correct context is given to both. The banning of teaching of intelligent design in science will remain.

"However, a new subject, philosophy of science, will be introduced, where topics such as the origin of life, the existence of God, and the contest of religions will be permissible topics for study at schools."

John leapt for joy as the phone rang again from his father.

"John, congratulations *twice* today. It looks as though you might have your job back."

"Dad, I hope you're right, but I am enjoying the moment!"

John put the phone down and explained what had happened to Jane.

"Congratulations, John. You have come full circle!" remarked Jane. She put her arms around John and hugged him. John, bemused, held her back gently, and then kissed her.

**

John walked in front of his old school. He remembered the day he had been sacked from there, and took the letter asking him to return to teaching from his pocket to make sure he was not imagining the dream he was living. His friend, teacher Bill Rose, was walking by, and when John caught his eye, he ran over with a large smile across his face.

"John, John, the giant killer! I'm so glad you're coming back to us. It's been the talk of the school. Look, your class is waiting for you. They're practically holding their breath. Go, go now! I have to fly anyway. I'll catch you later."

Bill strolled off, and John quickly marched into the school he loved to teach in. Before long, he walked into his classroom to cheering from his students. John blushed as he walked to the blackboard and wrote the words:

"From Dust to DNA. Remember, man, that thou art dust, and unto dust thou shall return."

The class grew hushed. John smiled, turned to the class and proclaimed:

"I came, I saw, I conquered."